Three For A Girl

Isabel Fielding
Book 3

Sarah A. Denzil

THREE FOR A GIRL

Sarah A. Denzil

Copyright © 2020 Sarah A. Denzil

This is a work of fiction. All characters, events, organizations and products depicted herein are either a product of the author's imagination, or are used fictitiously.

Cover Design by Damonza

Also By The Author:

Prologue
CASSIE

Newmoor sounds more like a nursing home than a prison, but the barbed wire on the walls reminds you where you are. There's no creeping ivy snaking up the bricks, this is a building with hard edges, devoid of any softness, formed by squares and rectangles with sharp corners. A security guard waves me through the first gate and directs me to the carpark at the back of the institution. Those sharp-edged, red-brick buildings are ahead of me, like lego blocks smashed together, and I wonder whether those are all the different wings of the prison. I can't see any inmates, though I can see part of the outdoor area where prisoners can exercise.

There's a warmth to the mid-May air. This is the first week that I've noticed the temperature rise and suddenly summer doesn't feel so far away. I back the car into one of the spaces, foot trembling on the brake pedal as I turn slightly too sharply. It takes me three attempts to get into the space, and afterwards, I stop for a moment to check my reflection in the mirror and take a deep breath. I have the questions ready in my pocket, but if I dwell on who I'm meeting, then my knees weaken with nerves.

What will she be like? I've read so much about her. Every newspaper article, Wikipedia entry, even a criminologist's study, but I've never met her. I've never met anyone who kills.

Outside the car, I pull my hair into a quick ponytail, getting the hair away from my neck. I don't want to arrive with a sweaty glaze across my forehead. I want to appear calm and collected. After a hasty vocal warm up, which I find calms my nerves, I make my way through the strange roads to the entrance to the prison. I have the prisoner number ready; I've tried to dress in a way to make the search easier, with no metal underwire in my bra, no zips and so on. My heart patters nervously. In a way, this is like going on a first date, I think. And when I'm patted down by one of the officers, it's like a *third* date. And then I realise that my mind is rambling on to calm the bubbling nerves.

"Can I see your bag, love?" she asks, raising two pencilled eyebrows. I take in her widely set shoulders, round middle and cropped hair and pass it over with a smile. Most of the officers talk in a similar way workmen do when they're fixing the plumbing or cleaning out the gutters. Lots of "loves" and "sweethearts". It has a soothing effect on me. Like I'm in the presence of my favourite aunty.

She seems surprised when I give her the prisoner number. "Oh. How do you know her?"

"To be honest, I don't actually know her," I reply. A heart-beat passes and I wonder whether to tell her. "I'm playing her in an upcoming movie."

Those pencilled eyebrows lift high up her forehead. "There's going to be a movie, is there?" She tuts her disapproval.

"It doesn't start shooting for at least six months," I say.

"Still, it's not long after, is it?" Now that my bag is clear, she leads me through the prison towards the visiting room. "For the victims' families I mean."

"We're going to be very respectful. The director is mindful of the gravity of the situation."

She nods, already disinterested. "Well, you're her first visitor in a long time. There she is. Isabel Fielding." The woman presents Isabel to me with a sweep of her hand.

My mouth goes dry and my vision tunnels. For a fraction of a second it feels as though there is only me and her in the room. She meets my eyes, an open expression on her face. There is nothing remarkable about her at all. She's a medium build with medium brown hair, slightly olive skin, warm eyes. Her expression isn't exactly blank, because there's a slight smile on her face, it's... neutral.

If I was choosing where to sit on a bus, I'd sit next to her. If she was working in a shop, I'd feel fine about approaching her with a question. If I was lost, I'd choose her to ask for help. On the other hand, I wouldn't notice her in a crowd. I could walk past her several times and never remember the exact features of her face – the slope of her nose, the curve of her mouth. I'd probably forget her name if she told it to me.

And yet... she's the most dangerous female serial killer for decades. Possibly ever.

"Off you go then," the officer says, all but shoving me towards the table.

It pulls me out of my thoughts and for the first time I notice the rest of the room. There are several small tables filling the space. Each one is filled with family, friends and inmates. Isabel will not be behind glass. She will be sat across from me. Tentatively, I walk closer. My heart is hammering, and I know I should walk faster, because I have multiple questions to ask and limited time. I may never get this opportunity again, which means I need to study her mannerisms, accent, the way her body moves.

Isabel watches me, too, with eyes that follow me as I walk towards her. Is she sizing me up? My heart beats harder until I feel like it could burst from my chest. Finally, I sit down.

"Thank you for allowing me to visit you," I start. She's silent. Blinks once. "I explained everything in the letter, but I thought I would introduce myself further. I'm Cassie Keats and, umm, Neal, Neal Ford, the director, cast me to play you." I break for a moment to suppress a nervous laugh. "In the film, I mean. I thought I'd come to meet you and maybe ask you a few questions if that's all right."

She nods once, moving her head down and up in a particularly measured and languid manner.

"Great, thanks. How are you today? Are you being well looked after?"

She blinks slowly, and then leans forward, making me lean back. "Do you have a picture of the person playing Leah?" she asks. Her voice takes me by surprise, too. Soft, with a Yorkshire lilt. Almost melodic. "I'd like to see that."

"Yeah, I guess so." I scroll through my phone for a picture of Jess, the actress cast as Leah Smith. When I find a flattering one, I turn the screen around so that she can see it.

Isabel cranes her neck and lets out a long sigh. "She looks nothing like her. *You* look nothing like *me* either."

"Well, we were talking about a touch of prosthetics. Maybe false teeth. I'll make my hair colour match, obviously. But you can do a lot with mannerisms and accents."

"Go on then." She smirks. "Say something in my accent."

"Oh, I don't know—"

She starts to laugh and her expression changes so suddenly that it makes me physically jolt. This is the first

4

glimpse of the woman who carved bird wings into the backs of her victims; someone who murders for the sheer fun of it.

"I'm teasing you," she says. "It's quite boring in this place. I don't have much entertainment here."

I clear my throat and try to bring the interview back on course. "I heard that you still sketch. Do you draw birds?"

She shakes her head. "Not much anymore. It's landscapes now. I send the pictures to my mum. It reminds me that there's a world out there." She nods to the whitewashed stone. "Beyond the walls."

"She hasn't visited you for a while, has she? Your mum, I mean."

"I believe I've been disowned because of bad behaviour. Not even little bro wants to come." She picks at dirt beneath her fingernails. It's the first time she's avoided eye contact with me, and I wonder whether this is significant.

"He's been released from prison now, hasn't he?"

She nods.

I want to ask her why he falsely confessed to the murder of Maisie Earnshaw, but I decide that would be too much for our first meeting. Instead, I take the folded piece of paper out of my pocket and examine the questions I brought. Embarrassingly, my fingers tremble, shaking the note.

"Are those the questions?" she asks.

"Yes, is that okay?"

Isabel merely blinks, but I take that as a yes.

"Okay, well, I have to ask why you enjoy killing." I clear my throat because it's dry again. Isabel looks up, and her eyes shine. There's a slight pause where I turn away, intimidated by the strength of her gaze. When I turn back, it's in time to see her lick her lips.

"Let me tell you a secret," she says, shuffling her legs to get more comfortable. "My entire life has programmed me to be

5

who I am. My father was a serial killer and my mother is a drug and alcohol addict. We never received love, my brother and me. If we'd been loved, maybe I would never have started killing, and Owen wouldn't have started lying. If I hadn't found evidence of Daddy's murders, then maybe my brain wouldn't have wired itself to enjoy taking lives. Maybe I wouldn't be like this and the world would be better for it." She blinks again, and I notice that her posture has changed. Her shoulders have sagged, and her expression isn't neutral anymore, it's pitiful. Her eyebrows are scrunched together, her mouth pulled down. She stays like that, staring at me. I no longer stare at the table, instead I find myself pulled into her presence.

"Your impulse to kill is because of your upbringing?"

"That's right," she replies.

"You've been in prison for over a year now, Isabel. Are you beginning to look at your crimes in a different light?"

She opens her palms in almost a pleading gesture. "I didn't understand right from wrong, but since coming here I've begun to learn. Families lost daughters and sisters because of my addiction to pain."

"You see killing as an addiction?"

"Yes," she says.

"What about the time you were in Crowmont high security hospital? You were never violent then."

"No," she says. "But my thoughts were. Every single one of them. There's violence in everything, Cassie. It's merely the lengths you go to, to push that violence. For me, I used violence in the way I plotted and waited and plotted until the opportune moment came."

"You mean, the way you manipulated Leah Smith?"

"Yes."

"What is it about Leah? You seem obsessed with her."

6

"It was a silly fixation," she says. "Leah showed me a lot of compassion and it affected me. You see, I've never been given any compassion in my life. At all. I didn't understand what it was. That, mixed with the medication they had me on, which made my impulses worse, and the toxic atmosphere at Crowmont, basically made me even crueller."

I nod my head, wishing I'd brought a pen to make notes. My plan had been to observe only, but her answers are fascinating. "There is one important question I need to ask, because it might affect my performance. Are you gay, Isabel?"

"I have no idea," she says. "The only pleasure I've had of that kind has been through violence."

"You haven't had any relationships since being in prison?"

"I've been in the segregation unit most of the time," she says, following her words with a disinterested shrug. "They only let me out a few months ago."

"Was that because you were on suicide watch?"

"Yes."

"But you don't have that desire to take your life anymore?"

"No. I found a higher power guiding me to be better."

"God?"

"Yes. The chaplain here has been excellent at showing me there is another way to obtain love and maybe even to feel love. The love of God." She smiles, showing teeth. There's happiness on her face, spreading all the way to her eyes, that I'd expected to think of as cold. She doesn't have the unemotional eyes of a psychopath at all. She has warm eyes. I smile back before I'm aware of what I'm doing.

I decide not to push this subject any further. Her suicide attempts have been well documented in the news, from trying to hang herself with bedsheets, to an effort to cut her own throat. The religious aspect is new, but I'm not certain how sincere she is about it.

"What will the film be like?" she asks. "Will it be violent? Will they show you killing other women?"

"No," I reply. "It'll be about your escape from Crowmont."

"What about when I tortured Leah with my dad? Who's playing Tom?"

"He hasn't been cast yet. And, no, I don't think they are going to film that part. Whether they'll do a sequel, I don't know."

She cocks her head to one side. "How does the film end?"

"With you being caught and taken back to the hospital."

"You're rewriting history."

"The director feels that it's a bold choice. Film is a great medium to explore our own wishful thinking. If you'd been found right away, then Alison Finlay and Chloe Anderson wouldn't have died."

"Yes," she says. "So many lives ruined."

"I hear you're helping the police find your father's victims. That's admirable."

"The chaplain says that it's never late to atone."

I nod my head. And then the officers call out that our time is up. The large woman with the pencilled eyebrows returns.

"Did you enjoy your visit, Isabel?"

"Very much so, Miss. Cassie is great company. Time to go?"

"Up you come," she says.

Isabel turns back and smiles at me as she's led out of the room. My fingers uncurl from the edge of the table. I hadn't been aware I'd been gripping it at all.

Part One

1

LEAH

S eb presses a mug of tea into my hands and sweeps a lock of hair away from my face, the rough skin on his fingertips giving me a pleasant shiver. And that's the signal. That's what brings me back to reality when I recognise that I haven't been present in the room. He plants a soft kiss on my brow and settles back down on the sofa. The weight of him drags down the sofa cushions and I move closer to him.

"What time is she getting here?"

"In about an hour or so." My fingers wrap around the mug, dragging every bit of warmth from it. And then my hand tightens against the ceramic, revealing the white semicircle of the nail plate.

"Do you want me to stay?"

"No, it's okay," I lie.

Seb's eyes narrow as he assesses my lie, reading the tone of my voice that I always try and fail to hide. But it's not fair to keep asking him to be with me when he has a commitment to his family. God knows he's broken various family arrangements because of me.

"You should go and help Josh."

He grunts.

"His Pumpkin Patch was a great idea."

He rolls his eyes.

"It's best for the farm in the long run." I place a hand on his upper back, knowing that this is a sore subject.

"Bloody Pumpkin Patches," he says, finally, releasing his pent-up frustration. "We used to be a fully working farm."

The Braithwaites' farm was in decline before I moved into the cottage, and since then they've sold the majority of their chickens, a few pigs, and most of their cattle. Seb's older brothers have given up on the farm and both now work in York; Christopher is a supermarket manager, Jason a financial advisor. A lot of the income from the farm relies on Seb's mother, Donna, and his younger brother Josh, giving tours to schools and locals. Now Josh has set up the Pumpkin Patch idea, a part of Halloween that seems to be growing in popularity. Seb isn't too happy about that, but the prospect of wedding packages is causing a rift between the family. His mother wants to transform Rose Cottage into a rental for the bride and groom, and get planning permission to build three more cottages on the estate to provide accommodation for a full wedding party. But Seb wants us to continue living here together. He sees our lives laid out so clearly. Us. This cottage. Children. The farm.

But I'm more uncertain about the future and where it will take us.

"It's what makes money these days," I remind him. "And it makes children happy, don't forget about that!"

He grunts again.

I remind myself not to take his grumps too seriously. They're all for show. Seb has been nothing but attentive to the pumpkins he's grown in preparation for Halloween, which is

12

now less than a fortnight away. Every spare moment he has goes on those things.

I take a sip of tea to hide my smile. "Go on. Don't be late or your mum will blame me again." My jaw tenses just thinking about Donna. About her disapproval of me living with her son.

He plants another kiss on my head and a moment later I hear the familiar sounds of him pulling on his boots in the kitchen. I lean into the sofa and try to enjoy the tea while it's hot. But I end up putting it on the coffee table as soon as the kitchen door closes firmly shut.

If there was ever a time when a door opening or closing didn't make my nerves tighten, I can't remember one. Long ago, it was the sound of my father coming home. Now it signals solitude in the place where Isabel abducted me. Where I found James Gorden's severed head on my doorstep. The dead birds on the windowsill. The envelope containing the magpie illustration. It all happened here, but when I'm with Seb, I can block it out.

Whenever I'm alone in the house I can't sit still. I head into the kitchen for a cleaning frenzy, scrubbing the kitchen counter even though it's already clean. I bend down and clear out the dust bunnies behind the fridge, wipe down the shelves, attack the cobwebs in the corners of the room, and when the knock on the door comes, I almost fall from my stool. I'd forgotten all about Jess's visit. Which means I'm a mess now that she's arrived. Sweaty hair, dirty fingernails, the scent of bleach emanating from my body. But there's nothing I can do about it. I quickly run my fingers through my ragged hair and open the door.

"Hi," she says, smiling broadly. "I'm Jess."

"So nice to meet you," I reply, sticking out a hand. "Sorry,

I started cleaning and got a bit lost in my thoughts. I'm all scruffy now. Come in, though."

"Oh, don't worry about it. I'm a bit of a neat freak myself. It's nice to know other people lose themselves in cleaning. I was starting to think there was something wrong with me." She laughs, and I observe that she's nervous about meeting me, and it feels so alien for someone else to be intimidated by me.

I let out an appreciative laugh, partly to try and make her feel more at ease. "Can I get you anything? A cup of tea? Glass of water?"

"Water would be great, thanks."

I watch her eyes roam around the kitchen, the way they linger at the door. She must be picturing the severed head on the doorstep. Everybody does. Seb has to stop hikers from taking photographs of our cottage.

"It was so nice of you to let me meet you," she says. "It must be a pretty weird feeling knowing that your life is going to be depicted on screen."

"It is a bit," I admit. The tap splutters and water spills over the side of the glass.

"These situations are always weird. It can't be helped." She takes the water and smiles, not commenting on the damp surface of the glass. "But you have my word that I'll do everything I can to make this experience as painless as I possibly can." It's when her smile widens and small dimples form in her cheeks that I see the girl I remember from the TV show.

Jess Hopkins used to be a child actor, and a pretty famous one at that. She was the daughter in a long running sitcom, one I grew up with. I remember wanting her clothes when she was a teen, and how I used to pull my hair into a high ponytail because that was how she used to do it. All of a sudden, I'm not nervous because she's here to talk about Isabel, I'm nervous because she's Jess Hopkins.

"Do you want to go into the living room?"

"Sure."

She follows me in, and we settle on the sofa.

"Neal sent you the script, didn't he?"

"Yeah."

"What did you think?"

I rub my hands together for a moment. "It's very respectful, but not exactly true to life."

She nods. "The ending."

"Is there a reason why he changed it?"

"Well, the main reason is to be respectful about what happened to you. But also, because it's possible there might be a sequel if everything goes well." She lifts her shoulders as though unconvinced a sequel will happen. "And as you know, there's been a delay. There was a funding issue, but Neal has sorted that out now. It worked out for me and Cassie because we wanted more time to research anyway."

"And you still haven't cast Tom." Saying his name has a sombre effect on the atmosphere of the room. My missing son.

"That's right." She takes a sip of water and places the glass on a coaster. "It's a shame he's not here to meet. Have you heard from him recently?"

I shake my head.

She moves on. "This initial meeting is to help me get to know you a bit better. I know you've had a lot of trauma in your life and I obviously don't want to press you about that or make you feel uncomfortable, but at the same time it would be great to know more about you and how those experiences have shaped you as a person."

Her initial nerves seemed to have calmed, and she's so direct that it's almost disconcerting. I wasn't expecting her to tisraS A. Denzil

dive in like this, but then I'm not certain *what* I was expecting. She's also much prettier than me, slimmer, and has eyes that are a different colour. She moves more fluidly, like a dancer. Her accent is nicer than mine, like a middle-class TV presenter. I can't imagine her ever being me.

"It's... complicated," I begin. "I have countless conflicting thoughts about everything and how it's affected me. I suppose I should start with my mental health." I pause, staring down at my hands, at the grime beneath my fingernails, the red tinge of my battered fingertips. My skin will peel tomorrow because I didn't bother wearing rubber gloves.

"Why don't we go for a walk?" Jess suggests. "It's a beautiful day outside. I put on my boots in case, it'd be a shame not to use them."

I agree, mainly because it gives me time to avoid her questions as we put on our coats and leave the house. The cold air greets us like a swift, but gentle, slap across the face.

"The weather really turned this week," she says. "Lead the way, Leah. You must know all the best walks around here."

"Seb is the real expert," I admit. Intuitively, I take one of the paths he used to show me not long after Isabel escaped, when he'd take me on long, slow walks to help me heal. Even these fields, these moors, bring bad memories along with the good. I don't block them out like I often do. Jess is here to hear me talk about the bad times. I need to let them in.

"It must have been hard to be away from him when you were in witness protection."

"It was. I'd think about him a lot. He... he's a decent man and I don't think I would've made it through any of it without him."

"You should see the guy we have cast as Seb. Hot doesn't even begin to describe it." She smirks. "I have a strict rule

16

about not dating co-stars. It's going to be a struggle this time around."

She giggles like a teenager and for a moment it feels like we've known each other for years and all we're doing is gossiping about the fittest boy in school.

I allow my fingers to trail the yellowing leaves of a bush as we climb up the hill. With the bright sun overhead, I almost feel like it's summer again, and unzip my jacket. My boots dampen with the dew of the grass. Jess helps me as we scramble up a few rocks and find a nice spot to sit.

"I don't want to give Isabel too much power over me," I say finally. "But the truth is, she's still here. She's in my head. My dreams. I think about her far too often."

"I can imagine."

"I see her hurting my son every time I close my eyes."

"Tom?"

"Yes."

She nods.

We're silent for a while until Jess breaks that silence.

"I want you to know that I understand elements of what you're going through. Not in the same way. God, I would never claim that, but I went through things as a child that have forever changed me. And, yes, I still see his face when I close my eyes. I still feel the same pain."

"You do?"

She nods her head. "PTSD is a bitch."

"I'm so sorry."

"It's the reason why I wanted this part. I fought to get it. Neal wanted Anna Young from Seattle Stories, but I threw in my name and basically pestered him until I got the part."

"Anna Young? She's American, isn't she?"

"Her London accent was terrible, apparently. Otherwise I might not be talking to you now." She laughs.

"Did she go full cockney?"

She laughs again. "Yes, *full* cockney."

"I need to make a confession," I say, after we've stopped laughing at Anna Young's accent.

"Go on then."

I pick up a stone and bounce it on the heel of my hand. "I'm not happy about the movie." The stone drops to the ground and begins to roll down the hill. "Honestly, I think it's too soon. Far too soon. Decades too soon. This is going to feed Isabel's ego, and believe me, it's big enough already."

"I swear, I wouldn't be on board unless Neal had promised to be responsible about the way he's telling this story."

"No, you don't understand. Isabel isn't simply dangerous, she's incredibly intelligent. She's escaped one secure institution." I grimace, trying not to dwell on the fact. "She can manipulate or ingratiate herself to make people help her. You have no idea what she's capable of, no one does, not truly."

Jess nods. "I get it. But she's in prison now, and she can't escape prison. No one escapes maximum security."

Not without help, I think. Not without manipulating someone until they make a mistake. I was the one who made the mistake before, and it resulted in even more murders. My stomach turns and I try not to let my thoughts dwell on the lives taken.

But maybe Jess is right. Isabel is in a women's prison and she's one of the only Category A prisoners. She was even segregated for a long time, due to her numerous suicide attempts. I know that, in theory, there's no way she could possibly escape. But I also know how resourceful she is. How persistent. How patient.

"I think this film is irresponsible," I continue. "I said as much in an email to Neal, and it's why it's taken so long for me to agree to meet with you. But that doesn't mean I won't meet with you again. I, umm... I guess curiosity got the best of me."

"It gets the best of the best of us," she says with a laugh. "Look, remember that you're *here* and she's in prison. You survived. You're much stronger than you think you are."

I want to believe her.

2

ISABEL

"Fielding?"

5am and there's Rick the Dick yelling through the door, banging his skinny hand against the metal. I roll over in bed like I'm supposed to do, to show them that I haven't died in the night. Every single one of us has to do this at 5am and 6am. The 6am roll call is because of changeover. The night staff go, and the day staff arrive. Prison is almost as boring as Crowmont Hospital, but at least the inmates come up with wicked nicknames for the guards here.

Rick the Dick is the kind of long, thin man who leans over you and breathes coffee breath in your face when he talks. He's the sort who'll try to be your mate. Fat Jan isn't that sort. No, she's forever on guard, one hand perpetually hovering above her walkie-talkie like it's a gun. Then there's Gabby-zilla, Fat Elvis and Fiona Forehead. They're the main crew who never leave. Others come and go before the prisoners can think up a new nickname.

When the screws – yes, I'm truly one of the inmates now, even using the lingo – are satisfied with roll call, our doors are unlocked at 7:45. Breakfast is one slice of bread and butter.

Everyone here is fucking starving, that's why they all eat dehydrated noodles for breakfast.

I shuffle out of my cell and head down to the kitchen, receiving my toast and butter while Fat Jan watches me from the other side of the room. I see her pencilled eyebrows wherever I go.

"How are you today, Miss?" I ask her. The inmates seem to have adopted a schoolroom mentality towards the guards. When we're being polite, it's "Miss".

"Can't complain. Did you sleep okay?"

I sometimes wonder whether Jan has been tasked with keeping an eye on me herself, the way she follows me around with that sour look on her face, her back always straight, her large breasts poking forwards.

"That mattress is a torture device," I say. "Any chance of a new one?"

"I'll find out for you."

"Thanks, Miss."

"It's your big day today isn't it?"

I nod my head and smile. Then I finger the rosary around my neck.

"Well, hope it goes well for you," she says with a stiff nod.

"Thanks, Miss. I'm a bit nervous to be honest."

"I'm positive it'll be fine."

"Yeah, it's a big deal though, isn't it? It's not every day that you accept Jesus Christ and absolve of your sins."

Jan glances away when I say that. I can see the way her stomach flipped at the thought of my "sins". "I hope it goes well for you, Isabel," she repeats, her tone implying she hopes no such thing.

"Don't worry, I know it doesn't absolve me of everything. But it helps me see that what I did was evil. I don't want to be evil anymore, Miss."

"That's good, Isabel." She edges away from me, backing away like prey suddenly aware of the hunter before them.

"See you later then, Miss," I say brightly, making my way back to my cell with the toast. It's best not to leave the cell alone for too long when the inmates are milling around. Things get stolen all the time. Back inside my tiny room, I sit down on the mattress and wait, knowing I won't be alone for long.

It's Genna with a G who comes in without asking. But I suppose we've come to some sort of comfortable arrangement in that way. We've been cell neighbours since I came out of the segregation unit six months ago, which she wasn't happy about at first. No one wanted to be near the magpie murderer. According to the rumours, she's psycho.

"Got any noodles?" she asks, scratching her upper arms and pacing back and forth.

"On the shelf," I nod.

"Thanks." It comes out "fanks". "You all right?" She doesn't give me a chance to answer. "I'm right nervous. Can't believe it's come 'round so fast." She shakes her head and the greasy hair around her shoulders ripples back and forth.

Genna and I are being baptised together. It was her who told me about the chaplain and how she made a lot of sense. After going with her to the chapel to pray, I found that I had to agree. Genna is a drug addict. Believing in a higher power has some weight over her decision as to whether to take drugs again or not.

The problem is, her addiction is still the most powerful force in her world, and all she's done now is add an extra layer of guilt to her life.

"It'll be fine," I say. "Chaplain Ari will be there to help us. She'll tell us what to say and when to say it."

She sniffs and scratches her chin. "I know, but, right.

When I was four, I pissed myself in front of assembly, so I don't like this public talking thing."

"Well, I'll go first if you like."

"All right then, yeah. All right. That's better. What time is it again?"

"2pm." I take a bite out of my toast. She's asked me this five times in the last two days. "You know that."

She shakes her head again and then crumples the packet of noodles in her hands. "I know." Her eyes roam over the walls of my cell. "New picture?" She nods to a pastoral of a farm nestled in a valley.

"I did it yesterday in art therapy."

"Not bad. You should sell 'em."

"No, that's okay. I send some of them to my mum."

She grimaces. "What do you want to send them to that cow for? It's not like she visits you."

It's sweet that Genna with a G seems to like "having my back" but at the same time I don't quite understand why. Still, I can't suppress the smile her words ignite.

"At least it keeps me busy," I say, broadening that smile.

"It's the boredom, innit? Gets to ya."

"Are you craving, Genna?"

She nods her head too many times. "It's this fucking chris-tening, innit? How am I 'sposed to get through the fucking thing without a fix?"

"Do you want more noodles, Genna?"

She pauses, sniffs again. "Yeah, all right."

"Take what you need."

"All right, well. You're rich so it don't matter that much I guess."

"It's our secret, Genna. Remember that."

"Sure." But her eyes are glazed, staring at the packets of noodles. She isn't hungry, but she knows they can be used as currency in this prison. Money, noodles, cigarettes, chocolate. All can be exchanged for drugs.

"See you later, Genna."

She grabs as many packets as she can carry and hurries out of the cell. I finish my toast and pick up a book to read until it's time to go to work.

We have pointless jobs inside the prison. Some people work in the kitchen, others cultivate a vegetable patch, some even take care of a chicken coop on the grounds, but I'm a cleaner. The screws don't want me around knives. My weapon these days is a mop and bucket.

When the unit starts to come alive outside my cell, I know it's time to get moving. I leave my room, make my way along the corridors and watch people as they recognise friends from other units passing them along the way. Backs are slapped, cheeks are kissed, voices squeal in delight. None of these people want to leave because all their friends are here. They feel safe here, where they have a routine and know where their next meal is coming from. I'm the only thorn in their side, one of the few female serial killers locked up for life, a dangerous anomaly in their life of security.

"Keep it moving ladies." Today the screw watching us is a tall, skinny young man. Not Rick the Dick. I forget his name, but he's a try hard, and the inmates don't respect him. I see the side-eyes and chuckles directed at him as he makes his way through the prison. Soon he'll be potted and then he'll probably transfer.

Potting is not an activity that I take part in. Let it be known that I, Isabel Fielding, take umbrage at the disgusting practice where a guard is showered with collected urine, usually kept in a bottle or a bucket. Prisoners work together on this, blocking a CCTV camera, distracting the guards, and luring one away for the ambush. Then someone will throw the urine over their faces. Last time Genna with a G asked me to help and I outright refused. But, however disgusting I find the practice, I do applaud the ingenuity of the operation.

The day goes by quickly. I mop the floors, working rhythmically, mind elsewhere, on more important things. Owen sent me a letter when I was first brought here. Keep your head down and do what you're told, was the gist. He said that they'll hate me. They'll never trust me. But truth be told, I don't need trust.

Lunch is a basic sandwich, eaten with a considerably calmer Genna, who shares some noodles with me as a thank you. And afterwards, we make our way to the chapel.

"Look out, Fat Jan's about," Genna says with a giggle.

The most potted of all the guards, and yet she's still here, still throwing her weight around like the OG of the prison system. Genna taught me the term "OG".

"Fat Jan on the prowl, nothing but a foul growl," she adds, in a strange rap-like voice. Then she laughs again.

"I think maybe you need to get it together, Genna." I hiss. How did the task of keeping Genna lucid fall to me? I stare at the rest of the group stumbling into the chapel like zombies and see no one who could help.

"You're right," she says, slurring slightly. "Sorry, Izza."

I grind my teeth together. Of all the ways to shorten my name, which is a perfectly adequate name to begin with, she's chosen *Izza*.

"I'll be all right. You know me," she says. "You know me."

We walk up the aisle between the pews like two brides, or two mourners, I can't decide which is most apt. In front of us is the cross, built out of simple wood. No intricate carvings or depictions of bible characters. I find that I can't keep my eyes away from it, that it holds some sort of control over me. Symbols hold a special kind of power and this one suggests numerous topics. Life. Death. Resurrection. Guilt. Sins. Absolution. Atonement. The sight of it makes me meditative and, for the first time in a while, my thoughts drift back to Leah and the expression on her face when I told her the story of how I found out my father was a serial killer, the way she leaned into my cell at Crowmont Hospital, with pity all over her face. The sadness of it all.

Someone sent me a book through the post, but according to Jan, the sender remained anonymous. The book is about a drug addict trying hard to get clean. He slips, gets high, sells drugs to a teenage girl who ODs and dies. He feels so guilty that he almost kills himself. Later, he saves the life of the teenage girl's orphaned daughter and afterwards he spends the rest of his life doing good deeds to atone, even though he doesn't quite find peace. The addiction is always there to nag at him no matter what he does. When he wakes up in the morning, his first thought is always about drugs.

Will I have the impulse to kill all of my life? Or can I stop it?

I look around at the people in the room. I could steal a knife, or fashion one, and go to town in this room on these people. How many of them could I stab before I'm restrained? How many lives could I take? There's no death penalty in this country, I'd simply be kept in the segregation unit, probably for the rest of my life. But realistically how many could I kill? Three? Four? Five?

We take the nearest pew to the altar. My heart is fluttering in my rib cage, and it seems to me as though the chapel is filled with blood. Genna chews on the inside of her cheek and I nudge her with my elbow. We begin to sing.

Soon I'll say the words. I'll repent all my evil acts and promise to walk in the light. I'll begin to atone.

3
LEAH

Alison Finlay, the murdered woman, lays below me on the grass, her blood barely visible in the night. My hands are dirty with it, or it could be mud, I'm not sure. The ground is damp, my bare feet are wet. The knife lies nestled amongst the reeds of grass, its metallic edge finding a thin sliver of moonlight. Then a cloud drifts across the sky and the moon turns as black as the blood.

"Come away now, sis."

I turn my head to the left to see Tom's pale hand reaching for me in the darkness. Part of me wants to grasp it and pull him to me, but then I see the second person at his side. She's smaller than him, around my height, and there's no shock or fear on her face, merely a blank expression. Eyes as wide as I remember. A pleasantness to the shape of her mouth, as though she's about to tell me a sweet secret. Isabel. With her hand entwined with Tom's. But what I don't understand, is why.

I wake gasping for air, the sour tang of sweat lingering around me like vapour, the back of my neck still damp. Seb snores away, blissfully unaware of my tumultuous thoughts, missing the way my chest heaves up and down as I catch my breath. *Blood and mud mingled, the smell of rust, the light of the moon fading, and Tom and Isabel watching...* Pushing myself up against the pillow, I rest back against the headboard and massage my temples, trying to rub away the memory of the nightmare. The imprint it left on me. But I already know that this one is going to linger.

At least Seb is here. And, truly, I can't blame him for not waking. The man has been working himself so hard that sleep is more like a collapse in exhaustion at the end of the day. Transitioning from a working farm to events management is taking him every waking hour and he sleeps like the dead now. Not even my tossing and turning can disturb him.

The day had may as well commence, the dream was nothing but a dream, and I can't allow it to get to me. I get out of bed and walk slowly on stiff legs to the kitchen. Recently, I've often been waking to find my calf muscles cramped up, like I've slept in a curled-up position, tense as a coiled spring. I hobble into the kitchen and grab the pill bottles from the kitchen counter, swallowing down my daily cocktail with a tall glass of water. They may stop me from hallucinating, but they do nothing for the dreams that haunt me each night.

At 5am on a chilly October morning, the light outside is still as dark as midnight. Soon Seb's alarm will vibrate through the ceiling. I've mostly learned to adjust to a farmer's routine, but my stomach gurgles and complains about being up so early. I pour another glass of water and then grab some bread for the toaster.

Jess is visiting again today. I said we'd walk to the farm-house where Isabel tried to torture and kill me, which hadn't seemed so bad on the phone. Now, after the nightmare, even thinking about it makes the scars on my back itch. I remember sleeping on my belly for over a week while the scars healed. The swoop of the wings she carved into my flesh. I think of the way Seb runs his fingers along them, plants small kisses on them, softly telling me to retake the power from Isabel, to own those scars. Wear them. Be proud. Even Jess reminded me of how I survived. I'm out here, living freely amongst the beauty of the countryside, while Isabel is trapped in prison. But those thoughts don't make me feel any better.

The toast is buttered by the time Seb comes downstairs, and we eat quickly and quietly together. He kisses me before he leaves and stares deeply into my eyes, checking for any cracks. I nestle my head in his neck and whisper that I'm okay. And then he's gone, because we both know that he can't be with me every hour of the day. If I'm going to move on from my nightmares, the healing must come from within.

At least I have plans to see Jess again. It's been over a week since we last met and I felt a connection with her that took me by surprise. It's been a while since I made a friend. Hutton village isn't always the most welcoming place, especially for the nurse who accidentally released a serial killer into the world. I haven't made friends since being in Clifton. Even though I exchange emails with Mark, I haven't seen him since George's funeral.

The tears come on suddenly, and I find myself gripping the counter, bent over the sink, tears dropping onto the porcelain. And as soon as they come, I wipe them away, clear my throat and start tidying up the breakfast dishes.

These short, sharp moments of grief happen almost every day. Sometimes I cry for George, who died not long after finding new family members to love, other times I cry for James Gorden and Alison Finlay and everyone else who died because I made a terrible mistake, and sometimes I even cry for Isabel, who was failed a long time ago by the people who should have given her a happy, healthy childhood. But I always cry for Tom, and I always cry for me.

* * *

Jess arrives before lunch, dressed in a wax overcoat and rubber boots. I whip up some ham sandwiches to take with us. She has an aluminium bottle filled with water that makes a strange shushing sound when she unscrews the cap.

She picks up fallen leaves as we walk, takes pictures of the spider webs on the trees, the dew on the grass, feathers caught on barbed wire.

"I know it's super pretentious," she says. "But it gives me a lasting reminder of what this place is like. The feel of it. The soul of it."

"That's a magpie feather," I tell her. "I can't stand the sight of them anymore." I think about Tom with the feather in his back pocket. The dead magpie he tried to "save" and how strange all of that was. Then my mind drifts back to my dream, where Tom and Isabel were hand in hand, staring down at Alison Finlay's lifeless body. A shiver runs down my spine.

"Are you all right?" Jess leans over and places a hand on my shoulder, her eyebrows pulled together in concern.

"It's been a while since I came here, to the farmhouse. I haven't faced it for a long time."

"I'm so sorry," she says. "Maybe we can go back. Perhaps this is too soon."

"No," I reply, her concern lighting a fire of stubbornness, that I can do this, that I won't allow Isabel to ruin my life. "Come on. Let's go."

She nods, and we set off up the hill, tracing my footsteps back to that place.

"I don't remember the direction I ran away from the old house," I say. "It was so dark that I couldn't see anything. Most of the time, I knew I wasn't on the path. I could feel the uneven surface underfoot."

"You were naked."

"Pretty much, yeah. Covered in blood. Tom had stabbed David Fielding, killing him, and I was wearing his jacket. I had a mixture of mine and David's blood all over my body. God, I must have looked a sight." I shake my head, continuing slowly. "We were running away from the farmhouse. I thought she was unconscious but then I heard her, calling my name in her sing-song voice."

Jess lets out a long breath. "Jesus."

"We fought. I remember so much of it. I thought I would forget, but I didn't. I remember stabbing the knife into her thigh, the way we kicked and hit each other. She taunted me. Said I wasn't a killer."

Jess's face pales. She stares out at the moors, no doubt imagining the tussle.

"I told you, she's dangerous. She looks like a slip of a thing, like butter wouldn't melt. But inside, she's dark and twisted up."

"Do you hate her?" she asks.

My fingers wrap around the sleeve of my jacket and I twist it inside my fist. "Yes."

That moment in the cave, when I'd already stabbed her in the neck, and then I pushed her head under the water, feeling her thrashing body as she almost drowned. It was a moment I'll never forget. Jess is quiet for a few moments, and when I pull myself back from my thoughts, I understand why. I'd started walking faster and she was struggling to keep up with me. I slowed and allowed her to catch up.

"Sorry," I say. "I've grown so accustomed to these hills that I can storm up them now."

She laughs. "I guess I need to hit the gym."

During the last few minutes of the walk, we idly talk about how directors often ask for actors to lose weight before a role. "It's never a character choice," she says. "They just want you to look fuckable from every angle." One casting agent even told Jess that she should get a boob job because her "tits were saggy".

"I was eighteen years old," she says. "They weren't saggy, they were real."

That conversation brought us to the abandoned building, and I was glad for the distraction, because the enormity of it could have caused me to turn away and go back. Instead I stand up straight and face it without wanting to run away. My legs feel strong, like I could walk all over the grounds of it and barely tremble. But at the same time, the cold nips at my exposed skin here. I wrap my arms around my body.

"I got lucky that night," I say, as we slowly enter the crumbling building. I take her into the same room where Isabel tied me up and started to torture me in front of Tom. "If the pulley system they'd rigged hadn't pulled down part of the ceiling, I never would've escaped. And Tom wouldn't have made it out of David's grip to help me."

Jess takes a step into the centre of the room and stares up at the ceiling. She circles the room, taking in every detail.

"Do you mind if I take some photos?"

"No, go for it."

I force myself to watch her rather than let my mind wander back to that night. Jess's presence is a comfort in a place where such a terrible thing occurred. If I allow it, I think about Tom's scared face. The warm blood on my back.

When Jess is done taking photos she walks over and pulls

me into a hug. It's a welcome gift. The gift of warmth in a cold, cold place.

"I'm surprised Seb's family haven't knocked it down," she says as we make our way out of the building.

"There is a plan to do exactly that, but they've been too busy to arrange it recently. Meanwhile, we keep getting serial killer fanatics coming here to spend the night and post updates on Instagram."

Jess shakes her head. "People."

"If the place collapses on them, they'll no doubt sue the Braithwaites. Or try to. Josh comes up to throw them out most weekends."

Jess sighs. "They're scummy, don't get me wrong. But I kind of get it." She lifts her arms and looks up at the ceiling. "There's a weight to this place. The air crackles."

I roll my head from one shoulder to the other, trying to suppress a shiver. And we begin to make our way out. "If nothing terrible had happened here, it'd be nothing more than another broken-down building in the countryside."

She nods.

I take a deep breath when we emerge from the old building, enjoying the sight of the stretching moor, the hint of the Braithwaite's farm in the distance. "I'm glad we came."

"Yeah?"

"I have another memory of this place now. A better one."

Jess grins. "I'm so glad." She picks up a stone from the perimeter and slips it into her bag, then takes a gulp of water. "Have you had anymore thoughts about the movie? I can take any feedback to Neal."

I mull this over for a moment. "No, I still feel the same way."

"They've cast Tom now," she says.

My eyebrows raise. "Have they?"

"A fantastic young actor. He'll do a great job. Your son's legacy is going to be protected."

I close my eyes for a moment, wishing I hadn't told Neal about my past, but I felt it had to be represented if the film was going to be made. But I need to tell Tom before the movie comes out. I need to warn him, and I have no idea where he is. Not even DCI Murphy has been able to locate him. After sifting through sightings of young men with a birthmark, nothing came up. It's never the right young man with a birthmark.

"This is kind of awkward," she says, "but I need to tell you. We're going to start filming in three weeks. As soon as Freddy, the actor cast to play Tom, feels comfortable with the accent and the part. We're good to go."

I shove my hands deep down into my pockets, stretching the interior fabric of my coat. "Okay."

"I know you don't feel great about it, but I swear we're going to do right by your family. I swear it."

I have no doubt that she means it, and that her heart is in the right place. But ultimately, I'm not too naïve to know that the decision isn't in her hands.

4
ISABEL

"You're looking skinny, Fielding," Jan observes.

I suppress the desire to roll my eyes, and make a retort about her own weight, but instead I wonder what my father would have made of her. He hated those people with a modicum of power who thought they ran the world. The ones who have a jauntiness to their walk. Cocksure, chin high, nose up in the air. He wouldn't have killed Jan, because too many people would notice her disappearance, but he would have hated her. He would have imagined what it was like to take her life and then use that hatred on a poor homeless prostitute somewhere.

"Thank you," I say, suppressing all of those thoughts. "A few of the girls showed me a new work out."

"Oh, is that right? Well, it's clearly working." She shuffles some papers in her hands, still standing outside the cell. Screws don't come into the cell unless they have to. "You've got post, today. Lucky you. Is it your birthday?"

"No."

"Well, it seems that someone has sent you a card." She tosses the envelope onto the mattress.

It's been opened and the contents have been checked. Usually, when I get post, it's money from my mother. There's rarely a note, but if there is, it's particularly impersonal. There are no expressions of love or any kind of feeling, but she can't help but send me money even though I'm the devil child.

"Thanks, Miss," I say as she leaves.

As soon as she's gone, I remove the card from the envelope. The artwork on the cover is pretty. Three magpies on a telephone wire. *Three for a Girl*. Perhaps I'm the girl in question. Magpies, the tricksters. The squawkers. The thieves. The birds that feast on the eggs of smaller, less powerful birds. But also, a bird that represents friendship and loyalty. One of the most beautiful birds, in my opinion. Immediately, my mind goes back to Pepsi. My only friend for so long.

I open the card.

To my darling big sis,

I saw this card and thought of you. Remember when we went to that big estate mansion in North Yorkshire? There were magpies all along the branches of that old Oak tree. You were eleven, I think, and you tried to count all the birds with me. But I couldn't count them all because I was too young. Then Daddy told us to shut up and Mummy took a swig from her "special flask".

Do you remember the garden with the maze? I bet you don't, because you have a crappy memory. Well, I may have been young, but I remember all about it. Like how it was your birthday and you begged Daddy to go. I remember how you got lost and I had to show you the way. You kept going west, because you didn't understand where the sun would be in the afternoon, but I reminded you that we needed to go east. There were clues in the hedges.

I miss you, big sis. I'm glad I'm out, but the world feels like a mighty stranger without you. No one else understands how effed up the Fieldings are, do they?

Well, I'll come and visit you soon.

Stay east, sis.

Your little brother,
Owen

I pocket the twenty-pound note included and place the card on the tiny shelf beneath the barred window. There, now I can pretend that I can see the birds outside. Hear their song. I breathe deeply in, close my eyes and walk around Owen's maze, following it east, nodding my head as I understand his words.

"Helloooo."

With a sigh, I open my eyes to find Genna with a G standing in my cell, hands on her hips, greasy hair pulled into a high bun. The slick of that hair turns my stomach, and the sight of her neon pink scrunchie makes me want to grind my teeth. But we're "Baptism Buddies" and I'm not supposed to be imagining my fist connecting with her nose.

"You asleep, Izza?"

I shake my head. "What can I do for you, Genna?"

She begins to pace up and down the cell, ranting about Tina, a girl from another unit who has a beef with her. I can tell she's craving drugs, probably going through withdrawals after the last time she took them. Her energy is exhausting to watch. Her body moves jerkily, her hands clench and unclench. Every now and then she turns to me, arms passionately flailing, and I nod, pretending to listen, almost completely in Owen's maze, listening to the squawk of the magpies.

"Thing is, right, I owe her. And I haven't got nothing to give her, 'ave I?"

"Which is where I come in," I say.

She stops her pacing and stands before me, completely still, arms dangling at her sides like two floppy sausages.

"We're mates, aren't we, Izza?"

I resist gagging at the sound of my nickname. "Yes."

"Can you lend me a little something? Enough to pay off that bitch and buy a bit of Spice for later. I'm struggling, Izza, I am." Her eyes flood with tears and for a moment I think that maybe Genna is more dangerous than I give her credit for. She's always reminded me of Chloe, with the same weaknesses and the same ability to be led, but Genna has ways to manipulate back. The only thing is, she doesn't realise she's in a much larger game than she anticipated.

I roll up the sleeves of my hoody, pretending to think about her suggestion. "The problem is, Genna. You already owe me quite a lot."

She falters, begins to stumble over her words. "Oh... well, I know. I know I do, but—"

"But this time you'll pay me back? You haven't paid Tina back yet."

She takes a step towards me. "Please, Izza. She'll get me somehow; I know she will. She's tough."

"Tougher than me?"

A flicker passes over Genna's face. For the first time since we became friends, Genna looks afraid. The tears stop falling from her eyes, but her mouth contorts into a grimace. Now she remembers who I am and what I'm capable of. Exactly when I need her to.

"N... no. That's not what I—"

I stand up and watch her cower away from me. If I'm honest it's quite ridiculous because I'm smaller than ever, thanks to the prison diet.

"There's a way we can straighten all this out," I say.

Genna lets out a long, slow breath. "Whatever you want, Izza."

I want you to stop calling me that ridiculous nickname. I keep the words in my mind rather than blurting them out. Yes, I want her afraid, but I also want her to believe that our friendship is real.

"I don't want you to suffer, Genna. You're my friend. I can lend you whatever you need, you know that."

She laughs, but it doesn't sound like a genuine laugh. It's too high-pitched and breathy. "Why didn't you say that then?"

"Well, the thing is, I need a favour."

Genna pulls the sleeve of her jumper over her fingers and worries at the fabric. I see the loose threads that have been pulled out already. The ladder-like snags that are worming their way up the cloth.

"What kind of favour?"

"Chill, Genna, okay? It's nothing big. All I need is for you to find a few friends that might be able to help me out with a small request." I lift my fingers to the rosary around my neck and count the beads between thumb and forefinger.

"Wh-what are you planning?"

"Honestly, it's nothing to worry about." I placate her with the wave of my hand.

"Okay."

I reach into my pocket and hand her the twenty. "There's more where this came from. Tell that to your friends, too."

She snatches the money from my hands. But before she can go, I grasp her by the shoulder, tightening my fingers around her bones. If I bit into her neck, could I draw blood?

"There's something important that I have to tell you."

She nods. "Tell me then."

"No snitches. No rats. Loyal people only."

She nods again, her chin wobbling as she tries to hold back tears, genuine tears this time. I can see how she now knows she's managed to get herself much deeper into trouble than she intended.

"What's the name of your mate on D unit who feeds the prison chickens?"

"Sharon."

"Is she loyal?"

"She hates the screws as much as the rest of us. She can be trusted." Genna pauses. "If she has an incentive to be loyal."

"She'll get money," I say.

"Then, yes, she's loyal."

"She has access to the tool shed, right? For chicken coop maintenance?"

Genna nods. "The screws trust her to a point. But they count the tools at the end of the day."

"All right. Thanks, Genna. I'll be in touch. You can take some noodles on the way out."

A hiss of air comes out through her teeth as she shrinks away from me. Like the stale air of a pierced balloon.

I watch her leave, and then I take a sheet of paper to compose my own letter to Owen.

5

LEAH

Tom is twenty now, and I haven't seen him for over two years. A lot can change a person in that amount of time. I can't help but wonder whether he's lost the baby fat around his face, whether he's eating well and still working out, if he has friends, someone to take care of him when he's lonely. What music does he listen to now? Does he still wear those black t-shirts and skinny jeans?

The way we left each other is a constant source of pain to me. Being in that hospital, my body broken and weak, waiting for him to visit. The pain in my abdomen was nothing compared to the ache in my body that craved the sight of his face, the comfort of his presence. And then the realisation hits that he's left me without even contacting me to let me know he's okay. No Christmas cards. No birthday cards. Nothing.

But I can't bring myself to be angry with him for what he's done. Do I even blame him? He found out that his entire life has been a lie. He found out that he was born from incest. From a place of abuse. What did that do to him? I can't help but wonder whether that changed a fundamental part of who

41

he is. If those things had been forced on me all at once, wouldn't I want to escape, too?

I glance down at the piece of paper in my hands and consider all of this. Of what he's been through, of how much he must have grown since I last saw him, and of how seeing me might bring back a lot of the pain he probably wants to escape. If he wants to be left alone, should I respect his wishes? Over the last two years I've been checking in with DCI Murphy every week to see if there are any leads on where he might be. I thought he might turn up at Isabel's sentencing, but he didn't. Luckily, Isabel pled guilty, which meant that he wasn't required to give evidence, because I'm not convinced he would have come.

And now, DCI Murphy has finally found information that feels real. I hold the details in my hand. This is the first one that excites me. There have been sightings of men his age with a birthmark, but the physical description never quite matched. They were either too tall or too short, hair or eyes a different colour. As expected, after further investigation, it wasn't Tom. This time, however, Murphy sent me a picture from a CCTV camera, and it's definitely him. I have the address scribbled down on this scrap of paper. A few hours away in Newcastle.

But there's a chance that if I contact him, I'll make things worse for both of us. I place the paper down on the coffee table and back away, like it has an infectious disease smeared all over it. As though it's a bomb. I suppose there is an incendiary quality to the address. Contacting Tom could change the way he feels about me, either for the better or worse.

Later in the day, after Seb is finished at the farm, I show him the address and we talk about what to do next. We sit down for a dinner of lamb stew and talk about my long-lost son between mouthfuls, as though this is a perfectly normal topic of conversation for a couple. *Hi, honey, how was your day? Well, I got a lead on where my missing twenty-year-old son is. But he might not want to see me because I remind him of how he was conceived, and the fact that we've both been tortured by a serial killer. Great stuff.*

Seb mops up some gravy with a chunk of floury bread. "Is there a reason why you're hesitating?"

"Murphy keeps reminding me that Tom is twenty and old enough to live on his own. But now that I know where he is, I need to see him, but..." I can't find the words to express the situation.

"There's something you're not saying," Seb prompts. His eyes are so penetrating that it takes me a moment to exhale and tell him what's truly on my mind.

"What if Tom is happier without me?" I say, releasing what has been kept buried for a long time.

When I glance down at my plate, I see the stew is beginning to congeal along the surface. I've barely touched it and now it's going cold.

"What if he's miserable without you?" Seb counters.

"He wanted to get away from me."

"And I think deep down he probably regrets that. You've both experienced the kind of pain that no one else on the planet understands. I don't, and I never can, because Isabel never tortured me."

The blood drains from my face and Seb leans across the table to wrap his hand over mine.

"You feel like you don't understand what I went through?" I say quietly.

"No." He squeezes my hand. "I mean yes. What I mean is, I wasn't there that night. I didn't feel Isabel's knife or fight her father. I'm not the one she stabbed." He grimaces, as though he's in pain and a ripple of tension passes along his jaw. All of the pain is there. All the anger, too. "I wish I'd been there, more than anything I wish that, but I wasn't. And while I will forever listen to you and be here for you, Tom is the only person who was *actually* there."

Except for Isabel, I think.

"Tom must feel the same about the night in the farmhouse and the night in the caves. I think you should reach out to him. He left because he was in pain, not because he'd moved on."

"Oh, wow. You should talk like this much more often." I squeeze his hand back, allowing my fingers to then trail over his, enjoying the rough skin of his hands, staring into his thoughtful eyes that draw me into him.

"Why don't we go next weekend? I'll take the day off from the farm and we'll go together."

"All right." I suck in a deep breath. A week will allow me to straighten out my conflicting thoughts, to calm the nerves worrying my stomach.

He gets up, walks around the table and pulls me into his arms. Everything seems much clearer when Seb is around.

* * *

I wake with stones beneath the soft flesh of my face. Almost immediately, I feel the sore rawness of cuts and scrapes on my skin. When I pull myself up from the ground, I examine my arms and legs to find grazes all down them. The soles of my feet are dirty and bruised. And then Seb's panicked voice calls my name.

When I stand, I notice that my nightgown is torn. There's dirt all along the hem, smeared across the sleeve where I laid in the dirt. It takes three attempts to call back to Seb, my throat is so dry. But then his boots scuff against the crumbling concrete and his bulk comes into view.

"Leah, oh my God, I was so worried." He pulls off his jacket and wraps it around my shoulders.

"Did I sleepwalk?" My eyes roam the ruined farmhouse. "It's happening again." I don't say what I'm thinking, that this is the beginning of a slippery slope to insanity. That what is real and what isn't begins to blur, like everything is a nightmare.

Seb pulls me into his arms and strokes my hair to keep me calm, but for some reason it doesn't work this time. No, I don't want to be saved by him because my brain refuses to behave. What I want is to be normal. To not need to be comforted every time my brain has a meltdown, or I sleepwalk onto the moors, or I hallucinate insects crawling around the house.

"Come on, let's get going," he says, helping me take my first steps on my sore feet.

My arm slips into his. I try not to look at the room as we go, but all I can see is Tom caught in David Fielding's grip. Tom hand in hand with Isabel. No, wait, that bit wasn't real, that was a dream. See? It's happening already. I'm losing touch with what's real. The prescription is supposed to stop all of this.

"What's happening to me?" I mumble.

Seb feels the tension in my body. "It's okay, this is a blip. An anomaly. I bet finding out Tom's real address has unbalanced you a bit, that's all. We'll make an appointment with the doctor, all right?"

When he sees me wince at the pain each step brings, he picks me up and carries me home.

* * *

45

A night of sleepwalking never gives me adequate rest, and I end up curling up on an armchair to nap for a few hours. This time, when I wake, my cheek rests on my hand, and there's a cold cup of tea sitting next to a note on the coffee table.

Rest up, sweet. I'm nipping to the farm but will text you later.

I smile at the note and then carry the tea into the kitchen to pour out. I check my phone on the way, and there's a text from Seb, as I thought there might be. But there's also a missed call from Jess. I fire off a reply to Seb before jumping in the shower, wondering why Jess had called. We've already arranged to meet for another walk in a few days. This time, however, we won't be going back to the farmhouse. My lofty ideas of the trip there helping me to heal didn't work in the end. What I actually did was make myself worse.

"At least you're not hallucinating," I remind myself, before realising I'm talking to myself.

After the shower I check my feet and try standing on them. Now that the cuts have been washed, and the tiny stones washed away, they aren't quite as sore, but I quickly bandage them and then put on my thickest, most cushioned socks before going back downstairs to make some toast. While the bread is browning, I return Jess's call, but get her voice-mail instead. Perhaps she'll contact me later if it's urgent, though I can't imagine how it could be urgent.

The sleepwalking has put a different spin on my relationship with Jess. Perhaps the imminent filming of the movie has dredged up some strange latent feelings. That, along with finding Tom's address, is probably why I ended up at the old farmhouse last night. I chew on my thumbnail, willing my mind to stop dwelling on my nightmares. But when the toast pops, adrenaline surges through me. Annoyed by my own jumpiness, I butter the bread with such aggression that the toast rips apart.

Later, as the day slips into the afternoon, I decide that I can't mope around the cottage all day. Being here alone with bad memories puts me on edge. So, I head down to the farm shop to lend a hand.

It's a beautiful sunny day with the kind of low sun that offers a glow to the trees and fields around me. The leaves are so golden that I take a few quick snaps with my phone and upload them to an anonymous Instagram account I've been using. Most of the time I use it to spy on old school friends, but it's nice to use my creative side, too. That's what I do now, picking the right filter and lining up the composition in the way that I want it. After kicking around a few leaves, I find one that has rotted down to a skeleton and hold it up to the light. Instinctively, I know Jess would like this, so I text her the picture with a message asking if she's all right.

On my way to the shop, I change my mind, and head over to the pumpkin patch instead. There's the grand opening in a few days, and I know Seb will need a hand with the tents and decorations. I'll be helping with pumpkin carving on the day. Donna will be working on the face paints stall. There's even a spooky hall of mirrors coming to the farm with a few actors dressed up as ghosts to scare the children.

Seb's struggling with a plastic gravestone when I arrive, trying to artfully drape a fake cobweb over it.

"Want a hand?"

He tosses me the decoration. "What am I doing with this?"

I separate the strands out to create a thin sheet of cobweb

delicately arranged over the fake stone. Then I place plastic spiders all around it to complete the effect.

Seb's eyebrows shoot up. "I hope that plastic doesn't end up in the field."

"They're held on pretty well," I say. "I don't think they'll blow away."

He makes a *harrumph* sound and his shoulders sag.

"What's wrong?" I ask, immediately regretting it when I see his face turn red. Since living with Seb I've come to see the warning signs when he's about to rant. I turn slightly away so that I can start on the next gravestone.

Seb fails to pick up on my body language and launches into his rant. "What's wrong? I'm arranging what used to be grazing for a dairy herd with plastic spiders and a fake gravestone for Mr. P. Mortem. This is a joke. We'd may as well sell the place and be done with it."

"What's that, Sebastian?"

The sound of his mother's voice prompts me to concentrate even harder on my task. Turned away, I hadn't noticed her approach, otherwise I may have quietly sloped away before witnessing yet another argument.

"Oh, hello, Leah," she says, in an almost dismissive way. "Didn't see you there."

I raise a hand, sheepishly, before going back to the plastic spiders. I know better than to get into the middle of a conflict between the Braithwaites.

"You've been complaining about this all day," Donna says to Seb, arms folded, feet planted far apart, like two tree trunks that have been there an age. Her voice begins quite calm and rises with each sentence until she's near shouting. "Never stops. I'm starting to think you don't want to make any money. Or contribute to the village. What's wrong with making a little money and giving the kids a fun day out? Want us to sell the farm instead? Is that it?"

"No, Mam." Seb's head lowers.

"Get on with it then." She yanks a stray clump of cobweb from her jeans and rolls it up between her fingers. Though I'm trying not to stare, I can't help but notice the red flush on her cheeks. The same flush that Seb gets when he rants about what irks him. "You'll be the death of me, you sons. I'll die of frustration, waiting for you to get on with your work without whinging."

"He's taking some time to adjust to the new normal, Donna," I blurt. "You know there've been a lot of changes around here lately. It's going to take some time for—"

Her light grey eyes finally fix on mine and I wish I hadn't said a thing.

"This is a family matter, Leah. You have no idea what it's like to try and keep this farm going, so until you do, I suggest you shut up."

"Mam!" Seb said.

With my eyes down low, I move on to a patch of large pumpkins, arranging them by size.

"It's okay," I say, concentrating on my task. "She's right. I shouldn't have butted in like that."

"Aye, well," Seb continues. "Maybe you should. That's right, Mam."

"Choosing your girlfriend over your mother now?" She lifts and drops her arms in exasperation. "Why am I not surprised?"

And with that she storms off muttering to herself.

"I'm so sorry," I say.

"It's not your fault." Seb smiles thinly, and walks off to help Josh direct a trailer onto the field.

6

ISABEL

Thirty minutes in the cold air. The screws insist we get some vitamin D, even on such a grey, rainy day. I wander over to the wire fence and watch the magpies hop along the perimeter wall, twisting my fingers against the plastic-coated metal, feeling its thickness. The toe of my trainer gropes the bottom edge of it. And then I step away and turn to watch my fellow inmates instead walk around in pointless circles. There's barely any space to do anything else. Others cluster around one of the only benches in the exercise area. I grow bored and lift my face to the sky, allowing the drizzle to hit my skin. For a moment I imagine that it fizzes and hisses like acid rain. Or that it's thick and warm like blood.

When I redirect my attention back to the others, I see Genna pacing up and down with her hands pressed deeply into her pockets. She's only slightly distracting me from the clouds, the way the sun is peeking through at the edges. Somewhere nearby a seagull squawks; migrating south for the colder months. The adventurous, independent seagull. Enjoy your freedom, my friend. Do worthwhile things with it.

"Miss, you got a minute?" I hear Genna say loudly. I turn back to see her moving towards Jan.

The stocky woman approaches her, pencilled eyebrows lifted. "Yes, Genna, what's wrong, love?" All of the screws have a soft spot for Genna. She's the girl with potential, the kind who could have been someone if they'd been born into different circumstances. If the drugs hadn't found her. If she'd received more love as a baby. If. If. If.

"It's my toilet, Miss. It's a mess," Genna continues.

Jan places one hand on her hip. "You mean you've clogged it again. What have you shoved down there now?" Jan asks. "Magazines again?"

One of the other women comes over. Long face, eyes too close together. I think her name might be Topaz or something. "Miss, you got a minute."

I turn away from them both and continue along the perimeter. From there I can see the chicken coop through the wire fence. In D unit, prisoners are generally Category B or below, meaning they get a bit more freedom. They have better jobs, more choices for canteen, and the guards aren't as strict.

"What's the matter now, Crystal?" Jan asks.

Ahh, Crystal, not Topaz. I knew it was some sort of precious stone. I keep walking slowly along the fence, not bothering to look in the direction of the women now crowded around Jan. Behind me, there's the sound of boots scuffing against gravel. I hear the slosh of liquid. Another woman, Sharon, hurries over to me and passes me the cold, metal object, which I find is surprisingly heavy.

"The money is in my cell," I tell her.

Sharon nods, and I notice the hesitation on her face. I lift the wire cutters in a menacing way and whatever hesitation ebbs away to fear. She huddles away from me, missing her opportunity to stop what I'm about to put into motion.

I hear Jan cry out as I drop to my knees and begin my task. Her cries aren't for me, though, they're directed towards the women around her who have now "potted" her for the fifth or sixth time. Poor Jan has had urine splashed in her face once again. The dirty protest of the prisoners provides the distraction I need to break through this fence.

I'm getting out.

Working the wire cutters makes my palms ache. They're old and not as sharp as I would have liked, but I grit my teeth and cut upwards through the thick wires. There. That's enough. My new skinny physique is perfect for fitting through a small hole. Shedding my hoody, I wriggle underneath the wire.

But even now that I'm through, there are more obstacles to overcome and I can't stop even for a second. I'm already on my feet, sprinting as fast as I can, the cutters still in my hand.

East.

Follow the maze east. I use the sun as my guide while my feet speed across the tarmac. My rubber-soled trainers pound the surface almost as hard as my heart pounds against my breastbone. I want to laugh, to lift my head and scream up to the sky, but there's another wire fence to cut. I drop to my knees, work the cutters, going faster this time now that my muscles have loosened up. I wriggle through and am running again.

Behind me I hear yelling, but I daren't look back. Now that I've sprinted away, I can't tell if the shout came from Jan or a different guard. If I've organised this as well as I think I've organised it, the other officers on duty are now restraining the culprits of the potting. But it's the people watching the security cameras that I have to be wary of. Genna promised me that one of her friends was going to block as many cameras in this direction that she could. By either throwing clothes on them or smearing them with shit. But there's no way she could do anything to the perimeter camera. All I can do is move as fast as possible.

My plan was always one that relies on other people. Genna and Sharon for the wire cutters. Crystal for the potting. Owen for the rest.

I hurry through the visitor's carpark, still following the perimeter east. With any luck, the guards are so distracted, they haven't noticed the perimeter cameras. I bite my lip, concentrating on that high, perimeter fence.

But when I hear a voice, I realise that my luck is about to run out.

"Oi!"

There are boots thumping along behind me. This time I have to look back because I need to know how far away the chaser is. I can tell by the sound of the boots that it's one guard, otherwise those thudding footsteps would be louder. I whip my head around to see how close my pursuer is to catching up with me. About 30-40 yards away at a guess. I still like my odds of pulling it off, but I have to concentrate. That brief moment can't slow me down.

I assess everything I gleaned from that quick glance all while sprinting towards the perimeter. The guard is male. Young. About thirty. He was talking into his walkie-talkie. Asking for backup, no doubt.

My eyes scan the perimeter, now just a few feet away. My heart leaps up into my throat as I see the rope dangling down against the bricks. Follow the maze, east, Owen had said, and I had. Now here he is waiting for me. I'm so close to freedom, but I can't get complacent now.

I shove the wire cutters into the pocket of my joggers and throw myself at the rope, landing with my trainers against the bricks, and my hands on the rope. It holds my weight with ease, but the bricks are slippery from rain.

"Stop!"

But I don't stop. Concentrating hard to not slip, I pull myself up, walking my feet along the wall. My new slimmer size helps me, but I wasn't kidding when I told Jan about the new workout. What no one has noticed, are the numerous hours I've spent dangling from the frame of my door to strengthen my arms.

Once I make it to the top of the wall, I cast another glance towards my follower, who I don't believe has the physique to pull himself up by the wall. He's still around ten yards away, his arms pumping at his sides. But I'm already cutting the barbed wire out of my way. I turn quickly to give my pursuer a salute and then look out to the free world. As soon as my brother comes into view, I drop.

"Fucking hell, Is, I didn't know you were going to do that," he complains after roughly catching me. "Get in the car."

I grin at him and hurry to the passenger side. He gets in the driver's seat and releases the handbrake, the car already running.

"I had to drop. They're chasing me. They'll have notified local police already."

"Shit," Owen says.

"You must have known they would. What have you arranged?"

"Don't worry, I have a plan."

"Drive faster."

He sighs. "Be quiet and let me concentrate. Unless you want to drive."

I think about my terrible time in Leah's car, barely able to reverse out of the parking space, and laugh. A rush of exhilaration runs through me and for a second or two I can't believe I ever thought about ending my life. I'd been on the run then, alone, unable to function. But this time I have a plan, and I have my brother, and it feels like nothing can go wrong. I rip the prayer beads from my neck and toss them out of the window.

"Well done. They know which direction we came now."

"They'll know anyway, idiot."

Owen drives us through narrow country roads, empty apart from a few other cars going in the opposite direction. He's avoiding the town, which seems smart. I probably shouldn't be calling him an idiot, but he is my brother after all, and that's what big sisters do.

He rolls his eyes at me. Immune to the insults.

The only thing that would make this moment even better would be to have Leah here with us, along with a knife. I let out a long, euphoric breath. Life has options again. Life is more than the walls of that prison.

"There are clothes in the back," he says.

As he drives, I climb into the backseat and change sloppily into the grey trousers and smart blouse he brought for me, bumping around on the seat while Owen takes tight corners at speed. Then I tie my hair back and finish the outfit with a pair of black heeled pumps.

"Am I going for a job interview?"

"You're insufferable, sis. Won't you please be quiet?"

In the distance I hear the faint sound of sirens and another jolt of excitement runs through me. "Perhaps we can get pulled over and bash in the police officer's skull with the wire cutters," I suggest, holding them up to the mirror.

But Owen tuts. "Get a grip, Isabel. There are new passports in the back along with a ton of money from Mummy. Wouldn't it be better to go somewhere sunny? Somewhere with decent food?"

The way he says that makes me think there's a part he's holding back from me. We hadn't been able to communicate openly about the breakout, which means I don't know where he's intending to take us. "Where are we going?"

"I told you, I have a plan." He smirks into the mirror. "Trust me."

Owen knows better than to believe that I would ever trust anyone. "We're leaving England?" I suppose I have no right to be disappointed about this because it makes sense. But then it dawns on me what his plan actually is. "Oh no. Are we going to stay with Uncle Lloyd?"

"Don't pout, sister. But, yes."

Owen makes a sharp right, pulls over and opens the door. "Time to get out now."

For a moment I don't understand why he tosses the keys into the hedgerow, but then I see the Toyota parked on the edge of a long driveway, barely visible from the country road. He pulls another set of keys from his pocket, and the car bleeps as he presses a button on the key fob. I snatch open the passenger door.

"Did you pick up the passports and the money?" Owen asks.

I lift the bag.

"Good," he says.

And then he pulls the car out of the drive. This time he drives carefully and within the speed limit.

"The perimeter cameras will have picked us up, so you switched cars." I reach over and pat his head. "Clever Owen."

"It's what Dad would have done," he says.

"How did you get it here?" I ask.

"I paid a student fifty quid to drive it here."

"And he didn't ask any questions?"

"Not really. You know it doesn't matter, Isabel. I'm not

trying to hide my part in this, I'm escaping *with* you. Look, I know how much you want to kill that nurse and her brother to avenge father's death, but the best thing we can do now is leave the country."

"I know," I reply. "But Uncle Lloyd. You do know he's a terrible person."

Owen laughs. "Aren't all of the Fieldings terrible?" He takes a right turn onto a main road and I see the sign for the motorway. "We have our own Wikipedia page for every Fielding family murder. We're the Von Trapps of stabbing."

I smile at his joke, but deep down I wonder whether he understands what he's done.

7

LEAH

I wake before Seb, sneak down to the kitchen to make myself a cup of coffee. The sunrise comes gently, nudging through the windowpanes almost apologetically. I take my coffee and watch the dark sky fade into sunlight. It's a peaceful moment, beautifully bathed in October colours. I snap a photo and send it to Jess, but she doesn't reply again. Perhaps filming has started and she's too busy, but I'm still worried. We were supposed to meet yesterday, but she didn't turn up.

Behind me, the stairs creak and I know Seb is up. His feet slap against the kitchen tiles. Soon his arms are around me and he nestles his face into my neck.

"Good morning," he murmurs.

I rub his arm with my hand, warming his cool skin. "Good morning."

"It's nice to wake up to you still in the house," he says.

Then it dawns on me that the slight hurry of his feet on the tiles was due to panic. To waking up and finding me not in bed again.

"Sorry, I should have stayed in bed so as not to worry you."

"No, it's okay," he says.

"What shall we have for breakfast?"

"Hmm, whatever's quick. I need to be at the farm." He unfolds himself from around my body and moves over to the coffee pot to pour himself a cup.

"I'll come with you. I want to help on the big day," I say, turning my back on that glorious view. The farm opens the pumpkin patch today, and there's a lot to do, people to organise, fairground rides to set up, face painting and pumpkin carving stalls to arrange. It's also my big opportunity to prove to Donna that I can be part of the family one day, that I will work hard. That I'm more than someone who attracts trouble wherever I go.

"Come in an hour or two, there's no rush," he says, and takes a sip of coffee. "I'm going to jump in the shower and get ready." He takes his coffee with him as he leaves the kitchen.

I'm about to put bread in the toaster, when movement outside the cottage catches my eye. Tyres crunch over gravel, and when I lean over the counter to get a better view, I notice that the car pulling up at the end of the drive is a taxi. Who would be coming to the cottage so early in the morning? My fingers instinctively grip the surface, and I push myself so far forwards, that the edge of the counter digs into my hipbone. A car door opens. Someone tall and broad steps out. Behind them, another tall, but slightly skinnier person emerges. And then the two of them move around to the boot of the car.

My breath catches in my throat and I snatch my keys from the hook, fingers trembling as I unlock the door. The sharp, autumn air is like a bucket of cold water on my bare skin, I'm still in my pyjamas, but I don't care. I run down the drive in my slippers, hair pulled back by the wind. The broad man turns to face me. When his eyes meet mine, I stop and I stare at him. He raises a hand in greeting.

"Hi, Leah."

I don't even hesitate for a moment, instead I throw my arms around him and stroke his dark hair. Tears on my cheeks. His body becomes rigid, pulling me back to reality. I withdraw and move away, fingers twitching by my side, awkwardness clinging to my body like my pyjamas in the cold air.

"You're back," I say simply.

Tom nods his head. "I'm back."

There are uncomfortable, nervy moments in the kitchen. It's only as I'm helping Tom with his bags and paying for the taxi that I take notice of the man he's with. Not much taller than Tom. Slim-hipped and blond, in a t-shirt that sags at the neck, and an inappropriately thin jacket, given the cold weather. Tom introduces him as Dominic, and we shake hands. I can't be sure, but I think that Dominic might be Tom's boyfriend.

Dominic hangs up his jacket as I call Seb down from the bedroom. I offer them both drinks, fiddling with my hair, the fabric of my pyjama bottoms, completely on edge, with adrenaline running through me.

"It's great to see you," I say, staring at Tom, hoping I'm not being too intense. In comparison, his eyes flick from one side of the kitchen to another. "Where have you...? Where have you been living?" I stop myself before blurting out *where have you been* in an accusatory tone. Obviously, I want to know. I want to know why he left, and everything he's done since then, but I don't want to frighten him away.

"To be honest, I've moved around a fair bit." He shoves his hands deep into the pocket of his jeans.

I nod my head and start filling the kettle with water. I can't even remember if Tom said he wanted tea, but at least it stops me from standing around like an idiot.

"But you've been well? You've been able to pay for things?" My eyes quickly take in Tom's clothes and cleanliness. He's far from slovenly, he's shaved, and his hair is neat. He hasn't lost weight. But there's an edginess to him, a failure to be still. Even his skin moves. I notice a twitch underneath his left eye.

"Yeah I've been fine. I've been moving around, taking any kind of job that I could, you know, retail, warehouse, kitchen work. Even worked with a bricklayer for a while." He turns to Dominic and smiles as though they have an inside joke about Tom's time as a bricklayer.

"That's great," I say, with phoney enthusiasm, praying for the kettle to boil quickly.

"Is it okay if we stay with you?" Tom asks, just as I'm trying to think of another question to ask him.

"'Course it is. This is always your home. You know that."

"Seb won't mind?"

"Well, umm, we live here together now," I say. "But you can have your old room. I mean, both. You can both have it if you want. It's your room."

Seb finally comes down the stairs and stops dead in the doorway between the hall and the kitchen. "Tom. Good to see you, lad."

"Thanks." Tom nods slightly.

"Well, shall we take our teas into the lounge?" I suggest brightly. "Catch up on everything that's happened?"

Tom stares at me and for a moment his expression clouds. It's Dominic who jumps in to break the silence.

"That sounds lovely, Leah. Thanks so much."

I'm grateful for him sensing the tone of the room.

Seb backs out first, then the others, and I follow last after quickly pouring the tea, and arranging the mugs on a tray. Spilled milk gathers at the base of one of the mugs and I remind myself to take that one. Before moving on from the kitchen, I steady myself. My hands are shaking. For months and months, I've imagined this moment. Tom walking into the cottage, well fed and healthy, willing to talk to me. Willing to let me back into his life. Wanting to stay here with me. But now that it's happened, I almost don't understand how I'm reacting, as though my life has been turned upside down. Him leaving is what turned it upside down, this should be righting it again. Why doesn't it feel like that?

"Here we are." I place the tray down on the coffee table and hand over the mugs. "I'm sorry, Dominic, I forgot to ask if you take sugar."

"This is perfect, thanks."

"I still have your Imagine Dragons mug. Do you still like them?" My fingers grip the rim of the mug so hard I think it might shatter into a thousand pieces. Tom quietly takes it from me.

"I'm more into dance music now."

I perch on the edge of the chair next to Seb, not wanting to sit by Tom so that we're side by side. I want to see his face while we talk. "Oh. Well, maybe we can find a Skrillex mug."

Dominic laughs politely, but Tom barely cracks a smile.

I rub my palms against my knees, longing for the right words to start this conversation. To find a way in, like navigating an overgrown part of the forest, or a winding path through a steep ravine.

"I've missed you loads, you know. Every day. And I've been looking for you. In fact, DCI Murphy found an address, I think it actually is your address, and we were going to drive there tomorrow." I'm tempted to dig out the paper from the bureau, but in the end I don't bother.

"Right," Tom says.

"Why did you leave, Tom?"

Seb places a hand on my knee. A gentle reminder to take things slow.

"I needed space."

I want to ask him why he couldn't contact me and at least let me know that he was okay, but I don't, I give him time.

"Did you heal okay?" he asks.

For a moment I'm confused, and then I remember the three-inch scar on my abdomen, the temporary colostomy bag I'd needed while my bowel was resected after surgery.

I place a hand over the scar. "Yes. Everything's fine now."

"I'm sorry I left you in the hospital like that. There was a lot going on in my head and I needed time alone. I knew if I stayed that I'd be part of the *investigation*. That I'd be giving evidence and forced to go to more therapy, and I was sick of talking about it."

"I get that."

His eyes meet mine. "You do? You love therapy. You're the queen of therapy."

"I think it's important, yeah. But I understand not wanting to talk about things for a while. I get sick of it too."

"I didn't know you felt like that," he says. "I guess a lot has changed since I left."

"Well, we can get to know each other again."

8

LEAH

Even though it's an odd thing for a person to do after meeting their boyfriend's family, Dominic is happy enough to go with Seb to the farm and help set up the pumpkin patch opening, leaving me and Tom alone. We decide to get out of the house and stroll around the moors, looking out at the view across Hutton village.

"You look well," I note. "Are you still going to the gym?"

"Not really. Money was too tight for a gym membership, but I learned a load of body weight exercises."

"Like the plank challenge?"

He laughs. "Yeah. Are you still going to self-defence?"

"Whenever I get time."

The conversation goes on for a while, skirting around the edges, never quite straying into dangerous territory. We remain civil, if somewhat detached. Tom tells me that he learned how to make crepes on a stall at a county fair in Lincolnshire before they moved to Newcastle where there were more jobs. He worked on the stall last summer before getting the bricklayer job. He promised to make me crepes with chocolate sauce in exchange for allowing him to move in for a while. Neither him or Dominic have much money at the moment.

"Dom's parents are old fashioned. They're strict Christians who don't believe homosexuals go to heaven."

"Oh, I'm sorry," I say. "That must be hard."

"It just means that we can't stay with them."

The comment stings. Am I forced to admit to myself that I was Tom's second or third choice? That I'm his last resort when it comes to potential homelessness?

"Is that the only reason you came back? Because there was nowhere else to go?"

Tom seems to flinch at that. He looks away, over the moors. "No, it's not the only reason."

I decide not to probe any further. The more we talk, the more Tom's body tenses, and now his shoulders are hunched up and his arms are folded tightly across his chest. I suggest that we head down to the field and help Seb's family with the new event, because we can't talk through all of our issues in one morning.

"Seb doesn't strike me as the pumpkin patch kind of guy."

"He's not." I roll my eyes. "To say he's unhappy with the situation would be putting it mildly. But his mum is adamant that this is the way the farm will survive. And to be honest, I think she's right. The farm shop Christmas gifts section outsells the meat. People want to come here for a day out, and if they're willing to pay, why not? I'm going to try and convince Seb to do weddings next."

"You should make him officiate. It would be the quickest wedding in history."

We both laugh, and finally, my freezing inner core begins to thaw. *Tom* is *home*. The words feel strange. I move them around my mind, shuffling the letters, seeing how it feels. I take in the angles and colours of him, his birthmark, the creases on his knuckles. The dry skin at his hairline. My son. I can't believe it.

"The only thing is, if Donna and Josh convince Seb to help with weddings, it might mean us moving out of the cottage. Donna wants to convert it into a holiday cottage for the wedding party."

"Oh," he says. "Maybe that's for the best. Do you want to continue living in the place that reminds you of Isabel?"

"I love the cottage, but some days are hard."

"Well, we won't be staying long. As soon as I find a job and get a steady wage."

"Sure," I say, trying to sound nonchalant and no doubt failing. Ahead of us, the farm is in full view. There are tents, and bunting. Local vendors have their stalls set up. The bungee cord ride has turned on its music. Pumpkins of all colours are lined up along trestle tables, and others spread out among the fields. Everywhere smells like dropped leaves, and the scent of coffee drifts from the refreshments tent.

Dominic's face lights up when we approach, and I watch Tom carefully to see his reaction. It could be the emotional exhaustion of the day, but it seems to me that Tom is more mechanical. His face almost always impassive. Whereas Dominic is the exact opposite, his heart on his sleeve, his expressions belying any attempt to hide emotion. He's an open book.

"Seb showed me the biggest pumpkin," he gushes. "Honestly, Tom, you won't believe the size of it. You could hide in it." He turns to me. "Don't you think this is gorgeous? It's like being in an American movie."

At first, I laugh. And then I remember the film, and Jess, and the new actor who has been cast to play Tom, and now I know that I have to tell him. But I can't predict how he'll react. I clear my throat and turn to Tom.

"Actually, there's something I need to tell you. There's going to be a film made about Isabel at Crowmont."

"A film? What, a documentary?"

"Not a documentary, no. A proper acted film. I've met with the actress who will be playing me, but I haven't met the director. The director emailed me and I told him that it was a stupid idea. But it seems as though they've started shooting recently."

"Are you serious?" He runs his hands through his hair and stares out into the distance. "What the fuck?"

I wring my hands together, my throat dry, frightened of the sudden change in tone. Perhaps it was a bad idea to bring this up now. "Sorry, I didn't mean to upset you."

"So, in a year or whatever I'll be watching myself on screen? Watching Isabel torture us? Watching her living up in our cottage attic, waiting for us?"

"Actually, they're changing the plot. Instead of Isabel kidnapping us, she's going to be caught and taken back to Crowmont."

Tom kicks a sod of earth with the toe of his boot. "What gives them the right to change our story? That's *our* story."

"Hey, hon." Dominic places a hand on Tom's arm. "Hey. Come on."

Tom does seem to relax slightly but continues toeing the mud.

"I'm sorry. There was nothing I could do to stop it. I'm not happy about it either."

"You're meeting with the cast, though! Don't you think that sends a message? Look, you can't speak for both of us, Leah. You can't meet up with these people and not expect them to take advantage or think that they can do whatever they want."

"Tom, that's not what's happening. I'm not speaking for

67

you. And, incidentally, I would have told you sooner, but I didn't know where you were."

His eyes narrow. "You *do* resent me for leaving. I knew it. I knew this was all pretend, this nicey-nicey act."

"There's no act, Tom. I'm glad to see you and know you're safe, but you have to know that what you did had consequences. You left me. You disappeared and left me in hospital recovering from a major stab wound. If Mark hadn't been there to help me, I wouldn't have even been able to go back to the bungalow. I had to be wheeled around in a wheelchair for a week!"

Tom turns around and walks away. I start to go after him when Seb catches my arm.

"Give him a bit of time."

"I'll go," Dominic says.

I watch as Dominic catches up with Tom. They stop, exchange words, hug, and then Dominic comes back.

"He's fine. He wants some space for a while."

I let out a long sigh, watching him head out towards the moors. All eyes are on him. Donna stands with her back straight as a rod, hands on her hips. Recognition flashes over her face, and I can tell that she doesn't approve of Tom's arrival. She doesn't like her son being involved with us – the family tainted by *unseemly* tragedy. For a moment it hits me that some tragedies leave a stain. There's acceptable loss and unacceptable loss. Cancer, road accidents, unusual diseases: acceptable. Mental illness, murder, violence: unacceptable. We're the stains currently blighting the Braithwaites.

Forcing those thoughts away, I help Dominic arrange pumpkins in one of the tents, learning more about him as we work. He's twenty-one and recently dropped out of an engineering course at University. It was his father's passion, not his, and a couple of years away from his parents made him comprehend that. Since he dropped out, he came out as gay to them, only to be rejected and asked to leave.

"It's not their fault," he says. "It's the way they were raised. They can't see past the sin."

"You were raised that way too," I point out. "But you're not closed-minded like them."

He shakes his head. "I was for a while. I tried to repress it, prayed that I was wrong. I even started self-medicating. It was Tom who helped me."

His words make me smile. My Tom, helping others. "Yeah?"

"He's been through so much and he's trying so hard to get better."

"Getting better?"

"Yeah," Dominic says. "What with the drug addiction and everything?"

I stop what I'm doing and stand up straight. "Drug addiction?"

"Oh, I'm sorry, I thought you knew."

"No. I know nothing." My voice breaks and I try to pull myself back together before I crack even harder. "What kind of drugs?"

"Cocaine mostly," Dominic says. "And some alcohol abuse. That's actually how we met, in a narcotics anonymous meeting. Tom's been clean for several months now."

My eyes prick with tears. To think that Tom was going through all of this on his own. Addiction, meetings, his first love as well. I was there for none of it.

I clear my throat and make my apologies, the tent suddenly lacking air. I run my fingers through my hair and try to catch my breath. While I've been here with Seb, still haunted by Isabel and our father and everything else that has happened, Tom has been out there alone in the world. And I can't decide what's currently hurting me the most, the fact that Tom has been in pain and I haven't been there to help him, or the fact that he seems to have pulled himself back from the brink *without* my help.

Because what am I currently to him? A mother? A sister? A friend? I'm not convinced I feel like any of those things.

I set off walking in the vague direction I saw Tom leave. Seb is busy at a stall with his family, setting out a pumpkin carving station. It's 9am and people are beginning to filter in. Somewhere in the distance is the sound of a child's laughter. I squeeze my eyes tightly shut, trying not to think about how I used to make Tom laugh to distract him from our father's rages. A creeping cold sensation worms its way through my body when I think of those years, of the people who were our parents, of the things we went through. Seb was right, Tom is the only one who understands, and in some ways, it feels like he's chosen Dominic over me. But I have no right to think that. Dominic is obviously a very nice young person and I should be glad he and Tom found each other.

Finally, my clenched muscles begin to relax. I'm happy for him. How could I not be happy for him? And as I think that, I'm overwhelmed by the desire to pull him into my arms and hold him tight. I call his name as I climb the hills, slightly breathless, skin tingling from the cold air.

"Tom?"

It's only now that I notice I've been walking towards the old farmhouse again, which seems inevitable. My subconscious always brings me here. Perhaps it has called to Tom, too, with its twisted siren song. Can memories draw you back? Even the worst ones?

My boots catch on a stone and the sudden jarring takes me by surprise. A few tiny pebbles trickle down the steep slope behind me. The wind whooshes through short reeds of moor grass. I call Tom's name again, and even though he doesn't call back to me, I have the growing sensation that my son is inside that dilapidated building. I enter it, always with trepidation, with my heart hammering. My footsteps breaking the silence.

I follow through the rooms, expectant, knowing by instinct that I'm about to make a terrible discovery. It's like the time I woke in the night and knew there was a change in the cottage before I found the open door. *Something is different.* Perhaps it's the scuff in the plaster on the floor, or the metallic tang in the air. This isn't the place I remember from my nightmares, it's much worse.

"Tom?"

I consider turning back, but I can't. My feet are destined for this course. I continue on through the next doorway into the room where Isabel tortured us.

And there he is, my son, standing still, his head angled down. At his feet is a red stain. An old pool of blood. My stomach flips over, and I almost back away. I almost turn around and *run*, and not stop running until I reach the farm, like I did that night, but instead I tiptoe up to Tom, and I place a hand on his shoulder, gently moving him away from what he is staring at.

He's compliant. He steps back with the guidance of my hand, and finally I see what he's staring at. I almost crumple to the floor. I almost lose myself. But I don't, I take it in. The blood, the torn flesh, the nakedness of the body. The head turned up, staring at the ceiling, the horror on the face of the person who is now nothing more than a shell, a *body*. The hair sprayed out around her, legs at an angle, arms out wide, breasts almost blue in death.

Jess.

Jess is dead. Her eyes are glassy, and her mouth is fixed in a grimace. She'll never smile again.

Slowly, somehow managing to not be sick, I pull Tom away. We walk out of the ruins. I keep my arm around him. Then I take out my phone, and I call the police, all the while, my mind going over and over one fact: Jess is dead.

Part Two

TWO MONTHS LATER

9

LEAH

A name flashes on my phone screen, the same person who has been calling me for the last three weeks. Neal Ford. The director is determined to contact me, but I know what he's going to say, and I don't want to hear it. Two months after Jess's death, and he already wants to carry on with the film. He wants to shoot it in December, in the lead up to Christmas, with the ground frozen up. But I can only think of the friend I made and how soon it is since her funeral. I knew her for a short time, but I still grieve for her.

I'm guessing he's found someone who would be perfect for the role and now he wants to continue his *magnum opus*. No doubt he'll tell me that he's going to tell my story and that it will be beautiful. That he's going to honour Jess's memory with some pathetic dedication to her. None of it will be enough. None of it will bring her back.

I told them and they refused to listen to me. As soon as they started filming, Owen Fielding broke Isabel out of prison. Within days, Jess was dead, and both Owen and Isabel were lost to the authorities. I keep thinking about my walk with

Jess. Her gentle nature, collecting pebbles from the moors, taking photographs of the leaves as they were turning for autumn. Her humour, too, poking fun at the movie industry, doing impressions of famous directors. I knew her for only a short time and yet I miss her. Perhaps it's naïve of me to think it, but I saw a genuine friendship building between us both. She was going to play *me* in a movie and that was special.

The envelope icon appears on my phone and I open my inbox to find an email from Neal. This dance continues. He'll call me, I'll ignore it, and then he'll send me an email telling me how much he respects me and Tom. How much he'll ensure that the film will be careful not to attract Isabel's attention. That he's found a way to carry on.

How can he be so stupid?

It's morning, and Seb is already at the farm. They have a wedding at the farm in two weeks, and Donna is seeing the bride and groom today to discuss the planning. I've been working in the shop and helping at events, but most of the time, I'm here in the cottage. I'm here, and Tom is at work, and Dominic is at work, and I'm alone.

Despite what happened on the opening day of the pumpkin patch, the event was a success, mainly because the police were incredibly discreet, and because the old farmhouse is far enough away that people at the farm didn't notice. But once the story broke, even more people came, curious and morbid enough to want to be near the action. Since then, Donna has managed to convince Seb to try the wedding events. But as a compromise, there's currently no accommodation for the wedding party, who instead will stay in Hutton using a discount with a local hotel, negotiated by Josh.

As I swing my legs out of bed, a sudden wave of nausea takes over. I hurry to the bathroom to be sick, flushing the vomit quickly away. Afterwards, I take a moment, confused by the sudden onset of the nausea. Could it be a complication from the surgery? If it is, this is a strange time for it to happen – two years later. I brush my teeth and hop in the shower only to be interrupted by Tom knocking on the door, also wanting a shower before he begins his shift at the gym

"You know I start at ten," he says grumpily as I slip out of the room in my towel.

After drying my hair and getting dressed, my stomach demands that it's breakfast, and seems perfectly fine after the strange sickness, so I wolf down some cereal, pour out a cup of tea, and sit down at the table. Then I finally open the email from Neal.

Dear Leah,

Something tells me that you're reading these emails, so I'm going to carry on sending them to you even though you don't reply to them or answer my calls. The movie is going ahead. It's been approved by the production company and we're going to start shooting soon. I promise you; this film will not be in bad taste. I know you think it will be, but it won't. Isabel Fielding hasn't been seen for two months. There have been no further murders. Every expert says that she's left the country with her brother. That means you are perfectly safe, and so is the cast. I wouldn't even consider making this movie if I thought any of the cast might be put in harm's way. Safety is absolutely *paramount* to my movie set. Ask anyone in the industry. They'll tell you I'm a consummate professional.

But I understand why you're concerned. This is about people, after all. I miss Jess every day. She was an absolute treasure, the best of people. We want to respect her memory. I promise you.

Please contact me. There's hardly any information for our actors to go on. If they could meet you and Tom once or twice, they could vastly improve their performance.

Once again, your loyal servant.
Neal Ford

I close the app in disgust. Most of the email is about himself, not Jess. I can't imagine anyone like that respectfully honouring another human being. No, I'm almost positive that this person is in fact cashing in on Jess's murder rather than respecting her death. Before his film was going to be a relatively unknown TV movie, now it has publicity. It has a buzz. The main actress *died* before they could even start shooting. The subject of the film *escaped from prison*. Of course, he's trying to rush it now, a "respectful" two *months* after Jess's death.

The thought of it makes me want to vomit again, but I don't.

Tom whizzes through the kitchen to say goodbye while I'm opening the web browser on my phone, once again checking for any updates about Isabel or Jess's murder. By the time Tom found Jess, she'd been dead for a day. Her clothes were found bundled in the corner of the room. There was no murder weapon and, according to articles in the news, very little DNA evidence. She was murdered in the daytime, but because the moors are so isolated, no one saw a thing. The worst part of it all, is that it was the day I was supposed to meet her. She was supposed to come to the cottage. What if

I'd walked up to the farmhouse to see if she'd been mistaken and thought we were meeting there? Perhaps I could have stopped it. Or, as Seb reminds me, I might have been attacked, too.

Or worse, what if I did meet her? What if I wasn't myself but the dark sleepwalker I know I can be? I've forever wondered what really happened to Alison Finlay, and there's always been a part of me that... that considers... I stop myself before my thoughts go too far.

It's widely suspected that Isabel murdered Jess. After all, patterns were carved into Jess's back, and she was left naked. That's what Isabel would do to her victim. She escaped from HMP Newmoor in West Yorkshire the day Jess died. Was it luck? Did Isabel go to the house to reminisce her time with me? Was Isabel in the area because she was coming to kill me? Imagine aiming to kill someone and instead killing the actor playing that person in a movie. It feels too far-fetched, too serendipitous. If Isabel wanted to kill me, she would come for me. She would come to my cottage. Unless she planned to kill Jess all along.

After Jess's death, it was reported that the actress cast to play Isabel, Cassie Keats, went to visit Isabel in prison. Perhaps that was how Isabel got the idea to kill Jess. In one of the newspapers, Cassie mentioned that she'd told Isabel of Jess's visits to see me. What if she told Isabel too much?

But then there is that other theory, one I hate to admit but have to face.

What if it was me?

I haven't stopped thinking it since I saw Jess's body. I sleepwalk through my days as I sleepwalk through my nights, believing that I'm a murderer.

My stomach flips again, and I head to the bathroom.

* * *

A few days after the email from Neal Ford, I get an email from Cassie Keats herself. At first, I consider ignoring it, as I've been ignoring Neal's, but then I decide to respond. Cassie met with Isabel before the prison escape, and I can't help but wonder whether talking to her might help me process what happened to Jess.

We arrange to meet on a Friday afternoon in Hutton. I'm recovering from the sudden stomach bug, and I still feel off-kilter. But it's a sunny day, and there's a touch of frost on the ground, sparkling, and my mood lifts when I head away from the cottage. The claustrophobic cottage filled with people. All men, too. I'm beginning to feel like an outsider in my own home. Meeting Cassie might be what I need right now.

I also can't help but admit that part of me hopes for that instant connection I felt with Jess. That rare and sudden budding friendship that happens once or twice in a lifetime.

Since Isabel escaped prison, we've had a police presence in our lives. For the first month, there was always an officer outside the cottage, which annoyed the rest of the Braithwaites because it blocked access for their tractors. Then it became a checking in situation. Either the police called at the house, or we called them to let them know we were still alive. The police are almost completely gone now, which makes me nervous. Isabel can play a long game.

There was a discussion about witness protection, but unfortunately, my face is too recognisable to completely disappear. I'd have to have plastic surgery or move to Peru or wherever, and I didn't want to do any of those things. No, I thought, let her come for me. I'll fight her. I'll finish what I started in the cave.

My nerves jangle when I enter the coffee shop. I order

decaf to try and remain calm. Caffeine will only enhance the anxiety. It's been a while since I left the cottage and met someone new.

She recognises me immediately and waves me over.

It's only as I'm taking my seat that it hits me. This person is going to impersonate Isabel in a movie, and that's going to be incredibly strange to watch. She doesn't look like Isabel at all, she's much more petite, and has delicate facial features. Although she's sitting down, she could be slightly shorter than Isabel. She has an easy smile and big, open brown eyes. Perhaps it's the eyes that remind me of Isabel. I suppress a shiver, remembering my first meeting with her. The pity I felt for her. The waste of talent that I saw.

"Hey, you must be Leah," Cassie says. "It's so nice to meet you."

"And you." I place my decaf down and realise that I don't know how to start this conversation. Luckily, Cassie takes off.

"Sorry to badger you with emails. I know Neal has been bothering you for some time."

"He calls me about twice a week," I admit. "No idea how he got my phone number."

Cassie rolls her eyes. "He probably nicked it from Jess's phone. He's a bugger. I'm so sorry."

"It's not your fault."

She bites her lip, and the simple childish motion reveals that she's younger than I first thought, and that she's just as nervous as I am. She shakes her head and some pretty curls ripple in the sunlight.

"I really appreciate you meeting me today," she says. "I know you're not a fan of the film, and I completely understand why." She sighs. "Basically, I wanted you to know that I'm doing this because I'm contracted, not because I want to. I'm not that happy to be working with Neal, to tell you the truth, and I hate the way he keeps calling you, begging for you to meet us."

"Oh," I say, surprised. "I didn't know you didn't want to do the film anymore."

"The alternative is to break my contract, which makes me difficult to work with in the future. It's early days and I can't guarantee my career will ever recover," she says. "I'm so sorry that it's going ahead. There's not much I can do about it."

"I heard he cast someone else to play me," I say.

"Yes. She's lovely, by the way, but, well…"

"She's not Jess."

Cassie nods, wraps her hands around her coffee mug. "Exactly. I can't believe we're doing this without Jess. It doesn't feel right."

"Have you said that to Neal?"

She tilts her head to the side in contemplation. "Not in those exact words. I'm pretty positive that he *understands* the way we feel. But that doesn't mean he actually cares."

"Can't your agent get you out of it?" I don't actually know how these things work, but I can't believe Cassie could be forced into a role she doesn't want to play.

"I could be blacklisted, and to be honest, I can't afford to turn down work, even if it's something like this. I need to pay the bills. I haven't taken any other work for about a year because of this film. It needs to pay off."

"God, I'm so sorry. It seems completely unfair."

She waves her hand. "Don't feel bad for me. Save that for Jess." She swallows and stares out of the window, and that child-like anxiety shows again. "That's the other reason I wanted to see you. Jess."

"Okay," I reply. "What do you want to talk about?"

"Well," she says. "The fact that her death is all my fault for one thing."

10
LEAH

Her admission takes me by surprise and I shake my head. "Why would you think that?"

"Because if I hadn't gone to visit Isabel in prison, she might never have escaped. And she wouldn't even know about the movie until it came out at the cinema. I sparked a change in her, didn't I? I made her obsess over the actors. I even showed her a picture of Jess on my phone. It's all my fault." She scratches at a spot on her arm, more aggressively than I'd like, and some nurturing instinct inside me wants to reach across and stop her from doing it. However, she stops on her own. "What I haven't told anyone, is that I went to see her a couple of days before she broke out. I mentioned how you'd been walking on the moors with Jess. I think she must have waited in the old farmhouse for her." A painful sob breaks through her words. I reach into my bag and fish out a travel pack of tissues.

"But how would Isabel know Jess would be there?"

"Because I told her." Cassie blows her nose. "I stupidly told her that you were meeting on that day. Maybe she got her brother to ambush Jess and knock her out. I keep picturing him dragging her up the moors." She shakes her head again. "I know it sounds stupid. It sounds impossible, doesn't it? A man dragging a woman up the moors to that old farmhouse. I guess I don't know how she did it. Or... even *if* she did it, not for sure. All I know is that my friend is dead."

Now I remember that I've seen Cassie before, at Jess's funeral. She was at the back of the church and on her own. She hadn't been standing with the director, which now strikes me as odd.

"You had no way of knowing what Isabel had planned. This isn't your fault, Cassie. Okay?"

"I'll never not blame myself," she says. "I can't help it. Jess is dead because of me." She crumples the tissue up in her hand.

"Can I ask you a question?"

She turns to me, as though I'm pulling her out of her thoughts. "What is it?"

"Why did you contact me now? Two months after Jess's murder?" If Cassie has been suffocating under her guilt, surely, she'd want to get it off her chest sooner.

"We're shooting next week. I dunno, I guess things are more on top of me than ever. I mean, I'm playing the woman who may have murdered one of my best friends. I... What am I supposed to do with that?" She raises her hands as though trying to figure it out. "I'm going to need therapy for years." She bites her lip and stares forlornly out of the window. "That's part of the reason, anyway."

"What's the other part?"

"Neal," she says, in a matter-of-fact manner. "And... doubt. And the fact that the two go hand in hand."

"Go on."

"I mean it when I tell you how guilty I feel. I swear I'm the reason Isabel broke out. I sleep with a knife under my bed every night because I'm convinced she's coming after me next. But sometimes I wonder how much I believe Isabel murdered Jess." She scratches that spot on her arm again. "Look, you probably think I'm crazy, but hear me out for a minute. Isabel and her brother left the country. *Everyone* was looking for them. The police, regular people, probably the army. They're the most wanted criminals in the country. So why would they risk their escape from the UK for the sake of killing someone Isabel hasn't even met?"

I lean back in my chair. "But you seemed so convinced Isabel was guilty?"

"I know," she admits. "And, like, eighty-five per cent of the time I *am* convinced, until I get these flashes of doubt. I don't know what it is. Maybe instinct. Maybe it's because I met Isabel a couple of times, I don't know, but sometimes I don't think she'd jeopardise her chance of freedom for Jess."

"She would," I say. "She's done it before. She had the opportunity to go free when she broke out of Crowmont, but she chose to come after me."

"Because she knew you," Cassie says. "She had a personal connection to you. Her feelings for you are so complex. She both loves and hates you. There's, I dunno, maybe some sort of desire from her." Cassie flushes red. "I don't know if it's sexual or not, but you are definitely someone she fixates on. Whereas she's never met Jess." I open my mouth to speak, but Cassie continues. "I know she was supposed to play you in the movie, which means you and her have a connection, but it still seems weak."

"You showed Isabel the photograph. Perhaps that was enough to excite her," I suggest.

She shrugs. "Maybe, yeah. But why not go for you? You were so close."

I don't want to tell her what I think, that perhaps Isabel

didn't kill Jess at all, that some dark part of my brain has made me a murderer in my sleep. Or that Isabel is saving me for later. I close my eyes and take a deep breath.

"Sorry, this must be hard."

When I open my eyes, Cassie is staring at me, her eyes almost animé large.

"It's okay. It's stuff I need to figure out, too." I rub my temple, trying to shift a burgeoning headache. "How does all this link to Neal?"

Her eyes dart around the room as though she's checking that we aren't being watched. She leans towards me. "Jess and Neal had a complicated relationship."

"They were together?"

She nods her head. "And it ended badly. Jess rejected him in the end and he threatened her career. It was nasty. But they were both signed on for the film and neither wanted to break contract, so they decided to carry on working with each other."

"Are you suggesting Neal is a suspect? Have you told the police?"

"I did mention it to the police, but they seemed convinced it was Isabel."

"Did you speak to DCI Murphy?"

"No, it was a PC, I think."

"Right. Well, perhaps I should mention it to DCI Murphy."

She taps the handle of her mug with a blue fingernail. "What if it leaks to the press? If he's innocent, I don't want to ruin his career."

"Cassie, this is a murder. You could be working with a murderer. If he's innocent, I'm certain he'll have an alibi, and everything will be fine."

"He doesn't," she says. "I already checked. He told me he

was working on the script at home alone." She shrugs. "And he knew Isabel had escaped, and that Jess was meeting you."

"How did he know that?" I ask.

"Neal has a contact at the prison. It's how he arranged my meetings with Isabel. They told him before the police announced her escape to the general public."

I remember hearing about Isabel's escape from prison. We'd missed the news report while at the pumpkin patch. I'd missed a call from DCI Murphy while reuniting with Tom. And then we'd found Jess's body. I think of Tom standing there, staring down at her naked body, completely lost in his shock.

"Wouldn't it jeopardise his film, murdering the lead actress?"

"Or generate an amazing amount of publicity, which it has." Cassie's eyebrows raise.

"I have to tell DCI Murphy about this. Will you come with me to the police station?"

Cassie shakes her head. "I'm sorry, I can't. Please don't give them my name." Her chair scrapes as she stands and scoops up her bag. "I have to go."

"Do you want to swap numbers? You can text me if you learn anything else."

"I'll email you," she says, hurrying out of the café.

I lean back in my chair, trying to decide what to make of my meeting with her. Not sure what to think about this new information about the director of the film. Trying to ascertain whether my darkest fears about myself are actually true, and if they are, whether I should turn myself in before anyone else is hurt.

* * *

While I finish my coffee, I call Murphy and tell him this new information about Neal Ford. As Cassie requested, I refrain from giving him her name, which he's disappointed about, but I stick to my guns. After hanging up the phone, I take a few minutes to sit and contemplate it all.

Unlike some of Isabel's crimes from the past, I don't know much about Jess's murder. As far as I know, she was murdered the afternoon we were supposed to meet. I'd waited for Jess, but she hadn't shown up at the cottage like she was supposed to. Then I'd called her and there'd been no answer. She never replied to my text messages. That's what I remember. I'd fallen asleep for about an hour on the sofa and woke from that with no dirt or blood on me. But at the same time, there have been occasions in my past when my memories haven't matched reality. Such as believing that my father had died, when he hadn't, and all of my conversations with Alfie outside Crowmont Hospital. A person who didn't exist. Merely a version of my father, haunting my thoughts.

What else do I know about Jess's murder? Tom turned up at the house the next morning with his boyfriend Dominic. After a cup of tea and a catch up, we'd gone to the farm to work together. Tom had become upset and walked away. I found him staring at Jess's body.

The two of them must have been travelling the day before, which means they might not have been anywhere near the cottage at the time of Jess's death. But I can't remember exactly what Tom said to the police when we gave our statements. All I remember is being pulled away from the crime scene, then the SOCO workers arriving in their white suits, the police taking photographs. Walking back down the moors to tell Seb, Donna and Josh what we'd found. Pretending not to be traumatised so as not to scare the children. Then going back to Rose Cottage and giving a statement, drinking tea, letting out the tears when I was alone.

Fewer children came to the pumpkin patch on the following weekend, but there was a much larger than expected group of adults. They bought souvenirs and kept staring out at the moors. Someone asked me for a photograph, but I refused.

Can I rule myself out as a suspect or not? I know there's darkness inside me, but I don't understand it or know how deep it goes. I want to be a decent person, but I'm in constant fear that my father's genes are my genes. How violent am I? What am I capable of? Should I be locked away?

What Cassie told me about Neal's involvement with Jess is worrying, as is his knowledge of Isabel's escape. What if he saw this as the perfect opportunity to get rid of an annoying ex-girlfriend, pin the murder on a serial killer, and get extra publicity for his movie at the same time? Cassie was right to tell someone about her fears.

But at the same time, Isabel is still a strong suspect. She was free, the victim was the person acting as *me* in a movie, and Jess was mutilated with wings over her shoulders. There are elements of this that don't quite add up, such as the spontaneity of it, the possible coincidence, and the fact that she didn't come directly to me. But without knowing what was going through Isabel's head at the time, it's impossible to know.

I take my spoon and stir my coffee. Jess's life was taken for such a stupid reason. Either she was the means to ensuring future success, or she was a plaything to a murderer. Or she was someone's psychotic fever dream. I quickly gulp down the last cold dregs and rush back to my car to cry at the steering wheel.

11
TOM

I hadn't wanted Leah to see the dead woman, but she'd walked in on me looking at the body. Apparently, Leah was close friends with Jess, and I've certainly seen her grieving for her. As usual, my mother connected with someone too fast and too intensely, exactly like she did with Isabel, and like she did with that old guy from the nursing home. Come to think of it, Leah has a habit of causing deaths. She's the sun to a solar system of murder. When will it stop? When will *she* stop it?

Two months on, and I'm restless. Sick and tired of living in that cramped house. I'm doing all the things that a normal person should do, and none of it satisfies me. With Leah and Seb's help, I've been working on a qualification that allows me to be a personal trainer, while training on the job at a gym outside the village. Now I help old ladies on the treadmill and run spin classes. I put a smile on my face and say "good job" like a grinning idiot in a movie.

After spending a couple of hours in the gym, I head back to the cottage for lunch. Dominic is meeting me there. He's still finding his feet in the countryside. Even though he's one of the cleverest people I know, Dominic has found it hard to find work. From bar tending, to helping the Braithwaites, to even starting the sports science programme with me, nothing seems to stick for him. Either the work dries up, or he quits.

I lay out a few sandwiches and make myself a protein shake. Dom breezes in, his trousers still muddy from farm work, his face flushed.

"Seb's got me collecting eggs and feeding the pigs," he says. "They're amazing animals. Well, chickens are quite stupid but funny. Pigs are great."

"You stink, hon," I say.

"I know, it's brilliant!" He plants a kiss on my cheek and heads over to the sink to wash his hands. "I've only got thirty minutes, Donna's a stickler. I don't want to get on her wrong side."

"I know this is temporary," I say. "But you clearly love it. Why don't you stay on at the farm?"

"Oh, I would. But they can't afford someone full time." He bites into his tuna sandwich. "You okay, Tommy?"

I sit down with my shake. "Fine, why?"

He watches me thumbing the chipped edge of a plate.

"That's why," he says. "You're on edge. You're craving a hit, aren't you?"

It annoys me that he knows me so well. And it annoys me that he's always so *kind*. Yes, I love it about him, but sometimes I wish he'd make a mistake or... I don't know, something. Anything to make me feel less like a piece of shit.

"No."

"Tom, come on."

"I'm not," I lie. The truth is, every part of my body feels like a taut violin string, vibrating, waiting to be bowed. Waiting to make music. I long for that powerful, invincible feeling that I once knew and loved.

"Okay, I am."

"When was your last meeting?"

"Last week."

"Honest?"

I nod my head and take a gulp of the shake.

"Good," Dom says with a long sigh. "As long as you're still going. You can do this, babe. I know you can. I'm here."

"I know."

"Do you, though? Because..." He places his sandwich down.

"What?"

"You're pulling away," he says. "Ever since we came back here. These last couple of months, you've been so distant."

"Sorry," I say, hearing the monotone in my voice. "I guess I've had a lot going on, what with finding that woman like that."

"I know, hon. I wish you'd talk to me. You know, about your thoughts and feelings, like most couples do."

A flash of anger washes over me. "No. No more sitting around and talking, I'm done with it all. Stop going on about it, Dom. Seriously."

His eyes cast down to the tablecloth. "Sure."

I tut at myself. "Sorry."

"No, it's okay. You're right. I pushed too hard." He offers me a thin smile.

I reach over and pat his hand. "You're such a good person. It's just... I don't know, sometimes I don't feel like I'm worthy of your goodness."

"Hey, that's the addiction talking, not you," he says. "You *are* worthy."

No, I'm not, I think. Dominic has no idea who I am inside. How dark my thoughts are. He has no idea what I've done and what I plan to do.

"I know," I say.

"I want you to know. I want you to be happy."

"I am, hon."

He seems sceptical, but he takes another bite of his sandwich and smiles.

Sometimes I wonder what Dominic's life would have been like to live. Those smiling parents, that perfect home. The middle-class haze of it all. No violence, no murder, no lies, no secrets. If I'd had Dominic's upbringing, could I have turned out to be a decent man? Or would I have turned dark inside myself?

Every now and then I think about her. Alison Finlay. The blood on my hands. Lying to Leah, making her believe she was the one who killed Alison that night. Watching Isabel's expression in the cave when she fathomed that it was me all along. Feeling pride deep down that I'd impressed a serial killer. The protein shake sits sourly in the pit of my stomach. There are days when I want to be good, but I don't know whether there's any left within me.

12

ISABEL

Here I am, stuck sweating under the maddening sun, my body dressed in the finest clothes. Red lipstick on my mouth. Hair pulled up into a bun. Mascara on my eyelashes. I feel like a clown, but it helps transform me into someone else. Though we're thousands of miles away from the CCTV in England, I still need to be careful. But luckily, I have some help in that area...

Firstly, there's the curfew, imposed by Uncle Lloyd, a man who likes to impose. Someone who likes to lay down rules and watch his followers follow. He says that it's the only way to live when you're part of our family, especially when you have the desires we desire. Because we're all alike – me, Owen, Daddy, and Uncle. Even Mummy to a point, though she would never actually act on it. In fact, neither does Owen, but he likes to play games every now and then.

Secondly, there's the way we look when we leave the house. My hair is red now, and cut into a blunt shoulder-length bob. My clothes are laid out for me each morning. Uncle Lloyd likes to check that I'm wearing the appropriate outfit, and if I'm not, he threatens to throw us to the wolves. We follow his rules or he turns us in. It's like being in prison all over again.

Owen has his arm slipped through mine as we make our way back to Uncle's house. It stands out amongst the small Thai fishing village, as the biggest and boldest. The temperature is strange for me, having been in a cold cell for two years. My skin sweats where it touches my brother. I feel it trickling down the back of my neck. I long for the moors around Leah's cottage, for the cold-water streams, the spongy grass, the grey clouds overhead. Even in summer it rains that drizzly rain that lingers in the air. Here, when it rains it's sudden, and it pours down from the sky in sheets. There's nothing to be done but hide indoors until it's over.

We take a left down a narrow street and I happen to turn back for a moment. There, behind us, is a man in tatty clothes, following not too discreetly. He's an older man, though I couldn't pinpoint his age, not here, where poverty and physical labour can add decades onto a person's appearance. The skin around his mouth seems slack, indicating missing teeth, and the rest of his face is cracked by wrinkles. I stop, and Owen turns to watch.

The man holds out his hands in a begging gesture and I take a few steps towards him. He bows to me, begging again, silently, lifting his fingers to his mouth to indicate food. I slap him and he stumbles back, shocked. There's a hard glint in his eyes when he lifts his hand to hit me back. I start to grin, waiting for the pain, but Owen catches the man's hand.

"I'll tell you what, old fella," Owen says. "Dance for us and I'll give you this." He produces a coin from his pocket.

The man stares at the coin, looks at me, and then shakes his head. Owen produces three more coins and now the man is more interested. I can tell that he understood enough English to know what Owen wants him to do.

The man begins to dance. It's a strange dance, one that lurches from side to side. All the time he stares at me, his dark eyes burning with hatred. But he wants those three coins.

After a few minutes, the man stops, and holds out his hand, waiting for the coins. Owen turns to me with a smirk playing on his lips. "What do you reckon, sis?"

"Not deserving," I respond.

Owen turns to the man. "Sorry, matey." He shrugs, grinning from ear to ear.

Now the man is very angry, he lurches towards Owen, his fingers grasping the hand holding the money. I watch for a while, before stepping in to shove him away. He finally slaps me around the face, but in one quick motion, I grasp his arm and bite it as hard as I can until I taste blood. The man cries out, but it's Owen who wrenches me away.

"Are you mad? He could have any sort of disease."

I wipe my mouth and lift my shoulders in disinterest. It was worth the risk to watch the man scurry away, clutching his arm.

"Come on. Uncle will be waiting for us."

Owen was right, Uncle Lloyd stands with his back straight, watching us walk in the door. His eyes travel immediately to my mouth, as though he already knows what I've done. My heart pounds as I see his eyes examine me. His arms are tucked behind his back. A military man, rarely around when I was a child because he worked and lived in other countries. But when he did visit, he left an impression.

"We bought pla tabtim at the market," Owen says, lifting

the bag. "And prawns, too. I thought Apinya could prepare them for supper."

"You're slovenly, Isabel," he says, his moustache moving up and down when he speaks. "There is lipstick all over your mouth. Do you want to attract attention? Do you want us to be investigated?"

"No, Uncle."

He lifts his chin. He speaks with a low, quivering voice, as though barely managing to contain his rage. "You know that is not the correct way to refer to me. Try again."

"No, sir."

"Better." He turns and makes his way into the art-deco inspired Thai villa that has caused quite a stir in this small fishing village on the Mekong River. Uncle Lloyd is the rich white man who throws them a bone every now and then. Like father, he's a self-made millionaire. Like father, Uncle is drawn to the people who won't be noticed if they disappear. But unlike father, Uncle sells them. He's a human trafficker, among other things. Officially he owns restaurants, ships fruit and vegetables, and even fish. Unofficially, he can find you whatever you want. A new cleaner or a sex slave. "There will be none of your nonsense here. I understand that your father raised you with a different set of principles, but in this house, you abide by mine. I will not have my operations damaged because you cannot curb your desires. Is that understood?"

"Yes, sir."

I watch his folded hands bob up and down at the base of his back with every step. We follow him through the corridors to the bottom of the staircase.

"Perhaps you had best get ready for dinner. I'll give the fish to Apinya." He holds out his hand for the bag. "Dinner at 7, Owen."

"Yes, sir," Owen says, nodding, no, practically bowing to our uncle. I suppress an urge to roll my eyes.

"Now, Isabel." He wraps an arm over my shoulder and I cringe away from him. Feeling the way my body squirms, makes him pull me even more tightly into him. He leads me towards the kitchen, our hips bumping together like two disjointed cogs. Finally, he releases me as we come to the kitchen. "Be a dear and pass me that knife." He nods to the kitchen counter, where his prize possession, a Japanese sushi knife, is hung up on the wall.

I walk slowly over to the knife, my heart racing. What I could do with this knife. The flesh I could flay. The patterns I could draw, and the blood that would seep from the wounds. It would be a waste on a piece of dirt like Uncle Lloyd, but I could still do it and it would give me the release that biting into that peasant didn't quite elicit.

But Uncle Lloyd is watching me carefully, my every movement, analysing me and assessing my thoughts. I wonder whether he's ever killed anyone. I know lots of his trafficked people have died during transport, either suffocated to death in a container, or drowned falling out of a pathetic little boat in the middle of an ocean, but has he ever stabbed or strangled someone? Does he have blood on his hands? Real blood?

I pass him the knife and he smiles, baring teeth. He knows what I'm thinking and he knows that I'm weighing my options. I could kill him now, but if he dies, we're alone in this country with no money and nowhere to live. That's why he's taunting me, because he knows he has his sweaty hand on my throat.

He plunges the knife into the fish and begins gutting it.

"Do you like it here, Isabel?"

"Yes, sir. Thank you kindly for your generosity."

He shoots me the barest of glances, flicking his eyes up to mine. He knows there's a hint of mocking in my voice. "I am being *very* generous, Isabel. But then you know I've always had a soft spot for you." He rips out the guts and dumps them on the counter. "But that doesn't mean you can do whatever you want to do here. I'm sorry, but like I said, I have a business to run."

"I understand."

He waits.

"Sir."

He smiles. "Good." He chops off the head of the fish. "Your father never understood restraint, but his cleverness and luck helped him out. You were unfortunate that you ended up with his affliction at such a young age. He should have at least trained you to be careful if he was going to be careless enough to leave his evidence where you could find it. If you were my daughter, I would harness your energies for another purpose. You're a very bright girl, Isabel. Resourceful, ruthless, violent. All of those qualities can be used in my line of business. It's such a shame you're not mine." He glances at me as though waiting for a response.

"Thank you, sir," I mutter.

Then he turns around so that we're face to face, and holds the knife out between us, it now bloody from the fish guts. "But you should know, that I am not someone to be crossed." He takes a step forward. The knife is inches from my throat. I consider whether I could be quick enough to snatch it from him, and recognise that I would not be quick enough. He is older, but he is military. "I can make you disappear, Isabel. No one will ever know you even existed." Another step forward, I can smell his sour breath, but I refuse to back away. "I'd sell you. How would you like that? And you'd be chained up and fucked by some old man." Another step forward, he rests the knife on my collar bone. His nose whistles when he breathes. "Hmm? How would you like that?"

I glance at the fish, gutless. "How would *you* like that to happen to me? Sir?"

"Go to your room, Isabel," he says, stepping away from me, his back stiff and the knife vibrating in his hands. "And think about what I said. Because it's all true. I can do that to you."

And I can do *that* to you, I think, still looking at the fish.

Supper is uneventful. We drink white wine with fried fish and spiced vegetables. Owen drinks too much and begins to slur his words. He taps the dining table relentlessly with his fingers until Uncle threatens to chop them off. I can tell that he needs a fix. I don't know what drugs he takes, maybe the same ones as Genna with a G, maybe not. Thailand would be an easy place to find drugs, but Uncle Lloyd won't have it. Owen will cave soon. Selfless is not a term I would use for Owen. Yes, he sometimes takes his *turn*, in the family. He distracted the police so I could get to Leah. He got me out of prison. But then I spent years and years in Crowmont being a well-behaved girl without any of the family to help me. Owen could never do that. The short prison term he served for perverting the course of justice was enough for him. This is nothing more than another prison and soon he will cave into his desires. Perhaps we all will.

Owen and I go to our bedrooms early, and across the hall I hear the sounds of his house music thumping. He's desperate to go partying, I know that much. Owen likes people, drugs, cruelty and stupid music. And that's all he likes.

Uncle Lloyd's bedroom is on the other side of the villa which means that Owen can get away with his thumping music. It also means that he can't hear whatever it is I'm up to. Which is fine for me. However, I'm aware that Apinya, Lloyd's faithful servant – or possibly slave – watches my every move.

Once Owen's music has died down and the house is silent, I change my clothes, dressing in black leggings and a black, long-sleeved top. I hide my red hair with a hat. Then I go over to the window to look out at the streets below. My room is above a veranda with a porch roof. If I can climb onto the roof and down the support beams, I can get out. I haven't quite lost the strength I gained in the prison, and the thought of disobeying my uncle sends a hit of pleasant adrenaline into my bloodstream.

Quietly, I open the window and scramble down onto the porch roof. Then I listen, waiting to see if I can hear Apinya moving around on the ground floor. It's silent. I drop from one of the beams, landing like a cat. Then I wait again. There are some security lights fitted around the outside of villa, but they tend to be set off by stray cats and dogs. As long as no one goes to the window, I'll be fine.

I take my time sneaking slowly around the outside of the villa, and my patience is rewarded. None of the lights go off. I'm free.

Even at night the air is warm and I long to rip away the hat, but I know I'll need it. I want to blend into the shadows. My uncle knows everyone in the village. His reach is vast, and his influence is heavy. If one of them sees me sneaking around the alleys, they'll tell him. They're too afraid not to tell him.

I know where I'm going. Back to the narrow street where we saw the beggar. I know that he lives there in a cardboard box with his ragged clothes and small black eyes. I think about the hatred in those eyes. The slap across my face. The stinging of my skin. I think about the pleasure it all gave me. The tiny release.

I think about who I am and who my family is. There was never any stopping who I became, it was programmed into me. A family of psychopaths raises more psychopaths. What else was I ever going to be? I think about Uncle Lloyd and those wandering hands of his. I think about the first cuts I made on Maisie Earnshaw and the way it released all of the tension that had been building up inside me. How it made me feel like someone new, someone in control.

And then I think about Leah. The way I talked to her in my thoughts. The slight respite that brought me when I was in hiding. Alone. I'd felt doomed. I'd felt like I had one last job to do before I died, and that was killing Leah.

And then my hand drifts up to the scar on my neck. I think about the way I woke up in hospital, my life saved by people who would rather watch me die. Leah in the cave, her face fixed in determination as she drove the knife into me. The moment of realisation when it dawned on me that Tom had murdered Alison Finlay for fun. Perhaps it was that moment that severed some part of the connection I had with Leah and made me dig into self-preservation rather than fulfilling that death wish hanging over me. Leah and Tom had a violent father like I did, and they both ended up just as fucked up as I am. I'd found it comforting.

Around the next corner I see him lying on the ground, a dirty bandage around his arm. I remove the small oyster knife from around my waistband. I took it from the supply cupboard while Apinya had her back turned. Easily hidden away in a pocket or tucked into a belt loop.

I walk softly, my shoes whispering against the compacted dirt. The man finally looks up when I stand over him, and recognition flashes in his eyes. Then comes the hatred. He's not afraid, he looks like he's been waiting for me. He lunges at me, and I lift my hand with the oyster knife.

As I stab him to death, I don't tell him that I'm thinking of someone else.

13

LEAH

Donna passes me the ceramic casserole dish filled to the brim with roast potatoes, so heavy that I have to place it back on the table to serve myself. I take one and she glances at my plate with a frown. I add a second. The portion I've given myself is a small one, whereas everyone else has piled their plates high. But that's the farmer's life, all the physical labour replenished by a satisfying meal. Donna doesn't seem to trust someone without an appetite, but usually I'm too nervous to eat a lot when I visit. Tonight, my stomach churns even more than usual. I'm tired, I want my bed, and I want to take something for the stomach-ache.

"Seb tells me that your brother and his boyfriend are still up at the cottage." Donna spoons on some extra cauliflower cheese.

I pass the dish to Josh on the other side of the table. My eyes linger on the empty places. Most of the brothers have left, only Seb and Josh remain. That must be hard for his mother. "That's right. They're looking for a place right now. But Tom needs to stay in the village because his clients are here, and unfortunately there aren't many places in his price range."

"Ah well," she says, stabbing a carrot, "it's a bare ten-minute drive to Beckforth."

"They love the village though," I reply, smiling as wide as I can muster, but bubbling inside and wishing she would at least try to hide her disdain for my family.

"Still, it must be very cramped."

I sigh loudly. "We make do."

Josh saves the conversation by changing the subject. "We've found a new supplier for the wedding chairs. They do the tulle covers that the bride wanted."

Donna nods her head. "You should see the barn covered in the fairy lights. It works. We have a chance to make a living doing this."

Seb twitches next to me and I place a calming hand on his arm.

"It's a shame they can't stay on the farm overnight," Donna says. "There's an opportunity to make real money."

The table quiets and I eat a few bites, ignoring the swirling going on inside my body. Perhaps it's time to admit to myself that I'm ill. Even when I met Cassie the other day I didn't feel right.

"Joe Hewitt has ten calves for a decent price," Seb says. "Dairy."

Josh leans back in his chair and sighs. "We're not touching dairy anymore. You know that. There's no money in it."

His mother nods while chewing on her beef.

"Dad always wanted us to get into dairy," Seb insists. "*You* know that."

Josh snorts. "Mum, tell him he's talking stupid."

"Listen to your brother, Sebastian," she says.

"I think Seb wanted a discussion at least," I add, annoyed

by the way they're ganging up on him. "He's part of the farm and wants to talk about—" Seb places a hand on my knee and I know it's a signal for me to stop talking.

"Look, all I think is that Dad would be pissed off about the direction the farm is heading. All these events and—"

"Seriously? This again?" Josh says. He drops his fork onto his plate. "Why don't you fuck off and marry your psycho-magnet girlfriend? Go somewhere and live happily ever after. Far away from here, preferably."

"What did you say?" Seb pushes his chair back and stands, leaning low over the table. Arms rippling with tension. I try to take his hand, but he yanks it away from me.

"Boys," Donna says, her voice a muted warning.

"I'm right though, aren't I? Has anything damaged the farm more than her?" he says, pointing at me. "She brought that psychopath here. She ruined everything and wrecked our reputation. And her bratty brother doesn't even pay rent."

"What reputation?" I snap. "If anything, you get more attention now. People actually want to get married here because it's famous."

"Yeah, fucking weirdos."

"Weirdos with money," I shout. I push my plate away and shake my head. "I think we should go. Looks like we're not welcome here."

"Yes, go. Please. Get out of our cottage and take your freak family with you."

Seb dashes around the table before I can stop him. Josh's jaw tightens as Seb's hands grasp his shirt collar and rams him up against the wall. The sudden aggression makes my head spin. I'm back with Isabel, a knife in my hand. I reach down and pick up the knife for carving beef. All I see is the threat against the man I love, as Josh pushes back against Seb. Donna's chair scraps against the wooden floorboards as she stands. Sweat breaks out on my forehead. *You're not a killer, Leah.*

"Stop this right now." Donna squeezes herself in between her two youngest sons. "That's enough."

Seb backs away and the tussling ends. I unclench my hand and the knife drops to the table, the clattering breaking the tense silence. Every face turns to me.

Gently, Seb takes my hand and wraps an arm around my shoulder. My legs feel like jelly as he leads me out of the house. Cold, crisp air hits us as we leave.

* * *

The first thing I do when I wake is throw up. Then I eat four slices of toast and make a doctor's appointment. Seb kisses my sweaty brow on his way out of the cottage.

"You're still going to the farm?" I ask, concerned about the previous night.

"What else am I going to do?" he says while pulling on his boots. "How are you feeling?"

"Okay now. It comes and goes."

"You're seeing the doctor?"

I nod my head.

"Call me, won't you? I want to know you're okay." He strokes my hair, softly pinches my cheek.

Suddenly the kitchen is full of men. But they file away one by one. Tom hurries through and leaves with a brief wave of his hand. Seb follows, after kissing me goodbye a second time. Only Dominic hangs in the doorway, leaning against the frame.

"Cup of tea?" I suggest. Since the sickness bug I haven't bothered going to work in the farm shop. Instead Donna has been manning the shop most days. She doesn't seem to care if I work there or not and I don't feel inclined to help right now.

"Yeah. But a quick one. I've got a job interview in an hour."

"Oh, fantastic! Whereabouts?"

"Actually, it's at Crowmont Hospital. Is that weird?"

Hearing that name almost makes me drop the mug, but I manage to compose myself. "No, not at all. It's actually a very nice place to work. What position are you going for?"

"It's a reception job. Part time, but it's better than waiting tables."

"Yeah, definitely. Oh, I'm so pleased, Dom. I hope you get it."

"Thanks."

I note the slight dullness to his eyes, and the way one finger taps against the wood.

"Is everything all right?" I ask. He steps into the room and his shoulders begin to slump as though he's about to cry. I pull up a chair. "Here. Sit down for a moment."

While Dom sniffs and rubs his eyes, I put the kettle on and drop tea bags into two mugs.

"Sorry about this," he says. "God, I'm such a loser, crying in front of you like this."

"Hey, no you're not." The kettle boils and I pour the hot water over the tea bags. "You're looking at the queen of loserdom here. And my therapist does *not* allow me to say that about myself, even though I objectively have the worst luck in the world." As I take the tea across to the table, I worry that the joke didn't land. But Dom offers me a weak smile, probably out of pity.

"Thanks," he says. "You're a great sister, you know."

I drop my gaze. "Oh, I don't know about that."

"Good mother then." He places one hand on mine and nods. "Tom told me. I hope that's okay."

I keep staring down at his hand, realising that there's something not quite right. Then I notice Dominic has a bruise all around his wrist.

"What happened?" I ask.

Dom pulls his sleeve down. "Oh, nothing."

"Did Tom do that?"

He sniffs and stares out of the window.

"You can tell me if he did, because I'll believe you. I love Tom, but there were times when he could be quite violent with me, too. When we were living in Clifton-on-Sea. We've both been through a lot and he has a lot of issues to work through."

"It's okay. It's... consensual."

"What does that mean? You can talk to me," I ask as gently as I can. "I want to make sure you're both okay."

He wraps both hands around his mug and holds tight. "It was just an experiment that went wrong. Can I... can we not talk about that bit?" He folds his arms, covering the bruise.

"Sure," I reply. "That's completely fine. But you were crying. There has to be a reason why you're upset."

He pinches the bridge of his nose before he answers, getting his emotions in check. "I think Tom is going to dump me. He's been distant and moody. He doesn't seem to like having me around anymore. I still love him, and I love *you* and even Seb. If he does dump me, I have nothing. No job, no family. No friends."

"I've been there," I say, patting him on the arm. "I haven't always been there for Tom. There've been times when I was out of our awful childhood home, but Tom was still stuck there. I went to live with a boyfriend in a squat." Dominic raises his eyebrows.

"Yep, it was as awful as you might imagine. And then again in Clifton when Tom left. I had a friend, Mark, who managed to keep me sane - until Isabel arrived anyway - but apart from that, I had no one. Until I came back to Seb." I smile at the thought. My anchor. My rock. "But my point is, you're strong enough to keep going. I know this because you're kind and thoughtful and those qualities attract people. And no matter what, I promise I'll be here for you. If things don't work out between you and Tom, and even if you decide to move out, I'm a phone call away."

"Do you mean that?"

"Dom, I'm a woman in my mid thirties with a psycho-pathic stalker, a sort of mother-in-law who hates me, and one of the most recognisable faces in the country. Believe me when I tell you that I can't afford to turn away friends."

Dominic laughs at that and I begin to relax. But then his laughter fades and he holds the mug tighter. "I think Tom is keeping secrets from me. I don't know what it is, but I think it's big. It's one of those secrets that get between you and them. The kind that makes you feel like you don't truly know the other person."

The expression on his face is so sincere and so yearning that it elicits a thud in my abdomen. A new anxiety that hits me beneath the skin. And for some reason, I feel like this sensation and my concerns about how Jess died are all connected. I bite my bottom lip, before noticing that I'm copying Cassie's tic from the other day.

"If Tom is being abusive, you need to tell me," I say.

Dominic shakes his head. "It's nothing like that, I swear." But his eyes don't meet mine. "I need to get ready for that job interview. Thanks so much for this chat." Again, his eyes don't meet mine, and when he stands up, a cold sensation runs over my skin.

14
LEAH

After Dominic leaves for his job interview, I hop in the shower and get ready for my doctor's appointment. Dominic's words keep playing through my mind on a loop. A mental image of his downcast, sincere expression remains clear in my mind. The bruises on his arm and whether he was telling the truth about where they came from. All of it links to Tom, his moods, his temper, his demeanour.

Despite us all living in the same house for the past few months, I rarely sit down and chat with Tom. Our relationship has changed dramatically since before Isabel came into our lives. He also has an incredibly busy routine that keeps him out of the house most of the day. He'll go to the gym around seven, then work with clients until the early evening. Often, he and Dom go out after dinner, to the pub or a club if they hit the next town over. Then they go to bed, wake up, and do it all over again.

He's young and that's the kind of life he should be leading. It should be fun. But I can't stop thinking about the fact that he's avoiding me. And then there are the AA meetings for his addiction, which we haven't once sat down and talked through. I can't stop thinking about Dominic's bruises, and the secrets he's apparently hiding. After what we've been through, it wouldn't be a stretch for Tom to be lashing out. There's no excuse for domestic abuse, but if I can let him know I'll help him change... If Tom is hurting his boyfriend, I need to find a way to save them both and I don't know how to do that, or even if Dominic truly *is* covering for Tom.

I drive out to Hutton on autopilot, almost taking the turning up to Crowmont Hospital. Isabel's escape is still a shadowy presence over the village, as much as it's a shadowy presence over my own life. My thoughts of Tom and Isabel jumble up until I find myself picturing my nightmares. Tom and Isabel hand in hand. Now that he's back in my life, I think I understand why. There's darkness in Tom that I've been trying to ignore. But that link between the two of them in my dreams is probably my sub-conscious telling me my own latent suspicions. Dominic's bruises may be the confirmation.

What am I going to do about this darkness? I know it exists in me, too. What I've been refusing to address for a while now is the fact that there's a common thread between me, Isabel and Tom: we're all capable of killing. Tom killed David Fielding to save my life. I may have killed Alison Finlay, though I'm not convinced I'll ever know for sure. I've almost killed Isabel twice. And then there's Jess...

I pull into the GP's carpark and squeeze into the last space. Coming out into the open always brings some paranoia. Even though my instincts tell me that Isabel isn't even in the country, I can't help it. Every part of me clenches up. I'm constantly checking behind me as I make my way in.

The GP is running late so I settle down onto an uncomfortable chair with an old magazine, listening to the sound of children bashing toys together. And it's in that moment that it hits me. The sickness. My heightened emotions. The exhaustion. And most damning of all, I haven't had my period for several weeks. I've never been regular, and stress is almost always the culprit, but this time it's coupled with the sickness. I feel a few beads of sweat break out on my forehead and my stomach lurches. One of the shiny-faced toddlers turns to look at me with unblinking eyes. I consider bolting out of the surgery. I can't be, can I? I can't be pregnant?

* * *

If there is a more humiliating process than sitting and discussing menstrual cycles with a man, I don't know it. The admission that, no, we weren't trying for a baby, and yes, I did forget to take one of my pills, and that yes, I did assume that my lack of period was due to stress, not any inability to know my body. The process is completed by a blood test, which feels like someone is intentionally violating my body as the needle goes in. I'm forced to clamp my hand over my mouth to suppress the urge to scream. It hurts, and I feel like a failure because of it, because I'm not one of those people who can make jokes with the doctor and pat their dressing with a wink. *Where's the lolly?*

And then, the worst of all. The talk about my antipsychotic medication.

"This is your decision," he says, as he gives me a leaflet to read. "But you do need to be made aware of the potential risks to the baby if you continue with your medication." When he sees the look of horror on my face, he backtracks slightly. "One thing at a time. Shall we wait for the results first?"

Rather than get in my car and go back to the cottage, I decide to walk around to the local sandwich shop and order the biggest bacon sandwich they make. If I am pregnant, the reason I'm feeling sick, the doctor told me, is because I'm hungrier than usual. It's best to graze little and often now, so that the baby doesn't protest. I remind myself that I don't know for definite that there is a baby.

If there's a baby, I have to make a choice between potentially hurting that baby, or hurting myself, because not taking my medication would hurt me. It would stop me being able to be myself. It'd allow my mind to unravel. Goosebumps spread up and down my arms. I rejected the last baby I had. I allowed someone else to raise him, and then I failed to be there for him when he needed me. I don't have the right to bring another child into the world, to fuck up another human being.

A stone-faced young woman of about nineteen creates my bacon sandwich, plopping on tomato sauce and spreading it around with a butter knife. I hand over a fiver and take a bite while waiting for change. Then I walk back to my car and eat the whole thing without taking a breath, leaning down in my seat so that no one can see me.

As I'm huddled down like a squirrel over a nut, I see Tom walking along the street, dressed in his usual gym attire. It's not quite lunchtime, so it seems odd that he's not doing his personal training right now. Where is he going?

I wipe sauce from my mouth, brush away crumbs and climb out of the car once he's a safe distance away. From across the street, I see him disappear into the village hall. He must be attending a meeting. I'm about to turn away and go back to my car when curiosity gets the better of me. According to Dominic, Tom is hiding something. My heart races. More than anything, I want to be able to understand him. I jog across the street and slip into the main entrance.

There's a group entering a smaller room, all of them quietly exchanging pleasantries. Some are carrying takeaway coffees. Outside the door are a few chairs occupied by who I assume are family members of those in the meetings. Brothers, mothers, sisters, friends, all trying to keep their loved ones on the right track. I take a seat as close to the door of the smaller room as I can get. No one looks up from their phone.

There are muffled voices coming from inside the meeting room. Though I can't quite hear all the words, the rhythm matches that of a general welcome. Very gently, I prise the door open one more inch, and listen in, my heart beating hard.

Emotional stories are passed around the group. Young mums who have lost their children to the system because they couldn't take care of them. Older men who lost their wives and their jobs. Talent squandered. The ache of poverty and the itch of addiction. And then I hear a name that makes my heart skip a beat.

"Tom, would you like to talk today?"

There's a moment of silence that stretches agonisingly as I hold my breath. Finally, I hear him say, "Okay."

"I know you aren't the keenest to share, but I think it's important for you."

I hear the sound of a chair creak and then Tom clears his throat. He's nervous. I shouldn't be listening to this, but at the same time, I can't pry myself away.

"I've been clean for two years now," he says. "At least, I haven't used for that long. My thoughts, though. No one could call those thoughts clean, they're as dirty as they can get. I... I'm a bad person. I'm horrible to my boyfriend. I feel on edge all the time and it's like people are an annoyance to me now. I can't seem to love anymore. I can't open my heart. All I want is that powerful feeling my addiction gives me." I hear some murmuring around the room. Agreement. "I want to feel like a god. Though, to be honest, feeling anything would be nice. I'm so numb and empty now."

My breath catches in my throat and I brush away tears. This is my son admitting his depression.

"There's this big, gaping black hole inside me and there are times when I think only the addiction could possibly fill it. But that addiction makes me a terrible person. It makes me a... a..." He stops for a moment and I imagine him bent over his knees, close to tears. I want to go in there, to hug him and keep him in my arms. "I had a horrible childhood. My dad was this violent, abusive person. An actual murderer. And I know I've inherited all that darkness from him."

"You have the power to change all those things," the leader says. She has a soft voice. The kind of motherly, soothing voice that I wish I had. There's a stab of jealousy inside me, that this person gets to be the one who finds the right words and soothes my son when he's hurt. "There's light and strength inside you, too. What are you going to let win, Tom?"

"I don't know," he says.

"You do," she replies. "You know deep down that you can overcome this darkness. *I* believe in you. The rest of this group does too. You can do this." There's another murmur around the room and some even applaud. I imagine the shy smile spreading across his face.

My hands are shaking with adrenaline and emotion. I get up and walk across to the entrance, leaning against the stone, half in, half out. Cold December air lifts the tiny hairs on the back of my neck, cooling my sweaty skin. If the doctor is right and I am pregnant, the baby is making me hot.

The meeting goes on for another ten minutes and I stay away from the small room for the rest of it. Tom finally comes out, and when he sees me, he stops dead.

"I hope you don't mind," I say. "I saw you go in and

thought I'd wait around to give you a lift. Are you going back to the gym?"

"Were you listening?" he asks.

"No," I lie. "Come on. Let's go."

What a stupid lie. As someone utterly terrible at lying, it sits on my face and I know he can tell from his expression that I've betrayed his trust again. Perhaps it was worth the risk to finally understand what he's been going through.

"All right, I did hear some," I admit as we cross the road towards the car. "I'm sorry. I couldn't help myself."

He glowers at me, and I don't blame him.

"I wish you'd say those things to me. I wish you knew that I'm here for you. Always. No matter what you've done."

I unlock the car doors and we get in. Finally, I reach over and touch his forearm. "Tom, can I tell you something?"

"I guess I can't stop you."

"What you said about inheriting that violent side from Dad... I relate to that more than you understand. After you left the cave to get help, I stabbed Isabel in the neck and almost drowned her. I held her under the water until she passed out and it was DCI Murphy who stopped me from committing murder. She wasn't a threat to me at that point. There was no *need* to kill her, but in that moment, I wanted to watch her die. As soon as she put you in ropes, I wanted her dead. Sometimes I even fantasise about it."

There's a sharp intake of breath from Tom. He doesn't look at me, he stares straight ahead.

"I have Dad's violence in me."

"You think you killed Alison Finlay, don't you?"

The blood on my hands, washing away into the sink. "Yes."

"You didn't, Leah."

I turn to him. His eyes are dark.

"How do you know? I don't even know. My mind is so fucked up. I still sleepwalk and I don't know what I'm capable of doing when I sleepwalk."

"It was Isabel."

"We don't know that."

"It was Isabel," he repeats. "And even if you did hurt someone in your sleep, it wouldn't be your fault. You aren't consciously hurting someone. And fucking hell, Leah, who could blame you for trying to kill Isabel. Someone needs to kill her. She's a menace. She's incapable of serving time. If this was America she would've been put to the death penalty already. She'd be fried."

"That's..." I shake my head. "That's beside the point. I still had it in me to try and kill her. That's part of me."

"You're not a bad person, Leah," he says. He closes his eyes and leans his head back against the headrest. "I'm sorry I left, because I think what I did messed with your head. Trust me, you're not a bad person, and I know more about that than you think."

"Have you been hurting Dominic?"

"Physically? Yes, sometimes I'm so angry I... I can't help it." He slumps over the glove box, head in his hands, and I rub his shoulders.

"Perhaps you need some specialist anger management therapy. We could ask the doctor what we can get on the NHS."

"Nothing is going to fix it."

"Tom, you heard those people in there. You have the strength inside you to be a better person. We can work on this together. We need help, Tom. I'm just as violent as you are."

"No, you're not. It's me who's like Dad. I can't change my genes, can I? I inherited this. I was doomed from the start."

"Don't say that."

"Why not? It's true."

When I start to cry, he's the one to comfort me.

"I'm pregnant, Tom. If I keep this baby, I'm passing on our genes to another generation." I shake my head. He stares at me with a frozen expression, completely still. Finally, he pulls me into his arms and I cry on his shoulder until I don't have any tears left to spill.

15

ISABEL

The sound of the blaring television comes from what Uncle Lloyd calls the snug. From outside the room I picture him sitting on the sofa, arms and knees spread apart, his forehead gleaming with sweat, eyes transfixed on the screen. I can't tell what he's listening to because it's in Thai, but it sounds authoritative. I try to tip-toe past, but his voice booms out.

"Isabel, come here please."

As I head into the room, I let my fingernails dig deep into my flesh to stem the building frustration. He is sitting with his arm draping along the back of the sofa, exactly as I'd imagined. Even though he gestures for me to sit, I hover between the television and the door hoping that this – whatever it is – will be over soon.

"Do you know anything about this?" he asks, gesturing to the television.

"I don't speak Thai, sir, so perhaps you could explain it to me." I smile as sweetly as I can. There isn't much to decipher. The picture on the screen is of a black plastic bag over a body.

The alleyway where I murdered the homeless man is clearly shown.

"There was a murder barely a mile from our villa," he says. "In fact, the body was mutilated with a knife. Which is exactly what you were arrested for back in England."

"Wrongfully accused, sir." I make my eyes go big, like a puppy dog, but I do it in a mocking way.

"Let's not play games," he says. "I know what you are."

"What's going on?" Owen steps into the room and lazily addresses the television.

I put on my best Scottish accent. "There's been a murder."

Uncle Lloyd practically leaps to his feet, leans over me and strikes me across the face with the back of his hand. I go tumbling to the carpet, grazing my knees and landing awkwardly on my hands, like a dog on all fours. I spit out a glob of blood onto his plush, cream carpet and then stand, wiping my face.

"Fuck. You. Sir."

"Get to your room."

"No."

"I will throw you both out of this house!"

"Go on then, it's not worth staying here, you aging, ugly, paedo."

"Isabel shut your face," Owen says. "I'm so sorry, sir. Let me talk to her and ensure none of this happens again." He grasps me by the elbow and marches me out of the study.

Uncle Lloyd follows us as we leave. "You'd better get her under control. Or I'll sell her to the highest bidder. I swear it."

"I'll cut the throat of anyone who buys me," I say.

"Shut up," Owen warns. He lowers his voice as he practically pushes me up the stairs. "We need his money. You know that." He bundles me into his room away from Lloyd and his nosy servant.

When he finally lets me go, I don't give him the satisfaction of rubbing my arms. "The man is a paedophile."

My brother dismisses the word with a wave of his hand. "You're a murderer."

"He used to molest me."

He simply shrugs his shoulders. "We're psychopaths and so is he. You're easily as bad as him. You murder at will, sis. What gives you a moral compass all of a sudden?"

I could claw his eyes out, but I manage to curb my frustration. If there's one person in this world I need, it's Owen. "It's not a moral compass, it's a matter of fact. He hurt me when I was a child and now I want him dead. I hate him and what he does."

Owen cocks his head to one side. "You spent too long with that nurse. Maybe stop mutilating people for pleasure if you've developed an appetite for justice."

"Maybe stop obsessing over money and recognise that Uncle Lloyd needs to die."

"I like money," he says. Owen's tone never veers from bratty. For the first time I find it completely infuriating and wonder what it would be like to mutilate him. "I can see your murderous thoughts, dear sister."

"Then you'd better stay on my good side."

Owen lets out a long sigh. "Arguing is getting us nowhere. Perhaps we need to develop a plan." He sits down on the bed and crosses one leg over the other. I take a seat in the armchair across the room.

"What sort of plan?" I pause and stare at the ceiling. "Wait." I lean over and press play on Owen's speaker. "I wouldn't put it past Uncle Lloyd to listen in on our rooms."

Owen simply shakes his head. "I don't think he's doing that. He would have heard you leave last night if he was."

"I was in my room all night, thank you very much."

"Save it for someone naïve, sis."

I stick out my tongue at him. "What sort of plan did you have in mind? Does it involve Uncle?"

"It involves us keeping out of trouble so we can use his money."

"That sounds boring."

"Hear me out."

* * *

For the rest of the day, I played nicely. I apologised to Uncle Lloyd and helped him prepare lunch. For some reason, he decided we should do it together. Once we started, I understood the real reason he wanted my help: showing off his skills with a knife.

"You do have impressive abilities, Isabel," he says as he cuts salmon into thin slices of sashimi. "I noted that most of your victims are women. But this time you overpowered a man."

I glance at him, sideways on. "Are you wearing a wire?"

"Are you wearing a wire, sir," he corrects; a smug grin spreading across his face. "Not very trusting, are you? The answer is no. You're already a criminal. All I'd have to do is call the British embassy." He laughs. "There's no need for a wire."

"Yes, well it's lucky no one knows you exist," I reply. "Mummy hasn't told the police, as far as I know, and I'm guessing that you've been out of the country long enough for everyone else to have forgotten about you. Daddy rarely mentioned you after you stopped visiting."

"Well, we had a falling out."

I nod my head. "Why was that?"

He ignores the question. "How do you surprise your victims? You weigh nothing. You're not physically intimidating."

"Small things hide easily. Weak people give in easily."

"You prey on the weak and vulnerable."

"A hunter finds the easiest target."

"Some like the challenge." He begins to chop the herbs, rolling the blade back and forth. "Leah Smith is that challenge for you, isn't she?"

"What do you know about Leah?"

"I know everything," he says. "I've always known everything." In one fluid motion, he drops the knife, grasps hold of my wrist and pulls my arm behind my back, pushing my face down towards the kitchen counter. "I've had people watching you ever since you escaped from Crowmont Hospital. My half-brother failed you." He leans down so that his face is close to mine. "With me you would have been magnificent."

"Let me go," I say, remaining calm despite the pain. My heart rate quickens slightly and adrenaline floods through me. Sweet adrenaline. My drug. But this is different because I'm not the one with the power. He is, and he always has been. Rage trembles through my body.

"Don't fight it. I want you to learn."

"Learn what?"

"Who is in charge. I want you to stop your silly murders. Carving bird wings into skin is so juvenile. If you worked for me you could achieve much more. I can make you rich. I can give your life purpose again. And perhaps if we do, we can arrange for a few of the women to come your way. Perhaps, once a month."

"What do you mean 'come my way'?"

"I mean you could do what you want with them. Chop them up. Carve your marks. Whatever." He releases me and I straighten up.

"You mean you'd give me a job and access to prey?"

He grins. "Exactly that."

"What about Owen?"

He leans against the counter in a strangely relaxed pose that I'm not accustomed to seeing from him. "Well, what about him? You know your brother better than I do. What will he want?"

"Drugs. Money. Parties. Money for drugs and parties."

Uncle Lloyd grimaces. "We can't have that. A man needs a purpose. Perhaps I can find him a job working for me."

"He wouldn't accept it," I say. "It's not in his nature."

"Then perhaps a small allowance, but not enough for excesses."

I lift my chin. "And what would be expected of me in return for this arrangement? What do you get out of it?"

He stares at me for a very long time, and then his finger traces the shape of my cheekbone. I let him move it all the way down to my jaw. And then I pull out the oyster knife. His blood sprays my face first. Once I've slashed his throat, his hands climb up to the wound, eyes almost coming out of his sockets in shock. I keep stabbing, both hands on the handle, throwing my weight behind the blade. It takes effort. It takes stamina. My wrists ache. A primal scream erupts from my throat. I used to dream of this moment.

When it's over, he drops to the kitchen floor, blood spreading over the expensive tiles.

I hear footsteps behind me and spin around to see Apinya hovering in the doorway. I expect a scream but nothing comes from her mouth. It's then that it hits me. She isn't a faithful servant, she's a woman forced into slavery.

125

Sarah A. Denzil

"You're free now, Apinya. Why don't you leave and go back to your family?"

She nods. "He keeps money in his desk."

"If you'd like to keep some, we can go there together. Now."

Her expression falls. "No. I leave."

"Good girl."

16

CASSIE

T he Christmas lights twinkle through the dark streets of York. There are tipsy people everywhere, walking to the next pub, standing outside bars puffing on e-cigarettes. Most of them without a coat, relying on their beer jackets to keep them warm. On the other hand, I'm not drunk and I regret not wearing a warmer coat.

Halfway along the street, I check behind me but there's just a group of guys laughing at a private joke. I'm not certain why I keep thinking Isabel is following me, but I can't help it. Even now I find my mind going back to the time I visited her in prison, and the way she leaned forward, listening to me talk about the movie, about how I was going to play her. It's almost an obsession of mine.

A group of women pass me, giggling excitedly, their heels clattering against cobbles. They jump into my taxi and speed off to their next destination. I wrap my arms around my body and head towards the restaurant. Filming starts on Monday, and Neal is treating the main cast and crew to a meal and a night out to celebrate.

The place isn't particularly special, though it is decorated nicely with a few faux chandeliers and linen on the tables, but Neal has a room especially reserved for us. I head down there and the group cheers when I walk in.

"Hide the knives, boys," Neal cries in his typical blokey manner, "Sweeney Isabel is in town." They erupt into laughter and I can't decide if they are laughing at me or with me. He grabs me and places a sloppy kiss on my cheek. Did he do the same to Jess?

"Hi everyone," I say, far too quietly to be heard over the din. I'm about thirty minutes late, and it seems that the group is already a couple of bottles of champagne in.

"We saved you a seat," Neal says, gesturing to the chair next to his. He pats the cushion and winks at me.

"Thanks," I say, shedding my jacket.

He pours me a glass and nudges it towards me. "You were amazing in rehearsals, darling. I can't wait to get the camera on you on Monday. You'll come alive even more, I know you will."

"Oh, I don't know about that," I say. "She's such a tricky character."

"You're fucking awesome. And I should know, I've directed Dame Judy. Trust me, I can see talent and you have it. Along with everything else."

Neal is a handsome guy with a big personality. With designer stubble and chestnut highlights in his hair, he could be mistaken as gay, but Neal has a wandering eye for women. Fresh from his divorce, he's an even worse flirt than before. I'm under no illusions that the rest of the cast and crew have been winked at and patted on some part of their body. His pretty young assistant eyes me with that blazing expression and I'm convinced that she's jealous.

I didn't want to come tonight. Neal makes me nervous. He sends jitters up and down my body. Who is he? What is he capable of? I keep thinking back to my conversation with Leah.

"Are you okay, Cass?" Neal asks, and his dark eyes express what appears to be real concern.

"I'm deep into this character," I admit. "There's a lot of darkness and pain. It's hard to shake."

"Then don't shake it." He sips his drink and around us the others seem to continue their night almost as though it's separate from ours. "Embrace it. To a point, obviously, but keep hold of it. *Be* her if you have to be. It'll translate, trust me."

"The psychological toll, though."

He frowns and lifts his arms as though to say, *so what?* "It's for two months. And then awards. Fame. Glory. Every actor goes through this to achieve greatness."

"You think there's greatness inside me?"

"I know there is. Cassie, you are important, and not only to this film, but to the world. You're going to be the next big movie star, trust me, I know these things." He leans closer. "I'm going to *make* you a star. I'll create you. This role will create you."

"That's what I want." I lick my lips before taking another swig of champagne. The bubbles hit the back of my throat and I suppress a cough. "But I'm worried about the backlash. Will I be vilified by the press for taking on this role?"

He shakes his head. "The press can go fuck themselves anyway."

"I'll need them," I say.

He whispers into my ear. "The only person you need is me."

* * *

The rest of the evening goes by in a blur of drinks and laughter. We order food and I pick at it, too scared to eat too much in case I put on weight. The champagne goes straight to my head. Neal talks to me for hours about Isabel and her family, her relationship with her father. We talk about the darkness inside her and where it comes from, the fact that it's almost preternatural.

Then we go to a nightclub. Neal buys the VIP area and we order bottles of vodka. One by one, the other members of the cast slip away. I chat with one of the producers for a while and he tells me not to take any of Neal's shit. We laugh and then he says goodnight. I stumble out of the club and I swear I see her face in the shadows. That open face, so average, so neutral. Nothing would ever frighten Isabel. Nothing would faze her. Neal is by my side and everything I said to Leah fades into the distance. He's going to make me famous. He's going to create me.

We get into a taxi.

"Do you miss Jess?" I ask.

Neal looks at me and his eyes glisten with every headlight. "No."

"Why not?"

"Honestly? She was difficult to work with."

"Because the two of you had a relationship?"

"No, not because of that. Because she kept trying to change the script." He sighs and stares out of the cab window. "You know what? I do miss her in some ways. But Jess wasn't as nice as she made out. She was trouble."

"Do you think I'm trouble?" I ask.

A forefinger slides down my face and he smiles. "No, you're too well-behaved to be trouble."

The champagne has loosened everything inside me. I lean

into him, thinking about the fame, the accolades, the part I'm about to play. Isabel wouldn't care what Neal had done in the past. Isabel would take her pleasure.

Neal's hand slips underneath my top and the taxi continues on to the hotel.

17
LEAH

I wake up thinking I'm bleeding, but I'm not. My dream had been about Tom's birth, except that the baby pulled from my body wasn't Tom. It was a baby with demon-black eyes. No iris. No pupil. No white eyeballs. Black.

There is a note on my pillow. *Let's have lunch today.* It makes me smile. Even when I sleep through his alarm, he thinks of me before he leaves. But the lingering memory of my dream makes the smile fade away. Yesterday, when he asked me about the doctor's appointment, I told him they took blood and that they were going to let me know the results. I didn't say what the blood was for. I didn't tell him anything about the possible pregnancy. Lunch together means I have another opportunity to tell him, but once I do, it'll be real.

The baby that might not be there makes me vomit before breakfast, but after a significant portion of bread and jam, I'm feeling much better. I tip out my usual medication dosage and then stare at it. I put it back in the bottle and close my eyes for a moment. With a shake of my head, I reach for the tea canister and then stop myself. This is it. This is the moment I acknowledge what is happening to my body. I move away from the tea and pour a glass of water while I wait for Dominic to finish in the shower. He's the last other member of the household left this morning and I want to check up on him.

But I get distracted Googling about my particular kind of medication and their possible side-effects on pregnancy, that I hear the back door open and close, missing my opportunity to talk to him. He hasn't even told me how his interview went yet.

The revolving door life at the cottage has to stop. There's so much to talk about and yet we're playing a game of chess with each other that allows us to avoid those unspoken things.

As I leave the house, I come to find that the possibility of the baby makes everything I do feel extraordinary. As I walk down to the farm shop for my shift, it feels like I'm doing it for the first time. Stacking shelves is strange knowing that there's a person growing inside me. Every time I serve a customer, I can't help but think that I have a secret they don't know about. They could never guess that I'm pregnant by looking at me. Sometimes I feel like blurting it out. *My life has altered forever, and you don't even know*. The more the morning progresses, the more I believe this baby exists, and that it's the new normal for me.

At around 11, Josh comes in with some fresh meat for the freezer. It's awkward seeing him again after the disastrous lunch the other day. After working in silence, he comes closer, rubbing his jaw, hovering like a bee over a flower.

"I messed up, Leah."

I want to say, *yeah, you did*, but I give him time to continue.

"I let all of my frustration out on you and that was a shitty thing to do. I'm so sorry. Look, I've apologised to Seb and we've cleared the air, so I want to do the same with you."

133

"I appreciate that, Josh," I reply.

His face relaxes. "And that's a weight off my mind." He rubs his jaw again. Out of all of Seb's brothers, I think Josh is the most like him, both in looks and personality. It's probably why they clash. "You must hate us right now. Or at least you must be wondering what you're stuck in the middle of." He laughs. "Sorry about that."

"You were an arsehole the other night," I say, smiling to let him know that I'm being gentle. "But you weren't wrong. I've brought a lot of stress on you all."

"None of that's your fault," he says.

"Yeah, well, sometimes it doesn't feel that way. Look, I don't want to overstep my place or anything, but I came from a family that no one should have. Take it from an outsider, it doesn't matter how dysfunctional your family is, you still love each other. That's what matters, and I'm glad to be a part of it."

"You're right for him, you know." He grins. "Mum won't admit it. In fact, Mum probably won't think it, either. But you are. You see the thing is, he wouldn't stand up to her before. He wouldn't have stood up to Dad or me either. But you've given him a spark, you know."

"Is that a good thing, though?"

"It makes him a pain in the neck, but it's a good thing."

"Thanks for saying that."

"Not a problem." His grin broadens. "When are you two going to make it official then?"

"What?"

"When are you going to join the family for real? How long has it been now? Two years? It's about time, isn't it?"

My face flushes bright red. "Oh, I don't know about that."

"The barn's all set up ready for when you do know." He

taps his forehead with two fingers in a salute. "Right. I'd best get back to it."

When he leaves, I can't help but mull over his words, both about whether I'm a positive influence on Seb, and whether we'll ever get married. I'm still undecided about both.

About half an hour after Josh leaves the shop, I have the phone call from the doctor's office. I'm pregnant.

* * *

"Tom texted me about giving him a reference," Seb says as we take plates of cheese and crackers into the lounge. "They've found a flat, apparently."

"He texted you?" I lean over to read the message.

"It makes sense," he says. "He'll need a reference from someone who isn't family.

"But I didn't even know they were looking at a place today." Yet another secret.

"He'll tell you later. He knows I'll tell you anyway, so it's not like he's trying to keep anything from you."

All this talk of secrets makes my heart thud. Seb has no idea that I'm keeping the biggest secret of all from him. And now it's official, I'm pregnant with my second child, only this time the child was made from love rather than hate. Whether that makes a difference, I just don't know. Seb starts flicking through the channels on the TV, his plate balanced on his knees. I think about my secret, and then I think about my dream. Little baby Tom with those black pools for eyes. I regret what I said to him in the car, that our father's genes are being passed on. I made it seem like I agreed with him, that I do believe he inherited them. That can't have helped him, especially after what I heard him say at the group meeting.

I wish I didn't believe we weren't both damaged by what

may have been passed on from our parents. I wish I didn't hold that in my heart, but I do. I turn to Seb, to the father of my unborn baby, and his brother's words come back to me. That loving, dysfunctional family of his. My baby will be half them, half me.

"I'm pregnant." The words spill out of my mouth like overflowing liquid. Fast. Bullet quick.

He drops the remote and stares at me, his face impassive for what feels like an age. Then he takes my plate, puts it on top of his, and dumps them both on the coffee table. He covers my hands with his. He pulls me into him.

"Are you sure?"

"I went to the doctors," I say. "That's why I've been throwing up."

His body relaxes against mine. "Leah, I'm so happy."

"You are?"

"Of course I am!" He kisses me and then pulls back. "But what about you? How are you feeling?"

"Tired," I admit. "Scared. Unprepared. Like having this baby might not be the right thing to do."

"What makes you think that?" he asks, gently squeezing my hands.

"Me. My family." I shake my head, trying not to break down. "I don't believe in evil. I think we're formed by genetics and our own experiences. But I've seen a lot of what other people would describe as evil and most of it has come from my father. He was horrible and violent. What he did to me was the worst thing anyone could do to another person. He violated me and killed someone I love. And now I have to face up to the thing that's worse than that."

Seb strokes my hair. "What?"

"That I'm like him. I'm ill, Seb. I have a psychological illness. Without my medication, I hallucinate and hear voices.

136

With it, I can live a normal life, but there's still something *other* about it. I'm capable of violence—"

"You're one of the gentlest people I know," he says, almost laughing at me.

I pull slightly away. "You've never been there at the worst moments of my life. You haven't felt someone else's blood on your hands. When I held Isabel's face underwater, I felt powerful and full of rage. You've never seen me like that."

"Leah, those were extraordinary circumstances."

"I know, but there's more."

His eyes are open and wide and completely full of love for me. "You can tell me anything."

"When Tom and I were in witness protection on the Scottish border, Alison Finlay was murdered by Isabel Fielding. The night Alison Finlay died, I remember washing blood from my hands when I was sleepwalking. I don't know where I went that night. I don't know what I was doing. Alison Finlay was a therapist who used our local support centre. She was killed close to where we lived. And that night I washed blood from my hands that wasn't mine." I take a shaky breath, baffled by my own words. The words that have been locked inside for so long. "What if it was me?"

Seb stands up so quickly that it shocks me. "No. Absolutely not. You're not a murderer, Leah."

"Wherever I go, people die. My mother, Isabel's father, Alison Finlay, and then Jess."

"You're not a killer, Leah."

"That's exactly what Isabel said to me before I pushed her off a cliff. I stabbed her in the neck and then I held her head underwater until she almost died. I honestly don't know what I'm capable of. And now I might have to stop taking my medication so that I don't hurt my baby. Who will I even be without the antipsychotics keeping me sane?"

"Leah, you did not murder Alison Finlay, and you did not kill Jess. This is all Isabel's influence. She's been targeting you for so long that you're doubting your own sanity again. But you're not a murderer. You've been pushed to the brink a few times, and in those situations you've reacted exactly the same way anyone else would under that kind of pressure." He sits back down and takes my hands again.

"Then where did that blood come from?"

"It was a nightmare."

I shake my head, disappointed that he doesn't believe me. "My clothes were stained the next day."

Seb hangs his head. "I'm sorry, sweetheart, but you have to accept that this was another hallucination."

"You mean like I thought James Gorden's head was a hallucination?" I snap. "Stop patronising me."

"I'll never believe that you could murder someone in cold blood," he says. "If there was blood, then there's another explanation for it."

"What explanation?"

His jaw twitches and he turns away. "I have one suspicion."

"Tell me." I have to physically move his face to make him look at me again. "Tell me."

"This happened when you were living alone with Tom and you were both going to the same place for your exercise classes and therapy."

"What's your point?"

"Tom will have also seen this woman."

My body goes cold. "No."

"He killed David Fielding. You told me about how he used the magpies to mess with your mind. He was violent with you and he left you recovering from a stab wound in hospital and disappeared."

"He couldn't."

"He could."

"Get out." Before Seb can say another word I'm on my feet backing away from the sofa. "He's my son."

"And a very damaged young man. I don't want to be saying this. But I can tell by your reaction that you've considered it as well."

"Shut up." I rake my fingers through my hair, dig the nails into my scalp. What Seb's saying is completely ludicrous. If Tom killed Alison, then he must have put blood on my hands and set me up to make me think I did it. Surely, he wouldn't be so cruel? No one could be that cruel.

"I don't want to leave you alone," he says, standing, coming towards me. "I'm sorry I had to say this, but you didn't kill Alison Finlay. That's not you."

I close my eyes and all I can see is Tom standing over Jess, staring at her naked body. *No. No no no no no no...*

"Leah. Come on. Sit down and breathe, okay?"

"Please leave," I say, staring at the carpet. "I... I can't look at you right now."

18
TOM

The flat is perfectly nice, with a small but functional open plan kitchen-diner. There's a separate room for the lounge, unusual for a one-bedroom apartment, and the view shows green pastures and dotty stone walls. Sweet, picturesque Hutton. Nothing bad could ever happen here. Could it? But being in this flat makes me feel like I can't breathe. Wherever I go I can't breathe. The cottage is even worse with Leah and Seb there. The meetings are probably the one place I can relax.

I don't want to, but I write down Seb's contact details on the application form. It's obvious that he's not my biggest fan, but a local name on my reference will go a long way. As I put down the pen, I notice Dominic looking at me from the corner of my eye.

"I'll give you both a moment," the estate agent says. "Enjoy the space. Get a feel for it." She opens her arms in a dramatic gesture. Every second of this viewing has been the estate agent trying to illicit a response from us. I return another thin smile, the same ones I've been doing all day.

"It's okay," Dominic says.

My attention snaps back to him. "What?"

"You're earning enough to live here alone. I think you should take it without me."

He's noticed the slow withdrawal; I didn't know if he had or not. When I first met Dom, he was this bright, innocent guy who had lived a relatively sheltered life until he came out. There was no dark past or hidden agenda. He hadn't known violence until he met me.

"Dom..." I start.

He sniffs. "I didn't get the job."

My heart sinks, I'd forgotten all about it.

"Sorry, I completely..."

"Forgot. I know. Because you don't love me anymore. But it's okay, I'm fine with it now. At least I won't have to deal with your temper tantrums when I leave."

I hang my head in shame, but part of me feels like it's an act, that there's nothing inside me. No emotions, no remorse. "Where will you go?" I ask. "Back to your parent's place?"

"No." He brushes away a few tears. "Not unless I want to be told I'm an abomination again. I have a cousin with a spare room. I guess I'll go there."

Is he expecting more from me? Some sort of protest? A declaration of love? All I can muster is a feeble, "I'll miss you."

He shakes his head and leaves some words unspoken. *It's for the best.* We're both thinking it. I don't blame him either because I don't give much to him. And I've hurt him, both emotionally and physically.

"I'm sorry it happened today, at this moment. I should have known to..." *Do it earlier.* I don't say it, but we both know this has happened because I didn't have the balls to dump him first.

"Better now than five years down the line," Dominic says. "Will you say goodbye to Leah for me? She's been so kind to me." He gets up from the sofa and pushes his phone into his jeans pocket. "I'm sorry for everything that's happened to you, but you need to stop blaming her for it all. You're lucky to have her as a mother."

I slowly nod my head. He has a warm, sensitive heart, but he has no idea what I've been going through.

"Take care, Dom, okay?"

He leaves, the same way as the estate agent. When she comes back into the room, I explain to her that I'll be taking the apartment alone.

* * *

By the time I get back to the cottage, Dom has already taken his things. I find Leah in bed, awake, but staring at the ceiling.

"Dom just left."

At the sound of my voice she sits up in bed, her body moving so fast that for a moment I think she's having a seizure. She places her hand to her heart and takes a deep breath.

"Sorry, I thought you heard me come in."

She shakes her head. Then she seems to register what I said. "Wait, what do you mean Dom left?"

"We broke up."

She pulls her knees up to her chest and wraps her arms around them. "You did? Oh no." There's a queer note to her voice. It sounds far away as though she's completely distracted.

"Are you okay?"

"Are you?"

"Yeah," I say. "I guess I saw it coming. I probably should've broken it off before now."

Her eyes narrow in confusion. "I thought you were both in love."

"I did, too, for a while. But maybe we're better as friends."

"Are you going to stay in touch?" she asks. I get the impression that she's testing me, analysing my answers.

"To be honest, we didn't discuss it. It all happened quite quickly."

"Perhaps you're in shock," she mutters, almost to herself.

"Yeah, maybe. One minute we're signing a contract for the flat, the next we're breaking up."

Leah breaks out of whatever spell she was under and opens her arms. "Here, sorry, have a hug."

I fold into her and it feels strange. Who is this woman to me? Is she my mother, sister, friend? It doesn't feel right being trapped inside her embrace, it's like there are snakes wrapping around my neck, squeezing the air out of me. That's what I could do to her right now. I could wrap my hands around her neck and keep going until her eyes bulge out and she squirms beneath me. I could watch the light fade from her eyes and then all my problems would be over. Because she's the one I want to kill, isn't she? Alison Finlay was a nothing. Leah is the one I want to murder. My mother. The person who gave me life, but who lied to me. Who left me in that house with *him* knowing who he was and what he was capable of.

She gasps when I retract away from her, and she cowers away. I can't stop thinking about the night she interrupted my nightmare and I tried to hurt her. I'd hated the expression of fear on her face, and I hate it now, because it's a reflection of me, of my soul, of the piece of crap I've grown up to be.

"I've found a place." My voice sounds flat even to me. "I'll move in tomorrow."

"Okay," she says, still staring at me like I'm the devil. "I... I'll miss you."

She's lying again.

God, there's another baby inside her.

I turn around and walk out of the room. *There's another life.* She'll love this child; not like she hates me. I walk into my room across the hall and begin tearing down all those band posters that I used to love. The last reminder of my childhood, of the boy I used to be. That boy didn't fight back when Dad would scream and punch. I screw the thick paper into balls. Leah all but admitted to me that she thinks Dad's genes have passed down to us. She thinks I'm a fuck up. She's scared of me. She knows who I am. I'm the devil.

She'll love that baby more than she loves me, and that's not fair. I was the one who took care of her when she was ill. I watched her sleepwalk. I saw her obsession with Isabel. I was the child she abandoned.

The sooner I'm away from her the better.

19

ISABEL

Hi Leah, I'm back. Does it bring you comfort to know that I am back where I belong, in good old Blighty? I cheered to myself when I breathed in the air for the first time. When the shipping container opened up, and I saw the familiar grey sky, I knew I was home.

Ah, Leah, it feels delightful to be talking to you again. I had a break for a while, because I had other things to worry about, but it feels like the right time to bring you into my thoughts, to hold you close, to figure out *what* I'm going to do with you.

Shall I tell you about my adventure? Well, after I killed my uncle, I discovered that he'd kept a lovely safe filled with interesting things. We guessed the passcode right away because the poor man had no imagination. It was our Daddy's birthday. Owen and I paid dear old Uncle's associates to get us out of that god-awful country and back here. We managed to persuade his second-in-command to dispose of the body. No one will miss my uncle, but especially not the man who gets to inherit his business.

We knew we couldn't fly into the UK, even with our fake passports, but they did get us to Greece, and from there we've been stowed away in lorries and shipping containers until we made it back. Owen didn't enjoy it at all. No toilets, not much food, and a couple of screaming children. But we made it. We're refugees in our own country.

Once we arrived in Felixstowe there was an awkward moment with one of the traffickers who recognised me. The man was clever enough to keep his mouth shut, but I knew from the glint in his eye that he was going to be a songbird.

We waited until night. We made it quick. And it allowed us to take a car. But we've had to remain in the shadows. As you know, this is not the best way to live, especially for Owen, who is quite the uptight princess. So, we decided to come and visit lovely Mummy, driving the songbird's car all the way up to Rotherham.

"What are you doing here? Did anyone see you?" Mum said when she saw us on the doorstep.

"It's 2am, Mummy, what do you think?" Owen rolled his eyes.

"What if I'd had a maid living here? What if I had a... a... friend."

Owen and I both laughed at that. Perhaps it was rude, but we couldn't help ourselves.

"Get in, quick. The police still monitor the house every now and then."

But we decide it's best we don't mention that I slashed Uncle Lloyd's throat and had his business associates get rid of the body.

God, Leah, I'd forgotten how white and soulless that house is. I hadn't been there since I was fourteen years old, after all. In fact, the last time I was there was when I killed Maisie. I wandered through the house, examining every beige cushion and white ornament. Mum hasn't changed a thing. She herself is quite different to what I remember. She doesn't seem to be in much of a fog anymore, but she is on edge. She wrings her bony hands. The injected collagen on her face seems to have sagged, giving her a strange, lopsided appearance. Her lips bulged where they ought not to bulge.

"Missed you, Mummy," I lied.

When she looked at me, the dark cloud of fear moved across her face like rainclouds. Then she grew very pale.

"I missed you too, sweetheart. Gosh, you look so different from the last time I saw you. So pretty." She reached out and touched my hair with trembling fingers.

"I cut it," I said. "And I dyed it black. Do you think it suits me?" I'd decided to ditch the red once we reached Greece. You can never be too careful.

"Oh yes," she said, but I can sniff out a phoney, Leah, and I knew she was bullshitting me.

"We should have showers," Owen said.

"Yes, go ahead," Mum replied.

Owen turned towards the hallway, but I placed a hand on his arm. "Wait a minute, we're forgetting something. Mummy, I think it's best you give me your phone." I held out my hand.

"Is that really necessary?"

"She's not going to turn us in, sis," Owen said. "She helped us get out of the country. She's in this up to her neck and I don't know if she can get out."

"Which means now we're back, we're a problem for her," I reminded him. "Phone, Mum."

She pulled it out of her dressing gown pocket.

"Could you show us where your house phone is? And the thingy for the internet."

"Router," Owen said.

"Yes, that thing. I'm fully institutionalised these days. I can *never* remember what anything is called."

We followed her around the house, gathering up anything she could use to contact someone. And then I took everything we found into the bathroom with me, dumping it in the sink. I even ran the taps. No, I don't trust my mother one iota, in the same way that I never trusted my father and I certainly didn't trust my uncle. Does that make you pity me, Leah? No, I don't think it does. It makes me like you. I know what you went through with your own family. And now you're left with no one but Tom, who is even more like me than you are.

After showers, we reconvened at the table and dined on half a box of chocolates and some cold deli meat from the fridge. Mummy's eyes kept drifting over to the knife block in the kitchen. I did the same, ensuring that all the knives were accounted for. They were. If she had a weapon, she wouldn't keep looking at the knives, so I knew she was unarmed, and we had full advantage over her.

"Did you know about Uncle Lloyd?" I asked, pointing hammy fingers at her.

"I've heard rumours about what he does in Thailand," she said. "But I don't know whether they're true or not."

"No, not about that," I said. "About what he used to do to me."

She shook her head. "What are you talking about?"

"Poor blind Mummy." I stuck out my bottom lip. Then I turned to Owen, who had a strange expression on his face. I thought he might be upset, but I couldn't quite tell. I tried to mimic his expression for a moment, wearing it to see how it felt.

"How did you miss everything, Mum?" Owen said, his voice is thicker than usual. "How did you allow this to happen to us?"

And it was in that moment that I knew what he was planning to do, or at least what he wanted to do. "Wait. No, no. We can't do that."

He regarded me with raised eyebrows and a frown. "We can do whatever we want to do, can't we? Isn't that the point of living this way? As fugitives."

Before we came, there'd been a big discussion about our next steps. Owen didn't want to come back to the UK at all, but we had to spend most of the money we stole from Uncle Lloyd on getting out of Thailand, which meant we needed another source. Neither of us are the most talented thieves, so we decided to come back to the one person we knew had enough for us to start over. Here, with her.

"If you do that, we won't have enough money to live."

Mum nodded her head up and down enthusiastically. "Oh, yes. I can get you money if you want it. There isn't as much that's liquid as there once was, but I can move things around. How about a hundred thousand? I'm certain we can make that disappear on the books and then you both have enough to start a new life."

"How much is in the house?" Owen asked.

I gave Owen a look that I thought conveyed my feelings on the matter, that I wanted him to drop this. We could not kill our mother. We may need her in the future, for one thing. I'm not as resigned to my own death as I used to be. There could be another way for me to live, with options that I didn't see before. Money is the secret ingredient to that life. With money we can go wherever we want. Once I've dealt with you though, Leah.

"It won't be enough," I said between gritted teeth.

Owen cocked his head to the left. "Shut up, big sis."

"I hate to hear you fight," Mum said, a forced smile on her

face. "Please don't. Isabel is right, I can help you. I love you both and I want you to be happy."

Owen exploded into laughter. "Do you hear this, Isabel? Lies. We've been nothing but lied to our whole lives."

"It doesn't matter. None of it. What matters is survival, and we won't manage that if we murder her," I tried to remind him.

Mum lets out a pathetic gasp. "Darling. Please don't hurt me. I'm so sorry for whatever it is that I did to you."

Owen snorted. "See, she doesn't even know what she did. She's so stupid."

"Exactly," I said.

He shook his head. "If Dad was alive, I'd murder him twenty times over for what he's done to us. He forced me to go to prison for you."

"That was your choice. It was our code, how we live," I said.

But he wouldn't listen to me. "I never wanted to be part of that code. I'm not psychotic like you. I don't enjoy killing and carving people up. Why should I pay for the way you and dad wanted to live your lives?"

"You didn't care much when Maisie died," I said, shocked by this sudden resentment.

"But I still didn't want any part of it. I never have. *You* and *him* kept dragging me into it. And *she*," he jabbed a finger at Mum, "is the worst of us all."

"Owen, no. Please. I've always loved you." Tears began to run down her saggy face. It was quite disgusting to look at.

"She isn't like us," Owen said. "She has a soul and she was a bitch anyway. We're broken, Is. They were so cold to us that we never developed a conscience and she is the reason why. Dad, too. They did this to us. They made us who we are."

"What's wrong with who we are?"

"I know that we're better than everyone else," he said. "But they failed us. We've been in institutions ever since you killed Maisie, and what can we do with that gift in those places? Nothing. Our lives have been taken away because they didn't teach us how to live with what we have."

"We can do a lot with a hundred grand, Owen. Stop being ridiculous, we're not going to kill her."

He stood up and started walking around the table. Mum screamed, rose, and made an attempt to run away. Owen pounced on her then, slamming her up against the wall. I hurried around to them both and tried to prise Owen from her. But he simply wrapped his fingers around her neck and squeezed.

Eventually, I gave up and watched my brother kill my mother. I didn't feel much as I stood there and allowed it to happen. It's strange. I could shrug my shoulders about the entire situation. Now we need to adapt to the fact that we won't be able to get enough money to set ourselves up in a different country. Now we need to change the plan.

But what does surprise me is Owen. Has he enjoyed this all along? Was he lying to me? He said that he doesn't have the need to kill, but I don't know what to believe. What to think. I can't help but wonder what else he's done, especially on the journey up from Felixstowe, when he left me in a cheap hotel at night and disappeared.

Mother is gone and we have a little money raided from our childhood home. Perhaps the fugitive life will suit me better this time around. After all, Owen and I have a friend to help us, but I won't say more. What I want to tell you is that I see magpies wherever I go. I keep counting them off, wondering how my luck will turn out, wondering what the world has in store for me. They all keep bringing me back to you. *Three for a Girl. Three for a Girl.* You, Leah. That's you.

151

20
LEAH

He had made no effort to hug me back. The entire conversation had left me reeling. How could a man who had at one time seemed so wrapped up in his first love, have ended up with no feelings about it whatsoever? In truth, I was glad when Tom gathered his meagre belongings and moved into his new flat. I was glad, and I never thought I would be.

My mornings have been routine. The morning sickness, the dry toast, the kiss from Seb, and then the quiet house. I tried texting Dominic to see how he is, but he doesn't reply. I miss his calming presence in the cottage, and our occasional home lunches together, watching *Bargain Hunt* on the TV. Since the pregnancy, Seb arranged for me to only work afternoons in the shop, but we haven't told his mum about the baby yet. I want to wait until the three-month mark.

Now that I've accepted that I'm going to be a mum, and after a meeting with my GP, I've decided to try a safer antipsychotic drug. The thought of having no meds scares me to death. As a former psychiatric nurse, I know what can happen. Even now, I'm aware of the fact that not all medication works for everyone. I could easily go back to being ill. I have this horrible feeling that something bad is going to happen. Sometimes I dream about Isabel standing over my belly with a knife in her hands and a wild grin on her face. Sometimes that person is Tom, but he doesn't have a knife, he just demands to know why I'm replacing him.

While stretching out my tired limbs on the sofa with a peppermint tea, my phone rings. For a moment, my heart skips a beat, and I realise that I don't want it to be Tom. I bite my lip out of guilt, and accept the call.

"Hi, Leah."

I know right away that the voice on the other end of the line is DCI Murphy. "Hi." I screw my eyes shut. *Please have found her. Please. Please.*

"We had a hit on CCTV footage today," he says. "It looks like Isabel and Owen have somehow returned to the UK. The CCTV camera was in Felixstowe."

"Do you have her in custody?"

"No."

My heart sinks.

"I'm sorry. I know this is a blow for you," he says. "I called you as soon as I heard. Leah, I think you and Tom need to move somewhere else right now. There has to be a reason why she came back to the UK."

"To finish what she started," I say for him. "To come after me."

"I'm so sorry. I didn't want this for you. I wish I had better news."

"How are we going to raise the money to move? Seb's needed at the farm."

"You have to find a way. She'll come for you. That seems

to be the only constant when it comes to predicting her behaviour."

"I'm pregnant," I blurt out.

"Fuck."

I can't help but laugh. "I think the word you meant to say was congratulations."

He joins in with the laugh, but I can tell he's still thinking about me, and Isabel, and probably about his failures. No matter what happens, Isabel manages to outwit him and the rest of the world.

"Congratulations," he says, trying to sound happy for me. I appreciate it.

"It's early days yet."

"I'll do what I can to keep you safe," he says. "Even if it means breaking the budget slightly."

"Thanks," I say. "Stay safe yourself. She could come after anyone connected with her past."

"I will, Leah."

"Did you ever check up on that information about Neal Ford? In connection to Jess's murder."

"He had an alibi," Murphy said. "He was with his ex-wife, apparently."

"Oh, right," I said. I remember Cassie telling me that Neal was at home working on the script alone. Either she was mistaken, she lied, or Neal is lying. Truth be told, I'd been going through so much that I hadn't given it much thought before now, and I decided to let it go for now, making a mental note to speak to Cassie soon.

I disconnect the call and stare at the television with unblinking eyes until the tears begin to fall. There was a part of me that had moved on from her and begun to hope. I thought she'd chosen life over her revenge. I thought she'd given up on her obsession with me. I was wrong. I'm always wrong.

The first person I call is Seb, but there's no answer, so I call Tom instead.

"Then let's get ready for her," he says. "We've put up a fight before, we can do it again."

I shake my head and tell him how ridiculous that is. But he doesn't seem to comprehend that he doesn't have the intelligence to go up against her. And that isn't an insult to him. She's smarter than us all. She's more resilient than us all. She's more relentless than anyone I know, and she has fun the entire time.

"How can I fight her now that I'm pregnant? How could I fight her anyway?"

"I'll do it," he snaps. "I can take her on."

The empty sound of his voice makes my skin go cold.

"What we need to do is meet," I say. "All of us. Me, you, Seb, DCI Murphy, maybe even Seb's family. We need to talk about what to do next. Make the decision together. We know exactly how dangerous she is, we know—"

"Leah, stop," he says. "You can't organise this. There's no point in going anywhere because she'll find us wherever we go. You know that people recognise you on the street. As soon as you lost anonymity, the papers published your name and they printed your picture at the trial. You're infamous. Someone will post your whereabouts online and she'll find us. Game over. Why not sit tight? Fight back for once."

I hang up and throw my phone down, hearing the plastic cover crack against the floor. That's enough from him, I think. He sounds toxic and hateful; I can't stand it. I bend down and retrieve my phone, which fortunately hasn't smashed, place it back in my pocket and pull on my boots.

* * *

A soft layer of frost covers the hedgerows. Even in a hat and gloves I'm freezing cold. Ice has formed over the puddles on the way to the farm. I pull a piece of bunting from the nettles, a remnant from the last wedding at the farm. It must have detached from the outside of the barn and blown away.

It surprises me to see that the farm shop is closed. Donna usually opens about 9am. I continue on to the farm courtyard, hearing nothing but the sound of the chickens in the courtyard, scrabbling about in the frozen mud. Even Seb's brother's dog, Patch, is missing, and he's usually bounding around, ready to sniff my fingers for potential treats.

"Hello?" I call, tentatively opening the door to the farmhouse kitchen. No one knocks here. This kitchen is the centre to the entire business. It's where flasks are filled with tea, Tupperware boxes are stuffed with sandwiches. Where minutes are stolen leaning against the table.

I hear voices.

"He wouldn't leave the car. It's not like him. If he wanted to stay out all night, he'd drive."

"Hello?" I say again, stepping through into the room. "Am I interrupting?"

"No," Seb says, offering me a smile that doesn't meet his eyes. "Nothing like that. Josh didn't come home last night."

"Oh, was he with Mags?" I ask. Mags is his girlfriend of six months. It's a complicated on again off again relationship that neither me nor Seb tend to get involved in.

Donna shakes her head. "I called her and she didn't see him. His truck's still out in the yard."

"Maybe he wanted to drink. Did he book any taxis last night?" I suggest.

Donna sniffs and wipes away a tear. "I didn't see him

come in from the fields. In fact, I went out to check and saw that he hadn't even finished fixing the fence he said he was going to do. The barbed wire is still all tangled up."

"Oh," I say, the tips of my fingers beginning to feel numb with fear. My mouth goes dry and the blood drains from my face. "Oh."

"What is it?" Seb asks.

It's the last question I want to be asked. I don't want to tell them, because then it makes it real and it makes my suspicions real.

"I just had a phone call from DCI Murphy. Isabel has been seen on CCTV with her brother." I swallow. "In Felixstowe."

Donna's body goes rigid and her eyes widen so that I can see the whites of them. Her hand flies up to her pale face and she lets out a sob. "We need to call the police."

Seb grimaces. "I'll do it now. When did DCI Murphy call?"

"Less than thirty minutes ago. I phoned Tom to warn him and then I came straight to you to tell you."

"I saw your missed call," he admits. "Sorry, I should've answered."

I walk over and slip my arm through his. "Hey, it's okay. I had no idea Josh was missing." The warmth of him is a comfort, but at the same time I can feel the tension running through him.

"When was Isabel in Felixstowe?" he asks. "How long does it take to drive here from there? I know it's down South somewhere."

"I don't know," I confess. "I guess the police need time to confirm the CCTV hit. It must have been flagged sometime over the last few days. I'll call Murphy and find out more."

Donna slowly lifts her hand from her face and points at me.

"This is all your fault. She's targeting us because of you."

Seb, who has his phone out and is dialling the police, gives her a warning look. But he doesn't say anything because he knows she's right. I let go of his arm.

"I'll go and call DCI Murphy," I say, slipping away into another part of the house. Anywhere that gets me away from that pointed finger.

Two hours later, Donna and I are sitting in the farmhouse kitchen waiting for Josh to either come home or call. Seb is at the police station, filing a missing person's report, and meeting with DCI Murphy to talk about Isabel. There was yet more bad news when I called Murphy to ask about the timeline. He believes Isabel has been in the country for at least three days. What's more, her mother was found dead yesterday morning.

I remember the time I met Anna Fielding; how obvious it was that she was on drugs. I remember coming away worried for her. And since then I've always thought of her as a victim, even when I saw that she'd contacted Tom on Facebook. I can't imagine what it must feel like to be murdered by your own family.

The kitchen is silent. We're sitting around the old, pine table with two untouched mugs of tea in front of us. I can hear myself breathing, hear the whistle in my nose. Every now and then she sniffles. When she speaks, I jump out of my skin.

"We need to get water to the trough in the paddock," she says.

"I can do that for you if you like."

"You're not strong enough to lift the tubs," she replies. I can't decide if it's stating a fact, or if it's an insult.

"No, I probably shouldn't lift anything that heavy right now anyway," I say, and then my stomach flips over. I close my eyes.

The long silence makes it clear that she noticed my phrasing. She's guessed why I can't lift anything heavy. I long for a hole in the floor to swallow me up.

"You're pregnant." She says it as though she's stating a fact, without any emotion. But I don't blame her, no doubt her head is filled with nothing but the disappearance of her youngest son.

"It's early days, but yes. I'm so sorry, I didn't mean to tell you like this. Seb and I were going to announce it once we passed the three-month mark."

She nods once. "He's always wanted children, my Seb."

"He talked about having a family?" I ask.

"Not really," she says. "But he doesn't have to. He was the one who took Josh under his wing, not the two oldest. He was the best big brother any boy could have." She begins to choke out her sobs and I move closer to her, wrap my arms around her shoulders. No matter what may have been said between us, I hate seeing her like this. I can hardly stand it.

Once she's finished, she pulls away from me and blows her nose on a tissue. "I remember the night you came flying down the moors, the blood all over you. Wild eyes, like those of a blast survivor. Seb saw it all and there was nothing more he wanted to do than take care of you the way he did Josh."

"I know. But I want to look after him, too."

"You should have killed her when you had the chance," she says, with a voice filled with hatred.

"I tried. I failed twice now, but I wouldn't fail a third time."

Her head bobs up and down in agreement, but her eyes are distant, focussed on the world outside. "If Isabel has killed my son, I will find it very hard to forgive you, even if you do give me a grandchild."

"I know," I say softly. "I know."

21
SEB

In a drab, grey room on a drab, grey day, DCI Murphy blinks at me once. "And you believe all of this?" I haven't had as much to do with the detective as Leah, but it's clear he thinks I'm mad.

"I do," I say. "I think Tom is a murderer."

"Talk me through it again," he says. He picks up a pen and makes a note. I have a different opinion of Murphy than Leah. Because he's shown her support over the years, she thinks he works in her interests. I don't think that's true. I think any man leading a nationwide investigation and has failed *this* many times must be an incompetent moron. But he happens to be the best we've got.

"I know I don't have evidence, but I trust Leah. What she told me implicates Tom, even though she doesn't realise it," I tell him. Murphy writes down another note. "Did you know that she sleepwalks?"

"I think she mentioned it in one of her statements, yes. She suffers with some psychological problems, too, doesn't she?"

"That's true. But when she's taking her medication, she's absolutely fine."

"Was she taking her medication at this point?"

I pause. There's no way of knowing if Leah was taking her pills because I wasn't there. But I know the woman I love. The woman I love has expressed no other desire than to be better. "Yes, I believe so. But I wasn't living with them. It was when they were in witness protection. She remembers washing blood from her hands. She's spent the last two years believing she murdered Alison Finlay."

"What?" he says.

I nod. "It's not true though. It was Tom."

"Isabel confessed to the murder of Alison Finlay. Why would she lie?" He taps the end of his pen against the notepad.

"I don't know much about psychology," I admit. "But don't people like her want attention?"

"Some do," he says. "Anyway, go on."

"I think Tom made Leah believe she killed that woman. I think he is the one who killed Alison Finlay, and then smeared the blood from his own hands on Leah. Maybe he whispered it to her when she was asleep, I don't know. But the thing is, the day," I prod the desk and it rattles, "the very *same day* that he arrives at our cottage, Jess Hopkins dies in the same way."

"It was the same day Isabel escaped prison as well."

"Yes, but she got out of the country so fast it seems unlikely she came to the farm and randomly killed someone like that. After all that obsession with Leah, why would she kill Jess rather than break into the cottage and murder Leah?"

"I have thought about that," Murphy admits. "The two women shared a lot of physical characteristics."

"There's no way that Isabel would mistake Jess for Leah. It wouldn't happen."

"She'd been in prison for two years," Murphy replies. "That's a long time not to see someone's face."

"Is it? Would you forget your wife's face after two years?"

"That's different," he says with a laugh.

I don't find it funny. I have to sit on my hands to stop myself jabbing a finger at him. "That murdering cow doesn't do anything but think about Leah. She plots and she schemes all because she wants my girlfriend dead. So why wouldn't she take the chance if she had it?"

Murphy makes another note. I want to believe I'm winning him over, but his features remain impassive.

"Leah even saw Tom standing over Jess," I add.

"But he wasn't bloody. We checked him."

"Coming back to the scene of the crime? Maybe he wanted to look at what he did the day before. Look, hear me out. This is important because my brother is missing and Leah is pregnant, and I need to protect them both. I never thought Tom was a bad kid, but killing David Fielding changed him. He became aggressive, especially towards Leah. She told me all about it. He was violent to her when they were in the witness protection programme. He even moved out and left her in that house alone. He left her alone when Isabel Fielding was chasing them. I've lived with him for two months and I've seen that dead, empty look in his eyes. I know he's not right in the head. My brother is a big guy, he couldn't be hurt by a ten stone girl like Isabel. Whereas Tom is tall, and he works out. He could do it."

"Thank you for telling me this," Murphy says. "I'm glad you did, it's all information that I needed to know, and believe me, I will follow up on it."

Hands back on the table, I watch as he gazes above my

head. "And you're going to look for my brother? He doesn't disappear like this, not without calling or texting us. This is all wrong." I remember another part of the tale I'd been piecing together. "Can you find out if Tom and Isabel were in contact while she was locked up? It all feels connected. She escapes, a woman dies, and Tom finds the body. She comes back to the country and *my* brother goes missing."

"As far as I know, Isabel didn't have many visitors or correspondence while she was in prison. Only her brother sent her letters, and I believe the actress playing her in the movie visited a few times. Nothing from Tom, I'm afraid."

"Still," my earlier conviction begins to ebb away, "he's suspicious. You have to check him out." When Murphy stands, I do the same. My insides feel twisted up and not right. I'm rambling more than I'd like, heart pounding, everything on edge. This is not who I am. This isn't how it was supposed to go, I'd felt so confident striding in here with all my information to tell.

"Certainly," he says. "I've got your number. In fact, I've got everyone's number, Leah's, yours and Mrs Braithwaite's too. I'll be in touch as soon as I have a development." The man smiles thinly. The kind of empty, exhausted gesture that asks another human to let them be. Normally I'd be fine with that, but my brother is missing.

However, there's nothing more I can do here. Staying to argue some more won't bring my brother home. No, there's somewhere else I need to go.

* * *

This damn village. As soon as I walk out of the police station, I see Tom on his mobile phone, standing outside the supermarket across the street. He nods to me and I decide I can't do anything but wait as he crosses the road to speak to me. The boy has grown over the last three or four years, shoulders twice the width, arms twice the size.

"Did Leah tell you about Isabel?" he asks.

I nod. "Did Leah tell you about my brother?"

His brow bunches and his mouth turns down. "What about him?"

"He's missing." I watch carefully to see how he reacts. Can I gauge his feelings? Can I spot a lie?

"Fuck. When did that happen?"

"Last night."

He shakes his head. "Your brother goes missing and Isabel is back. Jesus. That can't be a coincidence. Have you spoken to Murphy?"

"Yes, just now. I told him everything."

Tom shuffles the toe of his trainer against the tarmac of the pavement. "Fuck. I hope you find him. Maybe he had a heavy one, eh?" The slight laugh is empty and feels inappropriate given the situation. It takes all of my willpower not to throw him against the nearest wall.

"Did you know that Leah thinks she murdered Alison Finlay?"

Tom's shocked expression is exactly as someone would imagine. Jaw dropping open, the tiny shake of disbelief. "What?"

"That's what she told me. She remembers washing blood from her hands late at night. Didn't you notice?"

"No, I never knew."

"You didn't see it?"

"No." His voice is faintly quieter than before.

"Well, that confirms it then," I say.

"What?"

"It was a dream."

165

"Sure," Tom says. "Yeah, must be. Leah wouldn't hurt anyone."

"No, she wouldn't. Unless it was to save someone's life, like you did with David Fielding."

He doesn't say anything, simply watches with an impassive expression. The confusion is gone.

"That must have been tough to do," I prompt, still watching him with interest.

"You have no idea," he replies.

"I've never stabbed anyone in the back, no. I think I would if they hurt my family though."

Tom nods. "Anyone would. It's a natural reaction. Anyway, I have to go. I have a session with a client. I hope the police find your brother."

Rather than head straight home, I get in my truck and sit for a moment. A heavy lump sits in the pit of my stomach, and everything else feels twisted up, my heart blocked. Frustration builds and builds. What can I do about this? Is my brother already dead? I beat the steering wheel with my fists, trying to stop my mind from wandering back to the day Mum and Dad brought him home from the hospital. I was four years old. They showed me how to hold him, starting with a cushion on my knees, until I was stronger and could hold him in my arms. At night, Mum would take me to his crib so that I could softly say goodnight.

The rivalry had come later. We always had to have identical toys, but as the oldest I thought I should have better ones. As adults, Dad showed us all how to be farmers, but he did it in a hierarchical order, starting with the oldest. Josh was jealous I learned more before him. That Dad was able to teach me more before he died. We'd have blazing rows at times, but the next day I'd help him fix the tractor or he'd hold a cow while I tagged it. We were a team. A bloody dysfunctional one, but still a team. And now he's gone.

I sniff away unshed tears, put the truck in gear and reverse out of the space. Everything I said to Murphy was true, but it's obvious the man didn't want to hear it. While I've always appreciated the way he's protected Leah since Isabel's escape from Crowmont, I suspect the man is short-sighted. To him, Isabel is the one he's looking for. She's the killer. But in my mind, it's clear. Tom is fucked up. And now I need to prove it.

22

LEAH

When Seb walks in, the stress is evident on his face, skin an ashen shade of white. The exhaustion tugs at him, pulling at eyebags, darkening of the contours on his face. How can a man age in the space of half a day?

"How did it go?" I ask.

"I met Murphy at the village station." He sighs. "He listened to me, took details. He says they're going to look for him."

"Okay, well, that sounds promising. He's a good police officer and he knows Isabel. At least we have allies." I'm still sitting next to his mother with my arm around her shoulder, but I get up to hug Seb before going to fill the kettle.

"I went for a drive around after," he says. "Thought I might see him somewhere. Stupid idea."

"No, that was smart," I say. "We could have another search of the area later. I was thinking we could check out in the fields in case he fell somewhere and hurt himself."

Seb nods. "I'll do that now."

"The water in the paddock," Donna says, lifting her head for the first time.

He starts walking to the door. "I'll take it on my way."

"She told me." Donna stares at the back of her son's head, eyes barely focussed, rimmed red from her tears.

I freeze, the kettle half full of water. "I told her about the baby," I admit. "It slipped out. Sorry."

Seb slowly turns to face us, and I see all of his pain. This isn't how he pictured this moment, and it isn't what he deserves. I know deep down in my bones that what Donna said about Seb always wanting to be a dad is true, and I know that on some level he's imagined this moment. The proud moment of informing his family that he's about to become a father for the first time. But he's been robbed of that joy by my loose tongue. How could he enjoy anything while Josh is missing?

"Well, now you know," he says simply.

"Now I know."

"We can talk about the baby as much as we want in the future," I say, trying to inject some happiness into my voice. "Right now, let's focus on Josh and everything we need to do to find him. I'll get on social media and set up a post. Maybe it'll go viral and someone will have seen him. I need a recent photograph and I'll be all set."

"You can get one from his Facebook page," Seb says.

"Right. That can be my job."

Seb says his goodbyes and leaves the kitchen.

Forgetting the kettle, I go through into the house and dig out the Braithwaite's laptop. I get on with my task, finding a clear picture of Josh and creating the post. Then I contact his Facebook friends, hoping that they can shed some light on where he might be. Some reply straight away and express surprise. This isn't like him at all, they say.

After a while, I start to immerse myself in my task. There are plenty of social media sites to try and lots of people to contact. I even start to do some research on local businesses who might share the post with their followers. It's over an hour later when Donna comes into the lounge and places a cup of tea on the coffee table in front of me. Her eyes are still wet, but she has more clarity about her than before.

"I can't work that thing." She gestures to the laptop. "Useless. My own son is missing and there's nothing I can do."

I feel for her because I've felt the same sinking feeling of uselessness in the past. "Did you and Seb try hospitals this morning?"

"Seb called all the major ones first thing."

"You could try them again," I suggest.

"I don't want to block the line," she says. "In case he calls."

"You can use my phone if you like." I hand it over to her and she sits down on the sofa with a copy of the yellow pages, licking her fingers to flip the thin paper.

The rest of the day goes by in a blink. Seb comes and goes, checking in to see if we've discovered anything, then disappearing to finish farm tasks, rearrange appointments, and drive around in the truck. He takes Josh's dog with him, hoping Patch will sniff out his owner. But when he calls in, we have nothing to tell him. We learn nothing. All I know is that I feel a sense of dread building up and I can't shake it.

When the sun goes down, tea isn't strong enough anymore. Seb opens an old bottle of Bells and takes a swig. None of us can make conversation because we're so raw inside. I think of Rose Cottage alone on the edge of the moors. Now in darkness.

The landline rings and Seb's mother snatches up the phone. "Hello." The phone falls from her hand.

We both lunge for her at the same time, but it's Seb who catches her when she swoons.

"They've found a body," she says. "They've... They've found a..." The wail is so broken and hoarse that it will forever be in my nightmares.

* * *

We walk into the hospital together as the first snow of the season begins to fall. Seb and his mother cling to each other. He carries her weight, shouldering the emotional labour. I try to stay close to his free side, so that I can place a hand on his arm or back whenever he might need it, but I am not their blood, and I am not truly part of this, I can only watch on the outskirts.

We all know that this body is going to be Josh.

Bright lights wash over us, all the people milling around the foyer appear to be in hyper colour, and all I can think about is how there is no way this body is anyone but Josh. People don't go missing in Hutton village. The police don't find bodies unless that person has been murdered by Isabel Fielding.

I'm shivering all over despite my thick winter coat. We negotiate the corridors beneath the blinding lights until we find the morgue. Even the signs hit me hard.

A short man with a neat beard talks us through the process and then leaves us to decide who will identify the body. Donna lets out a small whimper, and even I find myself crying already. Seb's face is a mask of pain. He keeps glancing down at his shoes and clearing his throat.

"I need to see him," Donna says. "I need to know that it's him."

"Then I'm going in there with you." Seb nods firmly.

"I'll come with you," I offer.

"No. Family only," Donna says.

The barb cuts deep, but it's her decision and I respect that. This is her son we are talking about, and this is the worst day of her life. I take a step away; then all I can do is watch as they walk together into the viewing room.

The man with the beard shows me where I can sit and wait, which I do, with my hands clutching my knees. I've done this once before after Mum died. I saw her laid out on the gurney. The paleness of her skin. How bloodless she was. I think of Jess's blue breasts, the bruises on her body.

I need to see Tom after this. I need to know he's safe.

Seb and Donna are in the room barely two minutes. He walks over to me much more quickly than I'd imagined, no longer holding his mother. I stand, knowing immediately that something is wrong.

"It isn't Josh," Seb says.

"What?"

"It's Dominic."

The world tilts. I push Seb away in my hurry to enter the viewing room. I have to know. I have to be sure. And there he is. Those handsome young features frozen in death. Eyes closed, mouth still. He seems even younger now, without his clothes and mannerisms and slightly sad smile. I begin to cry for him, and place one hand on his cheek, feeling the ice-cold surface. It isn't fair that this happened. Dominic was a decent person with a warm heart, someone I already miss. Now I'll never chat with him over shortbread ever again, and someone will have to call his parents to tell them he's never coming home.

23

ISABEL

It's an old saying, Leah – one I've never bought into – that the definition of insanity is performing the same task over and over again expecting a different result. If that's insanity, then a movie set is completely crazy. Through the dirty glass window of Owen's latest stolen vehicle, I watch them do the same thing over and over again. The girl playing me, Cassie, gets into a car and drives it down the street. Then they spend an hour resetting lights and cameras and they do it again. Each time Cassie comes out of the car, the director hugs her, pulling her into his arms. Then he wags his finger at her and she stands there staring at her feet, taking whatever criticism he has. I'm not convinced I would take it.

They're filming outside a hospital near York, nowhere near the real Crowmont. It doesn't look anything like it either. They've printed a fake sign and stuck it on the driveway to trick people into thinking this is where it all happened. I've never been a fan of trickery, unless I'm the one doing it. But even I have to admit that there are times when I see a glimpse of Cassie in that car and it reminds me of me, with hair I dyed a shade darker to look like yours. Along with the weight I shed

173

to resemble you at a glance. She looks like both of us. We could be sisters, and maybe that other one, too. Jess.

Can you imagine what our childhood would have been like if we'd been sisters? Would we have had my parents, or yours, do you think, Leah? I think yours. I would've killed your father before he had the opportunity to abuse you, and that means Tom wouldn't have been born so I could have my sister all to myself. It would have saved your mother, too. Well, our mother in this reality. And she would have looked after us in that tiny house in Hackney. The three of us together. Ah, yes, I've already forgotten about the other two.

I think it would've been blissful. I think we would've loved each other. Or perhaps not. From what I've learned about people like me, we can't love anyway. But you would've been all mine and that's enough for me.

The movie set begins to pack away and I can see Cassie following the director around like a lost puppy. He has his hand on her arm, very firmly. I don't like the look of this man, Leah. I don't like him much at all. You might be surprised to know this, but I can recognise one of my own quite easily. This man has that hard glint in his eye. Tom does too, sometimes, but I don't know whether he's exactly the same as me. Owen, obviously. My father. My uncle. My mother when she's intoxicated enough, but it's not natural for her. She wasn't born a psychopath.

But not you. Never you. No matter what happens to you, your heart remains open and raw. I could burn your life to the ground – and believe me, I'm trying to do just that – and you'd get up and keep going. You'd blame yourself first, then you'd find someone else to nurse and life would go on.

I have to go now, Leah. The police are tracking us using Mum's money, which means we can't linger in one place. I'd imagine that scabby detective has told you about her death by now. I ought to kill Owen for what he did, but perhaps even I have a limit. Or perhaps I know that I need him in order to survive. We will adapt, anyhow. I must go and find him now.

I wish you were actually here to talk to. My imagination only stretches so far. But there is a present waiting for you. I hope you like it.

24

LEAH

I stagger away from the body. Seb pulls me into him and my back rests against his chest. I can't stop staring at Dominic laying on the gurney, his eyes closed, his face slackened by death. Seb's arms take hold of my shoulders and he gently turns me around.

He brushes away a tear on my cheek. "I'm so sorry."

"I thought he'd gone home to his parents. I should've checked. I didn't even ask Tom, I just assumed." I sniff and wipe my nose with the back of my hand. Seb passes me a tissue. "He didn't reply to my messages and I should've checked he was okay." I don't say it, but I think it... It's the same situation as with Jess. I should've checked on Jess when she stopped replying. I didn't push anything. I didn't spend much time finding out where they were and why they weren't replying. Why didn't I call Dominic's parents to check he'd gone home? Why didn't I make sure Tom did?

Seb leads me out of the room and he tells the coroner that the body is not that of his brother, that he believes it's Dominic Molina instead. The coroner merely nods and tells us he's sorry for our loss.

"We should go and get some coffee," Seb says. "Or something stronger."

Back in the waiting room, Donna pulls me into a quick hug. Unexpected, but welcome.

She wipes away a few tears. "I feel awful," she says. "I liked the lad, but I'm glad it's him. I'm glad it's not my boy."

I can't hate her for it, in fact there's a part of me that thinks the same. I lived with Dominic for two months. I loved his company, and I thought of him as a kind and thoughtful friend, someone whose company I cherished. But Josh was practically my brother in law and I would've hurt for Seb and myself if we'd walked into that room and found Josh's body on the gurney.

"I wish there was no one in there," I say softly. Then I wipe away the last of my tears and retrieve my phone. "I need to call Tom."

"Wait." Seb catches my arm. "The police may want to handle that."

"What do you mean?"

He sighs. "Dominic was Tom's boyfriend and they broke up a few days ago. The police will want to question Tom."

The realisation sinks in. My son is going to be a suspect. "I can't not tell him," I reply. "How can I sit and do nothing?"

"Just give it a few hours," he insists.

I consider ignoring him and calling my son, but I don't. I don't know if it's what Seb said about the police, or the unemotional way Tom told me that Dominic dumped him, but I put my phone back in my pocket. "Let's go to the canteen then. Let's get coffee."

"No," Donna says. "Let's go home."

After a sombre journey back to the farm, Donna goes to bed and we walk back to the cottage. I've never felt so exhausted. Not since the night in the cave have I felt so emotionally and physically drained, and I had been stabbed that night. It was the night Tom saved my life.

My son has saved my life twice. There is good in him, I know it. Yes, he killed David Fielding, but it was self-defence. There was nothing wrong with what he did that night, anyone else would have done the same. But can I deny that it changed him? Can I put my hand on my heart and say that Tom remained the sweet, thoughtful boy he was before that incident? Perhaps I can't.

As we walk past the hedge where Pye the cat lurks, Seb stops, and blocks my way with his arm. He sees it first: the white envelope poking out of the letterbox.

"Did you catch the post today?" he asks.

"It usually comes in the morning when I'm having breakfast," I reply. "I don't remember anything arriving today."

"Wait here," he says.

I do as I'm told, scratching my forearms, a sick feeling laying low in my belly. The earlier snow has transformed into sleet. Slate-grey in the harsh tinge of night. The hairs on the back of my neck stand on end. The letter box slaps shut when Seb removes the envelope from its grasp. He lifts it between finger and thumb, using a tissue as a barrier so as not to get his prints on it. There's no writing on the front of the envelope. Whatever this is, it's been hand delivered. Then he checks the door.

"Still locked."

I walk up the path to unlock the door and we go into the kitchen, warmth hitting my numb face. Once inside, Seb puts on leather gloves and gently opens the letter with a knife.

He unfolds the note inside and spreads it out on the table. As the paper unfolds, it reveals the wings of a bird. A magpie in flight, with a necklace dangling from its beak. Looped into the necklace is a wedding ring, probably my mother's, though it's hard to tell. Still, this is clearly a taunt from Isabel.

"It was her," I say, leaning over the illustration. "She killed Dominic and she might have your brother."

I expect Seb to agree with me, but he doesn't, he simply stares at the picture on the table, his shoulders hunched over. He's exhausted, we both are. He thought his brother was dead. Even now, after identifying Dominic's body, Josh could be dead somewhere, waiting to be found.

"We should pack a few things and sleep in the farmhouse tonight," he says.

"Okay."

"You nip to the bedroom and get us PJs and a change of clothes. Whatever else you need. I'm going to check the house."

"Be careful." I loop my arms around his neck and kiss him. Isabel hid in our attic for days waiting for the perfect opportunity to abduct me. Now all I can think about is him up there alone and it makes my heart twist. "Take a weapon."

He goes into the cupboard below the sink and grabs a hammer. "I'll be fine, don't worry. Keep your phone close in case I do find anything."

The house is unbearably quiet as I head upstairs to pack. I find myself analysing every one of Seb's footsteps to check he's safe. With each creak I wonder whether that was him or an intruder. Every thud. But as I zip up our holdall bag, Seb is coming back down from the attic, his face flushed.

"It's empty."

"Okay, let's go then."

We leave the magpie illustration on the kitchen table and make our way back to the farm.

* * *

The spare room at the farm has a lumpy mattress and I wake up with an ache in my lower back. Bending over the toilet to be sick doesn't help either. Then the smell of cooked bacon drifts up from the kitchen and my appetite comes back immediately. But before I head down to eat, I call DCI Murphy to tell him about the illustration.

"Do you have any good news I can pass on to Seb and his mum?" I beg. "Any possible sightings? Did Josh use his debit card somewhere?"

"Sorry, Leah. We have nothing so far."

"How is that possible in this village?"

"Well, we're trying to find out."

I'm about to end the call when I decide to ask him a few more questions. "Have you told Tom about Dominic yet?"

"Yes, a few officers went to his flat first thing this morning."

"And Dominic's parents know?"

"They're on their way to formally identify the body."

"Can you not tell Tom that I saw the body first?"

"Well, I can't withhold information if it becomes relevant to the case," he says. "But I won't tell him unless I have to."

"And you're going to question him?"

"We'll certainly take a statement. Are you all right, Leah? Is there something wrong?"

"How did Dominic die?" I ask.

"There's an autopsy scheduled for later today to determine cause of death."

"But... you must have had an initial investigation."

"We have theories, but the autopsy will confirm those. Leah, you know I can't give out this kind of information."

"Sorry, I know. Sorry. I just didn't know if he'd been murdered or not."

"We're treating the death as suspicious."

"Yeah, I saw that on the news. And what about Anna Fielding? How did she die?"

He pauses. "Well, it's about to be public knowledge anyway. She was strangled."

"Was she carved?"

"No," he admits.

"Maybe it's because it was her mother," I say. "Don't you think that's odd, though? Isabel nearly always carves bird wings into her victims."

He lets out a soft laugh. "You should work for us. We've noticed that too and have factored it into our investigation. Look, I know you're caught up in all this, but don't start doing detective work, okay? Let us handle that side. You stay safe." He sounds tired and drawn. I wonder how much sleep he's getting. Then it dawns on me that I don't care about Murphy's wellbeing, all I want, is for him to be sharp enough to catch her.

"You need to find her," I say. "This has to end. If you don't find her, I'm going to die, and my unborn child is going to die along with me."

"We're working on—"

"Do whatever you need to do, DCI Murphy. Bend the rules. Break the rules. Fuck the rules. *Find* her."

When he replies, telling me about how he's arranged for a team to watch us for our safety, I'm barely listening. There's a swirling in my head, the blood pumping hard around my body. I think I know what to do.

* * *

After breakfast, I tell Seb that I'm taking Isabel's drawing to the police station so that they can dust it for prints. Which is true, I do take it, and I explain to DCI Murphy about the ring and what it all symbolises. Then I drive to Tom's flat.

As I suspected, he's home rather than at work. When he lets me in, he's half-dressed and dishevelled like I woke him up. It's almost lunchtime.

"Did you find out about Dominic?" he asks. He genuinely does look terrible, with bloodshot eyes and grey skin. There's the scent of alcohol on his breath.

"You broke your sobriety," I say, and then I go into a mothering mode, gathering up dirty dishes to put in the sink. I fill Tom's coffee pot and wait for it to brew. "Are you going to any meetings today?"

He shakes his head and reaches for a packet of cigarettes on the coffee table.

"Tom, I'm so sorry about Dominic."

He lifts a cigarette to his lips and lights it. "I bet you think it was me."

I move closer to him, but not too close. Seb would be angry if I was here, next to the young man suspected of murder. "Why would you say that?" It's not so much of an exclamation than it is an authentic question. I want to know what he thinks we see in him.

"Because I'm a murderer," he says. And then he breaks down. "You hate me. You don't love me; you wish I'd never been born, and I wish that too."

Now I go to him, and take his face in my hands, lifting his chin so that our eyes are level. In that face I see a broken little boy who is so lonely that it splits my heart in two. "I would never wish that Tom. Never. No matter what you've done."

"I didn't kill Dominic," he says. "But I'm bad. I did an unforgivable thing." His voice cracks. "Do you remember how powerless Dad would make us feel?"

"Yes." Powerless to stop him, to make him stop hurting our

mum, to help him quit drinking, yes, all those things and more.

"Well, there was one moment that made me feel powerful for the first time. Like I could take on the world." He pauses and licks his lips. "David Fielding."

There's a chime in my mind, the familiar ring of his words. And then I remember what he talked about when he was at his AA meeting. He talked about how taking drugs made him feel powerful. Except... he wasn't talking about drugs. I remove my hands and stand up straight. Why didn't I figure this out before? Tom doesn't go to AA because he's addicted to drugs and alcohol, he goes because he's addicted to violence. There was something else he said: *I've been clean for two years.*

"Alison Finlay." My hand flies to my mouth. My throat goes dry with either fear or shock, I'm not sure. "I thought it was me. I thought I did it in my sleep, imitating Isabel because there was part of me that..."

"Loves her?" Tom says. "I know. I've always known that. Which is why I took advantage of it and made you think you'd killed her." His eyes drop to the floor and he rubs his nose, his body twitchy with nervous energy. "I replaced your medication. That's why you were hallucinating and sleepwalking more than usual in Scotland. Then I followed Alison home through the quiet fields and murdered her, making it look like Isabel's handiwork."

I find a chair to drop into. "No, Tom. No. You couldn't have. You were at home that night."

"I came in as you were sleepwalking, and then I smeared blood on your hands and told you that you'd killed someone. You were so out of it that it worked. I wasn't sure if it would."

My eyes fill with tears. "How could you?"

"I told you it was unforgivable." He takes a drag of his cigarette and flicks the ash into a mug.

"Why? Why that woman? She did nothing to you, to us." My hands ball into fists as anger and shock and sadness rushes through my body.

He pulls on his cigarette and shakes his head. "I was so filled with hatred. You brought Isabel into our lives and I wanted to punish you for it."

"That's no excuse."

He looks at me sharply, and I get a glimpse into the depths of his anger. I see it now. I didn't want to before, but I see the rage in his eyes.

"You never told me, *mum*. You never sat me down and told me how I was born. I had to find out by accident. That I was made through *incest*. I... I needed to let it all out, this rage. Killing David Fielding made me feel so powerful and I wanted to feel like that again."

I can't believe the things he's saying to me. How did I miss all of this? We're both silent for a moment, the sound of Tom smoking the only noise in the room. A last, terrible thought hits me.

"Did you ever want to kill me?" I ask, watching a tear roll down my nose and drop to the floor.

"Yes," he admits.

25
TOM

She doesn't seem afraid of me, but she is devastated. Her tears wet the floor while I find my own tears drying up. They were real, the tears I shed for Dominic. I wasn't faking them. But I had never been certain if I'd ever feel remorse for what I did. I was wrong, there is remorse inside me, banging on my bones, demanding attention.

But more than anything, I want my sister back. I want everything to be back to how it was before Isabel escaped Crowmont Hospital. Leah was ill when we were living in the cottage, but if she'd gone to the doctor's and been diagnosed, we could've had a happy few years there. I want to be blissfully unaware of who I am. I wish I'd never killed David Fielding. Sometimes I even wish I'd let him murder Leah, and then Isabel could've killed me. At least it would've ended it all before it began.

That's not the reality, though. Here I am sitting in front of my sister, confessing a premeditated and sickening murder to her. And there she is, wiping her eyes, trying to compose herself.

"I only ever wanted to be your mother," she says. "But it was taken from me. I was so young, and I felt so violated. Mum never believed that it was Dad who did this to me. She took over and raised you as her own, making you my little brother. I've made mistakes, Tom, countless mistakes. I shouldn't have moved out of that house, I should've stayed and protected you, but I thought I could get you out once I'd settled in a job. I had no idea what Dad was going to do." She takes a break because the emotions are too strong. I see her swallow hard. "You're right. I did bring Isabel into our lives and there is a part of me that loves her. I hate her so much, but we're connected by something... otherworldly." She shakes her head. "I can't explain it."

"You're attracted to her," I say. "She's smart, free, danger-ous. She's obsessed with you and that has to have some sort of effect on your ego, even if you don't over-analyse it." I watch her closely. I've never known if Leah's ever been aware of the effect Isabel has on her, but I suspect it's because of our father and the house we grew up in as children. It's a part of myself that I've also come to understand. Leah and I think love will come from darkness. From pain.

"I don't want you to be right," she admits. "But I think you are." She smiles thinly, not a trace of joy on her face. "When did you become so wise?"

"When you weren't paying attention."

"Well, I think it's safe to say you have my attention now." She leans back in her seat and rubs her eyes. "What do we do now? Do I know everything?"

I nod my head. "You do."

"What about Jess? Dominic? Josh?"

"None of that was me." A ripple of emotion runs through me. "I could never kill Dominic. He was the one who helped me stop."

"Did he know?"

I shake my head. "He thought it was drugs all along. I never told him about Alison. I think that's why he dumped me, because he knew there was this secret between us."

She nods. "He mentioned a secret to me. He was upset, you know. He loved you and he wanted to make it work. But I saw bruises on his wrist. He tried to make it seem like there was some consensual stuff going on, but I could tell he was lying. You were violent with him."

"I'm like Dad," I admit, throwing the butt of my cigarette into the mug. "Sometimes I can't control my temper."

She comes closer to me now and takes my hands in hers. It's surprising to feel her touch. I thought she would run out of here screaming. I almost forgot; Leah loves monsters. "Remember when I was drinking too much and you were scared for me. You convinced me to give up drinking so that I didn't turn out like Dad."

I don't understand where she's going with this, but I nod anyway.

"Well, now it's my turn to stop you from becoming Dad."

I lean away, confused. "I already am. I'm a murderer."

"A murderer who confessed, and who is working on their addiction, who's trying to improve."

"You're not going to call the police?"

"If I call the police, you'll go to prison," she says.

I pull my hands away from her. What did I want from this? Did I want her to turn me in? I'm not sure. "I think I belong in prison, Leah. I took a life just for the hell of it. That woman had family and I ruined all their lives. You're not going to call the police?"

She shakes her head. "You're my son and I want to help you be better. You're not lost, not yet."

What she's saying is insane. No one could forgive me for

what I did. But when I search her face, I see no trace of a lie, and Leah has never been a convincing liar. I can't believe she would protect me, perhaps that's because the woman who raised me failed to protect us both.

"What was Dad like when you went to visit him in prison?" I ask.

"He was like a... a shadow of who he was when we were young. Thinner, shorter... smaller in general. He wasn't the man we remember. He wasn't the *monster* we remember."

"You weren't scared of him?"

"No," she says, and she seems almost surprised by this admission, as though it only now occurred to her. "He was pathetic to me. I pitied him."

"Like you pity me?"

"I'm so sorry for everything you've been through. Maybe I'm not seeing this clearly. We've known so many psychopaths. You know, maybe that's not true. Dad isn't a psychopath. He's weak. He's pitiful. Isabel is a true psychopath, not you. I think maybe you tried to be like Isabel to make it stop hurting. But you're not her. You have love to give, Tom. I wouldn't be here if you didn't." She places her palm on my cheek, and for the first time she begins to feel like my mother. "I've been thinking about Dad ever since the pregnancy test turned out to be positive. I feel awful about what I said to you in the car that day, about how I'll be passing on his genes from one generation to the next. I think I made it sound like there was no hope for you, that you'd forever be a copy of his worst traits. But that was wrong. Tom, I think we've both inherited some of his darkness and I think we're idiots if we don't admit that to ourselves. And I think that's why people like Isabel are drawn to us, because we're people who could have turned out like her, but we didn't. We've been fighting against it. If you were like Isabel, you wouldn't feel guilt for killing Alison. But you do, don't you?"

Dumbfounded, I merely nod my head. I hadn't looked at any of these issues from this perspective.

"Maybe at one point you enjoyed it, but you were lost then. And I was lost, too. I think we can find who we are together, and we can't do that if you're in prison. No, Isabel confessed to Alison's murder and we're not going to rock that boat. But you need to keep going to the meetings. And I think you should stay with us for a week or so."

"Oh," I say. "There's a problem with that. Seb. I think he suspects me."

She gets to her feet and chews on a thumbnail. "I'll have to talk to him and smooth things out. He knows. He's figured it out for himself, and I think he thinks you've hurt his brother."

"I swear I haven't—"

"I believe you," she says. "Stay here for now and I'll try to figure it all out."

* * *

Dominic's parents have no desire to meet me. I try calling them using a number DCI Murphy gave me, but as soon as I explain who I am, they make their excuses and hang up the phone. They'll never know about Dominic's last months with me. They'll never accept who he was. By doing that they've robbed themselves of learning all about his amazing qualities. The way he managed to keep me on a lighter path, despite the darkness that had taken over. They'll never learn about how he helped to make me a better person.

Now that I'm alone again, I decide to head over to the next town to go to an AA meeting. I'd forced Leah to leave after we discussed everything about Alison Finlay. I'd wanted to be alone when I called Dominic's parents, not that it had any benefit. But being alone makes me want to drink, or go out and get in a fight, or whatever. Anything that numbs the pain.

Despite the centimetre of snow on the ground, the buses are still running. The early morning dusting is all anyone can talk about. I see the people in front of me browsing the weather report, paranoid that the snow will get worse and they'll be stuck. I don't care.

The meeting is the usual affair: bad coffee, weak tea, and uncomfortable chairs. There are six of us in total, all sitting in a circle like a discussion group. As always, we go around the room and each person gets their opportunity to speak. Finally, it's my turn.

"I drank alcohol last night," I admit. "I broke the promise to myself and I drank. But alcohol isn't my main addiction. Drinking doesn't help, obviously, but it isn't what strips away at me until I don't recognise myself anymore." I rub sweaty palms against my jeans. "My boyfriend was murdered. I found out about it yesterday."

There's a murmur all around the room but no one talks.

"I walked straight out of the door of my flat and I went to the nearest shop to buy booze. I wanted to numb myself, or to lose myself, I don't know which.

"I met my boyfriend when I was at my lowest. In fact, I was drunk then, too. Not the fun kind of drunk, either, the crying, shameful, throwing up on your own shoes kind of drunk. I was walking down the street without any money for a taxi and he helped me get home. He didn't know who I was, but he helped me into bed, made certain I didn't choke, and then slept on the sofa. The next day I moped around feeling sorry for myself while he made me hot drinks and told me things would get better. He'd recently been thrown out by his parents and had spent a couple of nights on the street. But now he had a job and things were looking up. When he smiled at me, it was like someone was shining a torch on me, or him, I'm not sure.

"And then he hardly left my flat, even though I kept telling him that I was no good. He helped me find a new job that I actually liked. He made me start coming to meetings. He was always by my side when I felt the worst about myself. I gave him so little in return because I convinced myself that I had nothing to give. I gave him nothing but pain. And now he's dead because of me, because of the life I chose to live. And it isn't fair. None of it. I want to say that I wish I'd never met him, because if I hadn't, he'd still be alive. But I can't wish that, because he saved so many lives and he doesn't even know it, including my own."

26

LEAH

Tom asked me to leave his flat so that I could give him space to call Dominic's parents. He wants to tell them about their son. About the relationship they had and the way Dominic helped him get through the bad times. My legs feel like jelly as I leave. I'm still reeling from his confession.

Tom killed Alison Finlay.

He didn't just kill her, he also tried to make me believe I'd done it so that I didn't suspect him. He replaced my pills and risked my delicate mental health. I don't know how I'm even going to process this.

I get to my car and sit in shock. Tom murdered Alison Finlay for pleasure. I listened to him, and I made the decision not to call the police. Does that make sense?

No matter what, he's my son and I love him. I meant it when I said that he isn't a psychopath like Isabel. I'm convinced of that at least. He loves and is loved. Isabel loves no one. She has no soul, no conscience. Tom isn't like that. Is he?

The last month has been one thing after another. Since I

discovered that I was pregnant, so much has happened, from Dominic's murder, to Josh's disappearance, to Tom's confession. I've cried more over the last month than ever before. There's been a lifetime of suffering.

I try to push away those thoughts, and check my phone for word from Seb or his mother. There's a text message from Donna to say that there's no news. But there's also an email from Cassie.

I hadn't given Cassie much thought since Josh had gone missing, but the email sitting in my inbox screams for attention. The subject matter: PLEASE MEET ME!

Dear Leah,

I'm so sorry to bother you. I read about your brother in law going missing. You must be so stressed out. I can't even imagine. But if you have half an hour to spare, I'd really appreciate it. I need to tell you more about Neal. I can't stay silent anymore. I can't keep working for him! You're the only person I know here and I need someone to talk to.

She proposes that we meet at the same place. I fire off a quick reply and she responds immediately to ask me to meet her now. I'm about to tell her that there's too much going on to meet today, but then I think that this might be the best kind of distraction. Perhaps listening to someone else's problems will help me calm down. Plus, I believe Tom when he tells me that he didn't kill Jess, and Neal's alibi sounded sketchy. If he had a part in Jess's death, is it possible he had something to do with Josh's disappearance, or Dominic's death? Any information could be useful now.

Because I'm already in the village, I arrive at the café earlier than Cassie. I order myself a latte and sit near to the door so I can see her arrive. While I'm waiting, it strikes me as odd that she's not filming today, because it always seems that the cast and crew work for long, hard hours and rarely have a break. This bit of snow might have shut production down. Or maybe they're focusing on a different character. Perhaps it's me and Tom in the cottage. Or the dinner I had with the Fieldings. The thought makes me shudder. Two of the people from that awkward dinner are dead now, and the other two are fugitives.

When she arrives, I note that she seems agitated. Her hands flutter around her face, moving strands of hair from out of her eyes. She orders a herbal tea and settles down.

Her voice is breathless as she speaks. "Thanks so much for coming. I'm so sorry about Josh." She sheds gloves and a thick scarf, dumping all on the floor.

"Thank you," I say, without going into any more detail. Dominic's death hasn't been reported yet and I don't want to spread the news around.

"If this is Isabel," she says. "God. I suppose it's our fault, for making this film. It's made her go crazy."

"Isabel has been mentally ill for a long time," I remind her. "But I did warn Neal about what the movie would do to her. She's a narcissist and this plays right into her hands."

"Yeah. I think he knows that." She grimaces, staring out of the window. Then seems to shake away a thought, lifts her cup, and takes a sip. The motion makes her sleeve fall down slightly, and I notice a bruise around her wrist. Very similar to the bruise that Dominic had on his wrist. The kind that almost looks like fingers wrapped around the limb.

"Are you all right?" I ask. It must be a coincidence, surely, but dread seeps into my bones like a cold night.

"Oh," she says, covering it back up. "It's makeup."

Relief floods through me. "It's so convincing."

"The team are great. They make everything look real." Her eyelashes flutter as she glances away from me and she scratches her wrist. This doesn't feel right.

I decide not to push it, even though my instinct tells me she's not telling the truth, or at least, not the whole truth. "You seemed a bit upset in the email. What did you want to meet about?"

"Did you tell the police about Neal?" she asks.

"Yeah," I reply. "I told them everything you said and I kept your name out of it like you asked. But the police told me he was with his ex-wife."

She nods. "An officer went to question him, asked him for an alibi. He gave them his phoney story and convinced them he's innocent. It's all a load of bullshit. He admitted everything to me."

"What?" I lean in. "He confessed to murder?"

"Yes."

"When did he tell you?"

Her gaze drops to the table. "Please don't judge me."

"I won't." I decide to hear whatever it is she has to say, but remind myself to remain wary of what she's telling me. Part of me wants to believe her, but at the same time, I know I can't always trust my own judgement. Perhaps I'm jaded after dealing with the Isabel's of this world, but much of what she says and does feels like attention seeking.

"It was in bed," she says. "He was on coke, completely out of it. We'd just finished..." she glances at her wrist, which is exposed again, and she tugs down her top. Her face flushes red. This time, she comes across as real. A young girl caught up in a tangled web.

"He did that to you, didn't he?"

"It's a game, that's all. A kinda kinky game" She gestures with her hands, giving a *no big deal* shrug of her shoulders. Yet again she reminds me of Dominic, passing off domestic abuse by making it all seem like a game.

"I'm confused," I say. "How did you and Neal become a couple? You seemed so convinced that he was a bad person. You met me and told me that he may have killed your best friend. I'm sorry, Cassie, but I don't see why I should believe you. First you say the bruise is makeup, then you say it's real, but it's from rough sex."

"I know it sounds bad. Please, please don't dismiss me." She reaches across and takes my hand, moving so quickly that I instinctively move away from her. "I want the same thing you want. I want to get the movie shut down, because I don't believe in it anymore. All these people are hurt because of the movie, because of Isabel escaping from prison."

"How are you going to get it shut down?"

"If Neal is arrested then the film will have to stop," she says. Her eyes plead with me. Big and round, like puppy dog eyes. She's a perfect fit for Isabel's character, with the same kind of open face that you instinctively trust. Cassie is so pretty that the effect is quite alarming.

I sigh. "I want to help you, but I can't trust you. These meetings where you tell me Neal is responsible, don't match up with your relationship with him. None of it makes sense and Isabel is out there murdering people. She just strangled..." I tail off, remembering that DCI Murphy gave me early access to this information.

"What? Who?" Cassie prompts.

"Her mother," I finish. "Anna Fielding."

Her hand flies to her mouth, fingers trembling. "Oh no. Moira will be so upset."

"Who's Moira?"

"The actress playing Isabel's mother. They met and Moira felt so sorry for her."

"Isabel's mother wasn't a saint," I say. "I'm not saying she deserved to die, but she was neglectful and turned a blind eye to what went on in that house."

"You don't think that a husband can trick a wife?" Cassie asks, wrapping her hands around her tea. "Isn't that what your father did to your mother?"

Someone opens the café door and the bell rings. I start, and then exhale. I don't know how to respond to that. I don't *want* to respond to it.

"Sorry," Cassie says. "I'm so sorry, that was completely tactless."

"It's true though. I've known too many women, including myself, who have been tricked by narcissists and sociopaths." As I say the words, I wonder whether I've been too harsh on Cassie's relationship with her director. She's so young, she could have easily been seduced by him. By the promises he made to her. "Tell me more about Neal. How did your relationship with him begin?"

"It was so stupid." She bites her lip, in that childish way I remembered from last time. "We were drunk. He kept telling me all about how I was talented, and he'd make me a star. I had a few glasses of champagne and I felt totally lit. Which isn't like me. I guess I hadn't eaten enough. We went to a club and then we got a taxi and I remember him kissing me. The rest is a bit blurry. But the next day we stayed in his hotel room talking about the future and the kind of roles he'll write for me."

"You don't remember if you had sex?"

She frowns. "No. All I know is that I woke up in his bed."

"What? In your clothes?"

She shakes her head.

"Do you think he could have drugged you?"

"I didn't at the time," she says. "But I don't know now."

"Cassie, do you have your phone with you?"

"It's at home," she says. "I forgot it."

"I think you should call your parents and stay with them for a while. Get out of this film, go to the police about Neal and most of all *be safe*. How old are you?"

"Twenty," she says.

"Do you have someone with you? A friend? A relative?"

She shakes her head. "I'm fine, I'm over eighteen."

"You're still a child."

"I'm over eighteen!"

"You know what I mean. This man is taking advantage of you. Even though you suspect him of all these crimes you're still with him because he made you believe you were wrong. He spun you promises and platitudes. Now you have a bruise on your wrist, and you're afraid of him. Isn't that true?"

She bends her head. "Yes, it's all true. I'll call my mum and go home. I thought I could do this. I think playing Isabel has messed with my head. Some days I don't know what's real and what isn't."

I hand her a tissue and she blows her nose. "You're not the first person to be tricked by a person like Neal, you know. And you certainly won't be the last." I reach over and rub her arm, feeling responsible for her, but at the same time completely overwhelmed by the situation. I can't take on another person's problems when I have several of my own. And yet I can't leave her here like this. "Do you want help getting home?"

"No, I'll be fine," she says. She lifts her head, mops up her tears and clears her throat. "Thank you for everything. Sorry I keep bothering you."

"It's not a problem. But promise me you'll go back to your parents."

She makes that promise and leaves shortly after. I stay to finish my coffee before heading off to my car. If Cassie wasn't so all over the place emotionally, I would suspect that she was trying to distract or manipulate me. But I think that her role as Isabel is making me view her in a different light. She even admitted that the role is affecting her psyche.

On top of that, I don't know what to make of her strange relationship with Neal. I know that creatives sometime live within a different set of morals, putting their art above everything else, but even still, the whole thing is odd. I want to believe her, but I suspect her to be a fantasist. Even so, I make a mental note to check in with her from time to time to make sure she's doing okay. Whether she's lying or not, she seems vulnerable, especially with Isabel out there. A narcissist might be particularly tempted to kill their own doppelganger.

27
SEB

The dirt is frozen beneath the snow. No matter how hard I hit the soil with the shovel, nothing is getting through. Fucking snow. Fucking farm. What's the point of having land with bad soil? Dad could never get any crops to take. We relied on beef farming back then, but it stopped making money. Then the climate changed and now the summers are too hot, and the autumn too wet. The world is changing, and like Josh always told me, I'm being left behind. If there was a stick in this ground, that would be me, a cold rod in frozen ground. Immovable. I'm the one holding back progress, complaining about everything. What happened to me? How did I end up here?

The dead fox looks at me with glassy eyes, a tongue lolling out of the side of its mouth. What possessed me to pick it up off the road and decide to dig a grave? What's the point? Someone ran over this creature and now I feel compelled to lay it to rest. Foxes are beautiful creatures on the outside, but unpleasant on the inside. One of the few animals that kill for pleasure. The entire Fielding family are foxes, and we're the sitting ducks waiting for them.

200

Eventually, the ground breaks, and I manage to go deep enough for an animal grave. A moment after I toss the animal in, my phone rings and I yank it out of my pocket, dirty fingers spreading soil on my jeans pocket.

"Yeah."

"Mr Braithwaite?"

"Speaking."

"It's Patterson Lester from Lester Investigation. I have some information for you about the person you wanted to find. Do you have a pen?"

"I'll have to call you back. I'm outside at the moment. I'll go to the house. It'll be five or ten minutes if that's all right?"

"No problem, I'm in the office all day."

I throw down the shovel without even bothering to cover the fox first and make my way to the house to find a pen, bracing myself against the cold wind. One week away from Christmas and the weather is about to turn. We'll be getting deep snow soon. Despite being a thick farmer who never bested a C at school, I know one thing for sure, we need to find Josh now.

Leah doesn't know anything about the private investigator I hired. But she couldn't know, because I hired them to find out if Tom was involved. While she was out meeting that actress, someone from their office told me a few interesting facts about the case. According to Lester's colleague, there were two sets of DNA evidence found at the scene of Jess Hopkins murder. One was a match for Tom Smith.

But it wasn't conclusive. The DNA wasn't found on the body, it was found at the scene. We all know that Tom discovered the body, which muddies the waters.

The second set of DNA turned out to be "inconclusive". Whatever that means. According to the investigator, it doesn't mean that the murderer wasn't Isabel or her brother, it meant that they didn't manage to find a match. This was the DNA found on the body. The DNA that matters.

I don't know what I was expecting or hoping for. Anything more conclusive than what he found, I suppose. But it was better than nothing.

As soon as I walk into the kitchen, Patch whines at me, disappointed that Josh isn't with me. I bend down by the mat and start removing my wellies.

"Mum, it's me. Where are the pens?" I shout, half bent.

"Hi."

I'd been so busy with my boots that I hadn't noticed him. But there he is, bold as anything in my family home. "What are you doing here?"

"Leah invited me," Tom says. He tucks his hands into the pockets of his jeans.

It feels like he's smirking at me, like he can get away with anything he wants to get away with. Before I know what I'm doing I have him pressed up against the kitchen wall. "Where's Josh you little prick? I know you're working with her."

"Get the fuck off me. What are you going on about?"

"Isabel. I bet you've been secretly writing to her, haven't you? You know where she is, don't you? Did you help her kidnap my brother? Or did you kill him together?"

"Stop being an idiot," he says. "I didn't do any of those things."

He pushes back, and he's stronger, until I tap into the frustration and grief. I lift my forearm until it's underneath his chin. Tom lands a knee in my abdomen and I lose part of my grip. But I still have enough resolve to keep hold of him as he squirms beneath me. I keep hold of him until I hear movement upstairs. Mum's still in the house, possibly listening to all of this, I drag him away from the wall by the collar of his jacket, and out of the kitchen door into the yard. It's then I let him go and square up, ready to hit that smug face of his.

He lifts his hands. "You were kind to me once. Remember? We used to get on just fine. Look, I'm not going to fight you." He dances away from me when I lurch towards him. He ducks to the left to avoid a punch. "Let me explain everything because you're half right, Seb. And then you can do whatever you want. Go to the police, smash my face in, I don't care. I've made a mess of everything." His face scrunches up into a grimace. I don't want to believe he's in pain, so I turn away.

"Go on then," I say. "Speak."

"I didn't kill Jess, but I did kill Alison Finlay."

His words send a chill down my spine. I was right. I was living with a killer and I was too stupid to know it. But when I begin walking towards him, he backs away.

"I was in a dark place. I know it isn't an excuse, but it started with my father. I don't know why I did what I did. I guess killing David Fielding changed me. It made me someone I'm not. I... I haven't hurt anyone since then. I swear. That's why I go to the AA meetings. I told Leah all of this earlier today because she thought maybe I'd hurt Dominic. I didn't. I loved him. I didn't hurt Jess or your brother and I've never been in touch with Isabel."

"Why should I believe a murderer?"

"You shouldn't," he says. "Call the police. I'll confess everything."

I consider it for a moment. "Did you make Leah think she'd killed Alison Finlay?"

"Yes," he says. "I did."

"And yet you claim you care for her?"

"I love her," he says. "But I'd just found out that she'd lied to me my entire life. You've no idea how much that hurt. All I wanted to do was numb the pain until I couldn't feel anything. I knew that if she remembered me coming home covered in blood, she'd know what I'd done. That's why I tricked her."

"And then you went on tricking her, with the birds."

His eyes open wider in surprise. "No, that wasn't to trick her. I got... I started to think I was like Isabel... They began to fascinate me. And then I met Dominic and I understood that it was all a lie. I wanted the pain to stop. That's all. For it to stop."

I don't want to believe him, but I know the life he's had. Fuck. This boy is pitiful. Strange and messed up, yes. But I feel sorry for him.

"Go on. Call the police, Seb," he says. "It's time I paid for what I did."

I take the phone back out of my jeans and stare at it. "I have a better idea."

He lifts his shoulders quickly, in a frustrated way, as though he wants this to be over once and for all.

"I hired a private investigator. The police are stretched, limited by budgets, but my guy has other methods. He thinks he's found where Isabel is. I'm going to call him back and get the address, and then you and I are going to go to that address. We're going to finish this once and for all."

28
LEAH

I climb into my car and turn on the heater, leaving it running for a moment while I warm up. As I rub my hands together for warmth, it takes me back to my first day at Crowmont in my old car. Not yet acclimatised to the slight edge to the Northern weather, anxious about my first day at a new job, and still reeling from Mum's death. It was the beginning of my illness.

After being diagnosed, I could never imagine voluntarily giving up my strongest medication, and yet I have, for my baby. It hasn't been long, but I often find myself wondering whether I'm in the grip of paranoia. And with Dominic's death, and Josh's disappearance, I feel more on edge than ever. So much so, that when there's a knock on the passenger window, I throw my hand up to my heart. But it's just Cassie waving at me through the window. She gestures for me to open the door and I oblige. Without asking, she climbs into the passenger seat.

"Hi, sorry to bother you again," she says. "I was about to walk back to my hotel, when I decided that I didn't want to be alone. It was such an intense conversation and I'm sort of struggling to process what we talked about."

Even though she talks like an actress, or at least there's a definite generational gap between the way we talk, and it grates on me slightly, I feel for her. But at the same time, I don't want to bring her into my life. I don't need another wounded animal to care for. "Oh, well, I'm actually about to go home—"

She interrupts me by pushing her sleeve further down her arm, to reveal the red welts all the way up to her elbow. I can't help it, I gasp.

"It's lucky that Isabel is always covered up," she says. "Or I'd have to answer a lot of awkward questions."

"Did you do this to yourself?" I ask.

Her eyes flood with tears and her face crumples into an emotional grimace. "Yeah. It was me. I've done it ever since taking this acting job. She's infecting me, Leah. The longer I play Isabel, the more I want to hurt myself. I don't know what to do." She wipes her eyes with her sleeves and clears her throat. "All I know is I can't be alone. Can I come back with you? To the cottage? I'd love to see it. I've heard so much about it."

"On one condition. You're not going to be playing Isabel anymore," I say. "You're going to quit this job and then go to the police about Neal. Whatever or whoever Neal is, he's at least a domestic abuser. Okay? All of these stressors are contributing to this."

She nods. "You're right. I thought it'd be kinda interesting to see the cottage after all the research I did. We never got 'round to filming the scene where Isabel hides in the attic. To be honest, it was one of the parts I was dreading the most. Being up in a dark, cramped space. I'm afraid of spiders."

"Maybe going to the cottage isn't such a good idea. Maybe

I should drive you to a family member's house? Or a friend's place?"

Cassie leans back in the seat and sighs. "Honestly, Leah, I'm getting so tired of your trite bullshit."

"Excuse me?"

There's sudden sunlight in my eyes, a flash of metal comes out of Cassie's sleeve, reflecting the light. I reach out to grab her wrist but she slashes my palm and then pushes the tip of the knife against my ribs.

"I learned a few other tricks from playing Isabel. I researched anatomy for one, so I know that my knife is now extremely close to your heart," she says. "I can slide this thin blade between your ribs and kill you in an instant. You won't suffer much, if that's a concern of yours. But I don't want to do that. I want you to drive back to the cottage so we can talk for a while."

My senses clear as the adrenaline hits. It was all an act. The tears, the bruises and self-harming, everything. I'd been right to question Cassie's mental state, because it turns out she was acting, badly. This whole meeting was nothing more than an attempt to gain my trust.

"Okay, Cassie, you're in control," I say, cursing myself for opening the car door. I'd sensed that there was something "off" about her, but I'd thought it was harmless attention seeking.

I wince as I place my cut palm on the steering wheel. Blood smears on the leather.

"Come on, let's go," she says.

I put the car in gear and begin to reverse out of the space.

Once we're on the village road, I decide to try and keep her talking. I've learned from Isabel how much psychopaths and narcissists like to talk about themselves. "Did you kill Dominic?"

"Yes," she says. "In his car of all places. Poor boy was sleeping in it close to the campsite outside the village." Her eyes constantly flash back and forth from the road to me. I wonder how well she knows Hutton and the surrounding areas. Perhaps I could take her somewhere else.

"He didn't put up much of a fight. In fact, he let me into his car one night. I pretended to be homeless with nowhere to go. It was cold and he took pity on me. Then I stabbed him."

There's no time to feel pain for what happened to Dominic. No moment to close my eyes and grieve that loss, to dwell on the suffering he felt at Cassie's hands. He was such a mild-mannered, kind person that it makes me feel sick that she did that to him. I press it down and pull myself together. I need to stay focused for the baby inside me.

"Did you take Josh?" I ask.

She smiles. "That would ruin the surprise."

I see the petrol station coming up on the main street and decide to take a gamble. "I need more petrol to get home."

"Liar," she says. "I can see the monitor."

"A bandage for my hand then."

"You're driving just fine. Keep going."

I grind my teeth together. She knows I'm stalling, that I'm trying to find a way to alert someone.

"Drive back to the cottage like a good girl. I know you've been stabbed before and I know you'll want to avoid that again."

There's a hint of slush on the roads, and overhead the sky is oppressively white. More snow is coming. There's nothing I can do but drive Cassie to the cottage, but if this snow comes, it'll make it even harder to either get help, or escape. Fear lays low in my body like an indigestible stone in my intestines. *Keep her talking.*

"Are you working with Isabel?" I ask.

"Not answering that," she says.

"Did you kill Jess?"

She smiles. "Yes, I did."

I don't know why this revelation shocks me more than the others. Jess and Cassie were actresses on the same film. They were friends. "Why did you do that?"

She presses the knife into the outer layers of my clothing, taunting me with her blade, in the same way Isabel would. The two of them are uncannily alike. It makes me want to throw up.

"Do you know how many young actresses auditioned for the part of Isabel Fielding?" she asks.

"How could I possibly know that?"

Cassie ignores my retort. "Two hundred. And I was the one who won the part because I wanted it more than anything. I have been trapped in a prison all my life, passed from one person to the next. Did you know that before I won my first acting role, I'd been in foster care?"

"No, I didn't know that."

"Yep. Well, my foster father made a deal with the director. He told the director that he could do whatever he liked with me as long as my foster father received all of my money. It was a TV advert. It paid pretty well, and the director did everything he wanted with me. I got lots of roles after that, but I never saw any of the money until I was eighteen years old and I moved away from that psycho."

"I'm sorry for the child who was treated so poorly," I say, trying desperately to listen to her story, but also watching the road for any sort of opportunity to get away. "But what does this have to do with Jess?"

"She was a traitor for one thing. She was in and out of a boring relationship with *him*."

"Neal?"

"Yes."

"But so are you." I point out.

"I have a reason for that," she says.

"What reason?"

"You'll find out soon enough," she says.

"Have you done something to him?"

"You're asking too many questions," she snaps.

"I'm listening, too," I say. "No one has listened to you before now, have they?"

She remains silent, but there's the barest twitch at the corner of her mouth and I wonder whether I've broken through a barrier.

"How does murdering people help with the pain of what you been through?"

That movement turns into a frown. "Pain?" she snaps. "What pain? No one can hurt me."

"That's a lie," I say. She presses the knife harder and I almost steer the car into traffic.

"Get a grip, Leah!" she shouts. "Watch it."

When the car is righted, she settles down again. A moment later, she begins to talk. "I've been a fan of Isabel's since she escaped Crowmont Hospital. Her childhood must have been abusive with the father she had, but instead of being a victim, she outwitted everyone. She lived on her own terms. I kept a folder on my laptop with every morsel of information I could find about her. My favourite of her kills was James Gorden."

"I don't understand how you could admire that. It was disgusting," I say. "You'd feel differently if you'd seen the aftermath."

"I doubt it," she says, and I believe her. "He had it coming. The guy was a creep with a weird fixation on Isabel. Why was a man in his thirties interested in a young woman convicted of a crime as a *child*? Because Isabel turned him on."

"No." I shake my head. "No, that's wrong. I met James Gorden and he wasn't like that. He was interested in true crime and nothing more."

"He was obsessed with her," she insists.

"He wanted to uncover the truth."

"You were obsessed with her too," she says, "otherwise Isabel wouldn't have been able to manipulate you like that. Isabel Fielding is the most sexualised serial killer of our times."

"Come on, Cassie. None of that is true. Isabel was a child when she committed her first murder, and since then she's been tucked away in an institution for most of her life."

"I know it," Cassie says, with complete conviction. "What Isabel does is a justified reaction to the persecution she's faced."

I shake my head. "I'm sorry, Cassie, but that's completely misguided."

Despite everything, I can still see the child in her, the one who bit her lip in the café. Yes, I understand that it was an act, and that she uses her large eyes to manipulate. But a part of me empathises with the girl stuck in foster care, abused by people in the entertainment industry, so powerless for most of her life. I can see why she idolised someone like Isabel. Someone who uses absolute power to her advantage. But I can't marry any of this up to Isabel's actual crimes.

Hurt people hurt people. But it doesn't have to be that way. My baby doesn't need to inherit the crimes of my father, I can teach him or her to break the cycle. Even Tom, someone with an appetite for murder, has the psychological strength to seek help. It's now, in this moment, that I finally reject the notion that psychological damage can't be overcome, no matter what Cassie says.

"Isabel had a choice," I say. "Just like you have a choice. What she did to Maisie might have been a response to her trauma as a child, but it didn't have to continue. She could have accepted help. She could have changed. But she didn't."

"The system failed her. Our world failed her," Cassie replies. "Why should she live within society's rules if society doesn't care about her?"

"Are you working with her?" I ask. "Do you communicate with her?"

Cassie barely reacts. The tiniest of blinks.

"What arrangement have you made with her?" I ask. "Why did you kill Dominic? He was nothing but decent; he didn't deserve any of this. He's not your foster father or the director of that TV advert. Did Isabel order you to kill him? Tell me Cassie." We reach the driveway to the farm and I almost keep driving so I can keep her talking for longer. While we're in this car she won't kill me.

To get past the cottage I have to drive agonisingly close to the main farm building. I crane my neck, searching for Seb's truck but it's gone.

"Isabel is manipulating you. It's nothing more than that," I continue. "There's no righteous cause, Isabel just wants to kill me, and you're a useful tool to help her achieve that. Wake up, Cassie. This is about her obsession with me and my family. I think deep down you probably know that. She wants to punish me and Tom for what happened at Crowmont, for making her recognise how alone in the world she is. It's all my fault that she can't have a normal life, don't you see that? She's stunted emotionally and she's blaming me for it."

"No, she's free," Cassie says.

I sigh and reduce the speed on the car, hoping that at least

Donna will notice me. Somehow, she'll know something is wrong and call the police. And then I remember... the police surveillance. Surely, they will be around somewhere. Impulsively, I jam my hand against the horn, depressing it and holding it down so that the obnoxious sound blares out. Cassie pushes the knife into my flesh and I cringe away from her, the sharp pain making me wince.

"Stop that!" She slashes the knife towards my hand and I let the horn go before she cuts my knuckles. The horn stops and so does the car while I catch my breath.

"Keep driving. Act normal now." Cassie is riled up by the horn. She didn't predict me doing that and the lack of control has irked her. That's good. Maybe I can keep doing that until she makes a mistake. And if she makes a mistake, I can take advantage of it.

The cottage comes into view and I immediately check around for signs of the police. They should have been following me, now I think about it. But because they blended so well into the background, I'd completely forgotten about it. When I check my rear-view mirror, there's no one there. And no one at the cottage. Where are the police?

Cassie notices me looking around and smiles. "The police got a tip-off earlier. Someone used Anna Fielding's credit card in a small village about thirty minutes out of York. The police are going there now to find Isabel and Owen. Which they will, because they know which hotel they're staying at. Well, they'll find... something."

"What have you done to Josh?" I say.

"Park here, Leah," she says. "Now we're going to get out of the car together and you're going to behave yourself, or I'm afraid I'll have to cut you even more."

I glance down at the blood in my palm. I can barely feel the pain, I'm so afraid of what's to come.

213

"The best part of this plan," Cassie says as she unclips her seatbelt, "is that Seb hired a private investigator. He found the address before the police did. He might be the one to get there first."

I want to smash her face into the glove box. Seb can't be the one to find his brother. It'll break him. My Seb, the man who feels so deeply, so instinctively. No. I can't bear it.

"Come on," Cassie says, and her voice sounds so eerily like Isabel that I double-take to make certain it's still her. "It's time to go in."

29

DCI MURPHY

The air is stale from numerous bodies squashed into a small room. This is not where DCI Murphy envisioned doing his detective work, in a tiny village police station with tons of officers cramped together. But here he is, working on a tiny shared desk in Hutton village. He'd come here to train and co-ordinate the local officers with how to deal with Isabel Fielding. After all, this is a place where graffiti was the main issue before she escaped from Crowmont.

But they were ready and willing to tackle the task ahead, and if he's honest with himself, he knows deep down that there's nowhere in the United Kingdom that feels advanced enough to deal with a threat like Isabel. A relentless, twisted individual who looks like a fifteen-year-old girl and behaves like Hannibal Lecter. Not only that, but she has a family with money. David and Anna Fielding might be dead, but she still has her psychopathic brother to help her.

It was only after Isabel and Owen left Thailand that he discovered they had an uncle living there. And then he discovered that the uncle, now deceased, was involved in some pretty disgusting crimes. Including the trafficking of young women. And at that point, it was the first time Murphy had felt any pity for Isabel Fielding. Lloyd Fielding had been found in two pieces: his body, and his penis. The latter had been disconnected and tucked into the pocket of his trousers. His body had been pulled out of the Mekong River by the authorities there.

"Sir, we've found something interesting."

Murphy looks up from his desk. The young PC is flushed with excitement, waving a piece of paper. His name could be Ridley, or Roberts; Murphy's not sure.

"Someone used Anna Fielding's credit card at a hotel. They must be getting desperate enough to make mistakes."

"Where?" Murphy asks.

"Outside York," says the lad.

"Good work." Murphy nods at the PC. Robertson?

The PC, whatever his name is, beams. For the last couple of months, he's been training the officers to research, research, research. To check CCTV over and over again. To utilise the systems in place and even to understand more about DNA evidence, which in itself had been complicated and inconclusive in the case of Jess Hopkins.

Murphy looks out at the room and sees they're thin on the ground. "We need to get the surveillance detail back from Leah and Tom Smith." He quickly calls both Tom and Leah to let them know that their usual surveillance will have to be pulled away urgently. Both phones go straight to voicemail. He doesn't have much time, so he tells them not to go back to the cottage, or to be alone. It's the best he can do in the circumstances because they don't have a moment to spare.

"Okay," he says, gathering the officers around him, "here's how we're going to do this..." And then he launches into a plan he hopes is detailed enough.

Isabel has slipped through his fingers too often and it can't happen again, not now that she's so close. He arranges for a team to surround the hotel, briefing them on the building, the exits, and the village. Then he makes a call to York, hoping to get snipers somewhere in the vicinity. Even if there's nothing left in the budget, he has to try. This *has* to be it. It can't possibly go on. The country has lived in fear of this girl for too long.

"Everyone know what they're doing? Vests on?"

"Yes, sir."

"Aye, boss."

A chorus of voices answers him. He feels apprehensive for his team. For the people under his care. Not for the first time, his stomach flips over. Isabel Fielding might be a slip of a girl, but what she lacks in physicality, she makes up for in intelligence. He's seen his colleagues underestimate her over and over again.

What is he missing, he wonders. What could go wrong that he hasn't accounted for? He climbs into the panda car. He never felt as though he'd made any mistakes when it came to this case, but he did know he'd been outwitted several times; by Isabel, her father, and her brother. But then so had everyone else.

And the case is confusing. The DNA evidence on Jess Hopkins, for instance. He'd seen the hair himself. It was the same colour as Isabel's hair, and roughly the same length, though he wasn't an expert. And yet the hair hadn't been a match. They were missing the root, and that made all the difference. Was it Isabel's hair, or could there be another young, female psychopath out there obsessed with Isabel's murders? Copycats did exist but mainly in American movies, not in Yorkshire villages. But perhaps that was his own bias skewing his police work. Perhaps this kind of thinking is exactly why he hasn't found Isabel sooner.

He isn't the one driving the car, giving him time to clear his mind before the raid begins. He'd called ahead at the hotel and was waiting for any updates regarding their movement.

He allows himself a moment to consider whether this feels right. Whether it sits right in his gut. No, he can't call it. He isn't sure. And yet, this could finally be it. He could catch Isabel at last, and make sure she doesn't escape this time.

30

SEB

There's no answer when either of us call Leah, and we're almost at the address. There's no turning back, no warning her about what we're about to do. If I die, there'll be no last words other than whatever I said to her this morning, which I can't even remember. Was it, *see you later, love you?* Or, *back soon?* I don't know. My thoughts drift to the baby not yet born but it's too much, I have to push those thoughts away.

The other cars on the road are an annoyance, the tiny bit of slush slowing everyone down. At one point a man in a transit van blares his horn as I cut him up at a roundabout.

Tom gestures at the road. "We want to get there alive."

I glance over at Leah's son, knowing how little I trust him. He murdered an innocent person and now he's sitting next to me in my truck. And beyond that, he's perpetually calm, to the point where it's unnerving. We're about to confront a serial killer and he's picking the edge of his fingernail.

"Try Leah again," I say.

Tom glances at me and seems about to retort, but then he takes his phone and does as I ask. "Still no answer."

"Something isn't right." I shake my head.

Tom's eyes narrow. "What do you mean?"

"I don't know," I admit. "A gut feeling, I guess. I think we're being played."

Tom is silent for a moment. Then he says. "There's an element of this that feels too easy. How did you get the address?"

"I told you, the private investigator got it."

"He told you in person?"

"No, over the phone."

"But you met the guy in person, right?"

His questions are getting annoying, but I try not to snap. "Yeah, I went to his office and had a meeting."

"Okay," Tom says. "When you were on the phone to him, did his voice sound exactly the same, or was it different?"

A tingling sensation spreads over my scalp. "I don't know. I can't... I think maybe I met someone else in the office and a colleague called me with the address."

"Was it the same number?"

I shake my head. "No, it was a mobile. There was a team of investigators. I just assumed a different member of the team called."

Tom nods his head and makes a *hmmm* sound. "I think we need to prepare for the fact that we might be walking into a trap. The person on the phone could easily have been Owen Fielding and you didn't know it."

I follow the satnav, taking a left onto another unfamiliar street. How often do I even leave Hutton? When was the last time I left the country? What the fuck was I thinking? A thick farm boy like me can't take on a pair of psychopaths.

"How would Owen know that I've seen a private investigator?"

Tom shrugs, glances out of the window like we're on a

220

jolly somewhere. "Perhaps he or *she* has been following you. Perhaps they've paid someone else to follow you."

"I don't know. It seems a bit far-fetched," I say. "How would they find the time to do all this? Wouldn't the police see them?"

"Seb," Tom says my name like a sigh. "Let me explain something important to you. You need to internalise this if you are going to come out of this alive. They are cleverer than you. They are more devious, cunning and resourceful than you'll ever be. They also have money. There's no way they could have got out of the country *and back* without using money. It's pretty impressive, not sure how they pulled that off. You are thinking inside the box like you always do and assuming that they'll play fair, because you play fair. But they won't."

I close my eyes for a moment, and then open them again, my fingers wrapped tightly around the steering wheel. The road before us is empty. We're heading to a remote location and my chest tightens.

"How do we win?" I finally ask.

"Honestly? I don't know. All I know is, if we see an opportunity, we take it. We don't hesitate or stop to question whether it's right or wrong. Take it. End it."

31
LEAH

I can't help but gaze over at the farm when I leave the car on the drive, longing for Donna or Seb or someone to see me from the estate. If only Donna could see Cassie's knife and phone the police. But there's no movement. The doors and windows are closed against the cold. Donna is in there, somewhere, alone. That is, unless Isabel or Owen has her.

I begin to walk up the path to the cottage when Cassie grabs my elbow.

"No, not inside," she says. "We're going somewhere else."

I know what she's about to say before she says it. "The abandoned farmhouse on the moors."

"Good girl."

"It's a bit obvious, isn't it? Quite *on the nose.*"

"Everything is a circle," she says. "It all comes back around. Like karma."

We start on a slow walk, stumbling on the wet ground. A few flutters of sleet come down from the bright white sky. The further up we go, the more we're engulfed in a mist of snow. The wet sleet turns into snowflakes. There's no way anyone

222

from Seb's farm would see us now. They'll see nothing but mist and snow flurries. I imagine Donna standing at the window with Patch the dog at her feet, hair messy from sleep, the icy sky looming over the moors.

"That kind of logic doesn't work in your favour," I say. "If you believe in karma, then you will be punished for this."

"I've already faced my punishment. I had years of it. This is my reward."

She notices that I'm purposefully slowing down, dragging my feet through the snow. She takes her free hand and gives me a push to make me walk faster. I bow my head to protect my eyes from the cold. The sight of the settling snow freezes my blood more than the cold. This is terrible for me. It makes the chances of being saved even slimmer. But perhaps I can save myself. *Keep her talking.*

"Can you tell me one thing, Cassie?"

"It depends what it is." She's slightly breathless from the hilly climb. Her boots slip as we climb over some of the rocks.

"What are you going to do with Seb and Tom?" I ask.

She ignores me, her eyes drifting away. Her indifference seems genuine, which makes me think that Isabel and Owen have something planned for them, not Cassie. If it was Cassie, then I could at least find out, even if I can't stop what's about to happen. I get the feeling that I'm not going to be able to predict anything that happens next. If I want to get out of this alive, and save my unborn child, I need to adapt to the changing environment.

Up above us, the old farmhouse comes into view. There's a dusting of snow on top of what's left of the roof. The gaping holes where doors and windows should be make me think of missing teeth. Behind the house, the sky closes in. Not only is it snowing, but it's mid-afternoon and the sunset is only an hour or two away.

"What are you going to do to me?" I ask.

"We're nearly there," she says, nodding towards the farm-house. "You'll find out soon enough."

"It's not safe in there," I say. "Most of the roof has already collapsed. The rest could go at any time."

"We won't be there too long."

I stop, not wanting to put one foot closer to that building. "What if someone comes? This isn't as remote as it used to be. You get all kinds of morbid people coming to this place."

"We know," Cassie says. "We've decided to cross that bridge when or if it comes to it."

"We?"

She grins and pushes me towards the ruins. I hold my breath as we duck under the archway and into the house. This is where my dreams bring me. Where my subconscious longs to be. As soon as I'm inside, I picture Jess taking photographs with her phone, picking up stones and putting them in her pockets. I see her closing her eyes and breathing in the air, tapping into her creative side. And then I see Tom in the corner, pinned down by David Fielding. Isabel walking up and down with her sharp knife, in her element, relishing in the power of it all. James Gorden's headless body in the centre of the room, strapped to a chair.

Finally, my mind comes to the present, and I take it in slowly.

First, Neal Ford is tied to a chair, pushed into the centre like James Gorden once was. There is a small stool to his left, and on it, Isabel is perched. Her hands are clasped on her knees as though she's posing for a school photograph. She smiles sweetly at me.

"Hello, Leah."

32

DCI MURPHY

When Murphy arrives at the address, he discovers it's one of those independent hotels. Not a large chain type with hundreds of rooms. This is a small B&B with a friendly old couple at the helm. Even though he rang ahead, they are wide-eyed with fear when he turns up with his team.

"Good afternoon, I'm DCI Murphy, we spoke on the phone," he says, showing them the relevant documentation.

The greying man nods his head slightly. He's short, round and a little red in the face, like a comedian from the seventies. Right now, this man has the appearance of a rabbit in headlights, frozen, and uncertain of which direction to turn. A woman, presumably his wife, stands next to him, her hand gripping her husband's. She's even shorter, with hair cropped short but blow dried tall. Her eyes are wet with a glaze of tears. These are people who love their business. They never wanted to help a serial killer.

"Now, this is all routine and we don't want you panicked, okay?" Murphy says, suspecting that the man and his wife aren't listening to anything he's saying.

They both nod in unison.

"Okay," he continues. "Do you recognise this woman as the person who checked into the hotel?"

Murphy shows them a headshot of Isabel.

"No," the man says. "I'm not sure. The girl was about that age, and had hair like that, but..."

"Her face is almost the same," the woman says. "But not quite."

Murphy strikes that as an odd answer, but he gives the photo to a PC. Perhaps they're too rattled to recognise Isabel right now.

"And which room did the person using this credit card check into?" Murphy asks.

"Room four," the woman replies. She passes him the key. "On the second floor."

"Thank you. Before we get you out of the building, I need to know if anyone has been in or out of this room today?"

"We haven't seen anyone," the man says. "But we aren't always on the front desk."

"What about the last hour?"

"No," he says. "I was here checking in a couple from about three-ish. I stayed and manned the phones for the full hour. No one left."

"Great. That's really helpful. Now, if you could go with my colleague here. Is there a private room that you use?"

"We have a lounge, yes."

"Is there any access out of the building from this point?"

"No, just the main entrance, and one we use for deliveries, which is next to the kitchen."

"Great, this is PC Fisher and he'll go with you to the lounge. Thank you for all your help today." Murphy turns to his DI. "We need a team outside the kitchen. I'm going to head up to the rooms."

"Yes, sir."

Murphy directs two officers to stand outside the lift doors. Then he nods to the armed officers. "Enter room 4 on the second floor, search the place. Check all exits. If the room is clear, we perform a systematic search of the hotel. Are you ready?"

He hopes this goes well. Though it's unlikely that Isabel and Owen will be armed, he can't rule it out. Especially knowing about their uncle and his connections to the criminal underworld in Thailand. If they managed to get back into the country illegally, what are the chances that they brought weapons with them?

The stairs creak under the heavy boots of the armed police. Murphy follows at the rear with the room key in his hand. Everything is set up professionally, and yet he has the unsettled gut of a man who senses something is wrong. This hotel is the perfect location for two fugitives. It's rural, out in the middle of nowhere, with two older owners and barely any staff. Maybe one or two other customers. And yet, Murphy still finds it difficult to imagine no one recognising Isabel and Owen's faces. That's when he begins to wonder if they have help from someone else. He took a description of the woman who checked into their room and it sounded like Isabel, but when he showed the couple Isabel's picture, they weren't sure.

Room four is on the second floor, and Murphy's heart thuds as he and his team reach the first floor. A couple of men filter off to warn the occupants of room two.

Murphy barely hears the knock. He'd asked those men to be discreet and they were following that order well. Yelling, and loud footsteps won't help them today.

They make it to the second floor and continue along the narrow hallway. Armed police go first. Murphy's eyes roam the floor, walls and ceiling, checking for anything and everything. Old wallpaper peels at the edges. There's a stain on the carpet. A red stain. Blood?

The men wait for him outside the door. His heart pounds hard, but he can't let it show. He can only hope they don't notice the sweat on his brow or the dark circles beneath his eyes, because he hasn't known exhaustion like it ever since Isabel Fielding first escaped from Crowmont Hospital. She has turned his world upside down. And perhaps now, he gets to catch her for a second time.

He nods.

DI Davies bangs on the door. "Police. We have a warrant to search this room. Please step away from the door."

Murphy quickly unlocks the door using the room key, which is an actual metal key that scrapes in the lock. He immediately takes a step away. Armed police edge the door open first, and cautiously enter the room. Murphy hangs back, knowing that these men are trained for this. They move silently.

The door swings open a few inches more and he gets a better view of the room. The first thing he notices is that Isabel isn't here. There's no creepy woman-child standing there to meet him with a psychopathic grin on her face. Instead, there's a man lying face down on the bed.

"Check the bathroom and the wardrobe," he says, making his way over to the bed.

The man's wrists are tied together and strapped to the bed. He's naked from the waist up, and his back is covered in dried blood. There's blood all over the sheets and soaked into the carpet. But the worst part to look at are the cuts, carved deep into his back, on almost every inch of exposed flesh. When Murphy moves closer, the stench of urine hits the back of his throat. He's almost certain that this man is dead, but he can't see the cause of death. The cuts are bad, but there isn't enough blood on the sheets and carpet to believe that he bled out. These are mostly surface wounds.

Standing over him, Murphy sees the gag around the man's mouth. The lacerations on his wrist from the ropes are minimal. He isn't a forensic expert, but it doesn't feel as though there was much of a struggle. Then he notices the syringe on the table. They drugged him. Makes sense. He's a broad-shouldered guy, and Isabel is a small woman. Owen isn't exactly jacked either.

Murphy takes another step closer to examine the syringe when he hears it, the soft, inhale and exhale. He bends down and presses his ear closer to the man on the bed.

"All clear," someone says.

Murphy's eyes widen. "The victim is still alive. We need an ambulance. Now." He pulls at the ties around the man's wrists, yanking them apart in frustration. The victim moans softly, half conscious. Finally, Murphy gets him lose, pulls away the gag, and helps him breathe. With a thought that makes him sick to his stomach, Murphy comprehends the fact that if they hadn't come sooner, this man would've slowly suffocated with his face buried in the pillow like that.

"Someone get some water," Murphy orders.

Now that he's away from the pillow he sees the man's features for the first time. Even though there are more wounds over his face, at the hairline and across his nose, it's unmistakable. Owen and Isabel kidnapped and tortured Josh Braithwaite.

33
TOM

S eb doesn't trust me, and I don't trust him. I don't like the way he keeps glancing over at me, that square jaw clenched like an actor in a bad western. I don't trust him to have my back because he doesn't have the ruthless edge he needs for this. He isn't a killer. One look at Isabel's doe-eyes and he'll pity her.

I decide not to tell him about the missed call from DCI Murphy. I don't know what Seb has told Murphy, because he's definitely told him something. Otherwise, I wouldn't have had the grilling I got after Dominic's death. Luckily, I was with a client at the time of the death. It would be too obvious to listen to the voicemail, so I can't do that either. Seb will immediately think it's Leah and start asking questions. Besides, I do want to know if Leah is okay, and leaving the line open means she can contact us.

Perhaps none of that matters because the satnav is telling us that this remote lodge at the end of a private road is our destination. Both Seb and I take in our surroundings. The lodge is one of those wooden kinds, built to resemble an American cabin. It sits on the edge of a dense forest. I read the sign: Priestley Grove. A tingle of fear worms its way down my spine as I replay Seb's words in my mind. *I think we're being played.*

Stop Isabel by any means necessary. That's the end goal here. Even if this is some sort of set up, we can still ensure that Isabel Fielding never stalks our family again. Seb parks the truck and pulls up the handbrake. I grab the hammer from under the seat. Seb unclips his seatbelt and picks up a short axe. The weapons strike me as the kind of thing a Viking would arm themselves with. Which seems fitting, because this is a primal, ancient act of justice. Handled man to man, or man to woman in this case. I imagine Isabel, and how much I thought I admired her for a time. The thought makes my stomach heave.

I look at Seb before stepping out of the car and see the mirror image of my own grim determination. My feet hit a thin layer of snow before I shove the car door closed.

We walk silently towards the lodge. Somehow, with only a nod, Seb communicates that I should go around the back. I break away and walk around the side of the building. If there is anyone in there, they must have heard the car. We're not surprising anyone with our arrival. I move quickly, wanting to get this over with.

The snow makes everything slower and more dangerous, especially in a place as remote as this. Luckily, I was wearing sturdy boots when I turned up at the farm, making the slippery terrain easier to negotiate.

There's no exit at the back of the lodge, but there is a window that I attempt to peer into. The curtains are closed apart from a crack about two centimetres wide. I lean closer to the glass, squinting through the drawn fabric.

An eye stares back at me.

I lean away, gasping.

"Wait!" I yell, running around the side of the lodge, feet sliding in the snow. "Don't open the door!"

But Seb is already in the process of yanking the door open. He raises his axe, ready to fight, when an explosive bang echoes through the clearing. The axe wobbles in the air. Seb's body judders as he jerks back, the big farmer staggering from a blow. I reach him in time to catch him as he falls to the ground. But as I lower Seb to the ground a second bullet whizzes past my ear. Heart thudding, breath caught in my throat, I look up at the lodge, the door still half open. I can barely see into the small building, but I can make out the shape of Owen Fielding holding some sort of gun. Not a handgun, but not big enough to be a shotgun. A sawn-off shotgun perhaps. He's reloading it and I don't have much time. I wrench the axe from Seb's hand and fling it into the room, through the half-open door.

The axe finds its target with a crunch. I hear Owen Fielding let out a cry and I'm able to breathe again. But I can barely see into the lodge and I don't know how badly I've injured him.

I yank the door to the cabin closed. Then I lift Seb's bulk and hook his arm over my shoulders.

"We need to go!" I yell.

"My brother," Seb gasps.

I glance at the bullet wound in Seb's shoulder, the way the blood spews from it, like a person coughing up water after almost drowning.

"He's not here," I say.

I could be wrong, but instinct tells me I'm not. We begin to move through the snow together, Seb staggering with the pain. I hear his breath gulping next to my ear, every movement agony for him. We hurry towards the truck, barely ten feet away when a third crack echoes through the snowy air,

Instinctively, I duck, almost dropping Seb. But this time, the bullet wasn't aimed at us, it was aimed at the car, shattering the windscreen. I swear under my breath and quickly redirect us.

"You need to move faster!" I say to Seb, whose skin is as white as the snow. I look behind us and notice a trail of blood and footprints left behind. Fuck. Fuck. Fuck. It'll lead Owen straight to us.

"Faster, Seb, or we're dead."

I find myself almost half-dragging Seb away from the car, but he finally begins to speed up slightly.

"Good," I say.

"You should... leave me," he says.

"Yeah," I grunt back. "I probably should."

I cast a quick look back at the lodge but I can't see Owen. The one advantage we have is that I hurt him with the axe. I don't know where I hit him, or how badly, but I know that it was bad enough for him to cry out. Perhaps that makes us evenly matched now.

The only place we can go, is into the woods, which is probably what Owen, and maybe even Isabel, planned all along. If there wasn't a chase, it wouldn't be fun. Would it?

34
LEAH

"You couldn't have brought me a seat?" I ask, nodding towards the fold-out camping stool. Neal's chair is the same style, and for a moment I get a strange mental image of Isabel and Cassie walking to the farmhouse with their camping gear like two girls going on a picnic.

"You're right. I'm so sorry. And you've had such a long day as well." Isabel smiles sweetly, like we're over-polite acquaintances arguing over who should have the last slice of cake.

She stands and moves closer to me, reaching out to touch my face like a child petting an animal in a zoo. As her fingers graze my skin, I try not to flinch. I try not to feel anything, but instead my face burns with shame.

"It's been too long," she says. "Have you missed me?"

"Do people miss their tumours when they're removed?"

She breaks the electricity in the air by performing an exaggerated wail, her hands moving underneath her eyes like a cartoon character in mid sob. And then she stops and smiles again.

"Why didn't you stay away?" I say. "You were free! You even left the country."

I notice Cassie moving out of the corner of my eye, tiptoeing around to Neal. A few snowflakes are beginning to come in through the gaps in the roof, some settling on his body. He begins a terrible, fearful moaning through his gag which Cassie ignores. Instead, she sits on his knee, tossing an arm around his shoulder. This must be what it was like to be in the Manson family, to be surrounded by this aggressive, female energy mixed with so much rage and hatred. Rage pretending to be love. Pretending to be a case worth killing for.

Isabel saunters back to her stool and crosses one leg over the other. She has the appearance of a primary school teacher settling into her chair to tell the children a story.

"Impulse control," Isabel says at last. "Neither me or Owen seem to be able to spend more than five minutes with other family members. We have a bad habit of murdering them, you see."

"I know," I reply. "You murdered your own mother."

Isabel shakes her head. "Don't believe everything you read. I didn't kill her at all." She opens her palms and spreads her fingers. "My mother was strangled. Do you think these small things can strangle a human being?"

"Perhaps you used a rope. A wire."

"That's called asphyxiation. And it's quite different." She balls her hands back into fists. "No, it was Owen. And he was not supposed to. Naughty boy."

"Why have you brought me here?" I gesture to the crumbling walls around us. I feel strangely calm, like I know the rules of the game, which I suppose I do, because I've played this game before. "Where are your special knives?"

She glances at the floor and Neal begins to make frantic, muffled sounds through his gag. He sees the pouch and he knows what's inside. Isabel's scalpels.

"You can't use those on me," I say simply. "I won't let you this time." No, I'm fighting for my baby's life. I've been face to face with this killer before. I've fought her before, and I can do it again. My only hope is that Tom and Seb are safe, wherever they are. The fact that Owen isn't here frightens me. What if Tom and Seb are facing off with Owen right now? Cassie mentioned the fact that the police discovered an address, and that Seb got the same address from his private investigator. Surely that means that Seb is in the same location as the police? But what about Tom?

"What makes you think that you have a choice?" Isabel says, leaning forward in her chair. She laughs once. A humourless bark. "I know what it is, Leah. It's that hopeful part of you again. We had this chat the last time we met, didn't we? We talked about how much you always hope. How you never lose that faith."

"I remember that chat," I say, trying to engage with her. "You wanted to die then. You were at peace with it. So why didn't you kill yourself?"

"Maybe, I was inspired by you," she says. "Wouldn't that be funny? If I would have happily killed myself, but I lived because of the way you've inspired me to live."

I don't say a word. Slowly, I begin to angle my body so that I can see both Cassie and Isabel without having to move my head. Neal's panicked eyes meet mine. I didn't notice before, but there is blood around his mouth. Someone has already begun to cut him.

Cassie notices me looking at him and smiles. "We thought we'd give him a beak." She hops off Neal's lap and bends over him. "Nod for me if you'll be good." He nods once. Cassie pulls the gag from his mouth and Neal begins to scream, out of pain more than any attempt to get attention. Cassie shushes him and he eventually manages to quieten.

What I see is so disgusting that I have to look away. The two of them have cut deep lines from his nose to mouth. In some places, his lips are completely torn.

My reaction riles Isabel. She leaps onto her feet and gets in my face. One hand clamps my shoulder.

"Stop it!" she shouts. "Stop pretending that this disgusts you." She moves her hand up to my neck and digs her nails deep into the flesh, gripping and tearing, and as she does this, she moves me closer and closer to Neal, so that my face is a few inches from his. "Do not close your eyes." Her other hand comes over my face to prise open the lids. "Look!"

The deep, guttural noises coming from me, are almost completely drowned out by the sound of Neal's pitiful cries.

"Don't feel sorry for him," Cassie says. "He was going to defile your name. He was going to make money from your tragedy. He slipped drugs into my champagne, and he did the same to my friend Jess. A few weeks after my eighteenth birthday, he insisted that I do a nude scene in his latest film, just because he wanted to look at me naked. He's a creep. A fucking, dirty, perverted creep. He hid it behind his neatly trimmed stubble and fancy shoes, and now we've made it so everyone will see. They'll never stop looking at you, Neal. You'll like that."

I can't stand it. Isabel's nails in my skin, her fingers on my face. I wrestle out of her grip and back away, towards the exit. She doesn't seem particularly concerned; she barely moves, and I keep backing away, and then turn to make a run for it. Behind me I hear a whistle, like a dog whistle. A body collides with mine. It almost topples me over but not quite. But it grips onto my back, clinging there. I try to shake the lump from my back, but it refuses to move. A moment later, I feel the blade at my throat. I feel the trickle of blood. The more I move, the more the blood trickles. Finally, I'm still.

"Bring her back, Cassie."

The weight slides from my back, and she removes the knife before shoving me back into the centre of the room. Cassie slips her hand in mine. We stand there, hand in hand, in some perversion of intimacy. Isabel glances down at my hands with a frown. This makes her jealous, I note.

"Why is she here?" I keep my eyes focused on Isabel but angle my head towards Cassie. "And why is he here? Shouldn't this be about the two of us?"

Isabel walks towards us and removes my hand from Cassie's. She extracts the knife from Cassie's fingers and regards it for a few moments, weighing it in her grasp.

"That's an interesting question, Leah."

Cassie begins to laugh, and Isabel smiles, and it seems that they're in on the same joke. Gently, Isabel tucks a strand of Cassie's hair behind her ear. They're both still smiling.

When Isabel's smile fades, she plunges the knife into Cassie's chest. Horrified, I watch her topple onto the floor. Cassie's laughter turns into screams. Isabel pounces on the girl, lifting the knife again. Cassie's hands fly up to protect herself, but Isabel cuts them and forces them away from her chest. Cassie starts to scream, crying *no* over and over again. Her face is twisted into a mime's imitation of tragedy, the shock of the betrayal contorting her expression. Isabel ignores it and the knife goes up and down and up and down until her hands are covered in blood, and Cassie is gurgling with it. Neal moans and yelps. I'm frozen for a moment, but then I recognise that this is my opportunity to run.

A few snowflakes land on my hair as I hurry out of the ruins. The cold air freezes my lungs with each breath. She reaches me, and it's with a feeling of inevitability that her body collides with mine. I feel the tip of the knife next to my belly and I stop.

"There you go, Leah. She's gone now like you asked," Isabel says. "We can kill the man together."

35
TOM

The visibility changes when we head into the woods; snow coming down in huge flakes, hopefully covering our tracks as we continue between the trees. Winter has stripped them bare, and snow even covers the ground beneath the branches. I decide to take a chance, stop, and quickly fashion a bandage for Seb's wound using the lining of his jacket. It takes a few moments when we don't have them to spare, but perhaps it will save his life. The change in visibility is good for us, but it's also good for Owen. He could sneak up on us at any moment. The snow muffles sound, covers tracks, and clouds the air.

I wrap Seb's arm over my shoulder and set off, checking behind us as we go. The snow covers our tracks like I thought. Seb's heavy, exhausted breathing is the only sound in the woods. He shivers next to me. How long before he bleeds out? I don't think the bullet hit anything vital, but I can't be sure.

I can't find a footpath, which means we could be away from anywhere frequented by people, not that anyone would walk in this weather anyway. The terrain is uneven. Our feet sink into rotten vegetation beneath the snow, but I continue on, half dragging Seb through it.

"Leave me here," he grunts. "Go. Get to Leah."

That's my last resort, and I'd be lying if I didn't admit that I've already considered it, but I don't tell him that. Leah means a hell of a lot more to me than the farmer over my shoulder, but at the same time, I don't want him to die.

We find a steep slope and limp down it to the edge of a shallow brook. On the other side of the water, there's a cluster of large boulders up another slope.

"Come on," I say, gritting my teeth.

Seb nods, seeing the path I've decided on. His face is turning a pale shade of grey.

We both gasp when we step into the freezing cold water. It sloshes up our shins, soaking our legs. Up we go on the other side of the stream. I keep turning my head to see if Owen is following. He has to be. The snow is covering our tracks, but he must have picked up on a deep footprint or a drop of blood. None of us are experts at this, but it's common sense.

I prop Seb up behind a large, fallen tree trunk lodged between two stones. I peek out again and watch for movement. Without taking my eyes from the woods, I dig my phone out of my pocket and pass it to Seb.

"Murphy's mobile number is in there. Phone him, text him. Call 999."

I turn the hammer over in my palm. This is all we have left. If I need to defend us, Owen has a sawed-off shotgun and I have a hammer. Bad. He can still shoot the thing, because he shot through the windscreen. Very bad.

It feels wrong to have stopped. Part of me thinks we should keep moving, but Seb is struggling. I hear him mumble on the phone and his voice is strained.

There's movement through the snow. A dark, thin figure stumbles out of the woods and I suck in a deep breath to steady the flutter beneath my ribs. This is it. Owen is coming.

"Murphy didn't pick up," Seb whispers.

"The emergency services?"

"On their way," he says.

I huddle against the cold as I watch Owen limp towards the brook. I think the snow has covered most of our tracks, but I can't see from my position. There must be some footprints on our side of the brook, but I'm hoping that Owen can't see that far. One thing I do know, is that I was right about his injury. The axe must have done some damage to his shoulder, because as he walks along, he occasionally touches it with his other hand. However, he's still carrying the gun. I don't know enough about guns to know if he needs to steady this one with his shoulder, but I hope so. It could seriously affect his accuracy.

"He can't see us," I say quietly. "And he's hurt."

"A fighting chance, then," Seb mutters.

Owen makes his way down the bank to the brook and then walks following the direction of the water. It offers us a small reprieve. He must not be able to see our tracks on the other side of the brook, and he's assuming that we followed the direction of the water. Owen isn't a hunter, as far as I know. He's a spoiled, bratty kid who likes to party, if what Leah told me is true.

This gives me hope. If he doesn't come back up onto our side, he'll walk past us completely. That means we could be quiet and stay where we are. On the other hand, I could attack him from behind as he's following the brook. With the falling snow covering a lot of sound, it might be possible to sneak up on him. Could I take Owen if it came down to a fight? He has a gun, but he's nursing an injury.

I promised myself that I'd finish this.

If I get to Owen and keep him alive long enough, he could tell me where Isabel is, and what she plans to do to my mother. This was a trap all along, but it was more than a trap, it was a distraction. I continue to watch Owen as he walks next to the brook. He's walking more briskly, now. He doesn't even bother looking over here. Is he even trying to find us? Perhaps he's completed the task his sister asked of him: distracted us for a while to allow her to kidnap Leah. Now Owen's survival instinct has kicked in and he's planning to run away. This could be my last chance if I want to remove one more murderer from the world.

I turn to Seb. "Keep the phone. The police will need it to find you. Stay here and don't move, unless Owen ends up coming this way." I remove my jacket and wrap it around him.

"Where the hell are you going?"

There's not enough time to explain. I head away from the hideout, and down towards the brook.

36

ISABEL

I sit her down on the stool and every part of her body is completely rigid. Her back straightens, her eyes are alert. Inside that mind of hers, anything could be happening. But mostly, I believe it's fear. Then I turn to the man on the chair. His groans are becoming a nuisance. I yank the gag back over his mouth and he yelps like a kicked puppy.

"What a squawker you are," I whisper to him. "Perhaps you're a magpie. Or a seagull. Something chatty."

When he finally shuts up, I move back to Leah and stand over her, which feels nice. Powerful. The longer I stare, the more her rigid body slowly crumples in on itself until her chin almost touches her chest. She goes from terrified to defeated within moments. This is nothing like the Leah I know and love. She used to be a fighter. I lick my thumb and remove a smear of blood from her cheek. Cassie's no doubt.

"You wanted it to be just us," I tell her. "Why do you look so sad?"

"That wasn't what I said," she replies. She lifts her chin and meets my gaze. "All I asked, was why she was here."

There's some steel in her voice. That's more like the Leah I know.

"Good point. I interpreted it somewhat differently than you. Clearly." I glance across at Cassie's bloodied body. The girl had outlived her usefulness anyway. Her main job was to act as a distraction for the police, check us into hotels, and bring you to me. She's done all of those things.

"I won't let you kill me," Leah says. "I have more to live for than you do. We established that in the cove, didn't we?"

"People change." I shrug. "I know I have."

"I don't and you don't either. Everything you said was true. You have no role in this world. There's no way for you to live and be who you want to be. You're a destructive force, and the world will always want you either dead or behind bars."

She seems convinced of that. It almost gives me an existential crisis. Have I changed? Or am I the same person who almost allowed Leah to drown me? I'm not sure. It surprises me that I don't know anymore. Should I even care? Whether I've changed or not, the outcome is the one that has been inevitable from the start. I get to finish what I started, but with a slight twist, which, thanks to Cassie, makes this even sweeter.

"Come here, Leah," I say in my softest voice. She's hesitant at first. She shakes her head and a few tears begin to run down her cheeks. "I'm not going to hurt you." Her eyes flick towards Cassie's lifeless body. Then she rises, body slightly crouched, as though she's preparing for fight or flight. She takes two steps and stands in front of me. "I want you to hurt him." I nod towards the director.

Leah's eyes follow my own to the man tied to the chair. Her brow furrows in confusion. This isn't what she expected to happen.

"If there's one thing I can't stand, it's a sex pest," I say in explanation.

"I can't stand people who kill children," Leah snaps.

"People?" I laugh. "I was a child myself when I killed Maisie."

"You don't get to make yourself a victim," she says. "Not after everything you've done."

"That's fair."

She seems surprised that I agree with her.

"I'm no victim," I continue. "I made my choices and I don't regret any of them. Not having a conscience helps greatly when faced with problems like this. I wanted to murder Maisie, so I did. I wanted to murder you, so I tried. Now I want you to indulge your own dark side and hurt that man. A man who drugs young actresses and whispers lies into their ears as he's fucking them, making them believe that he'll turn their careers around if they comply with whatever it is he wants. And whatever he wants is carnal, every time. He's a narcissist. Those women are there to act for him. He tells them what he wants them to do. When to take off their clothes, when to parrot the lines he's written for them, and it's not so he can create art, it's so he can get off on it."

Snow drifting in through the broken roof continues to blanket the director's head and shoulders. I watch him shivering, and then I turn to Leah. There's a flash in her eyes I can't read. Have I broken through, to that dark part of her personality that I know exists?

"He's the one who wanted to make a film about your life without your permission. He wanted to take you out to dinner, to buy you champagne and let you order lobster. But there would be an exchange, wouldn't there? Isn't there always? You eat and drink while he talks and talks. You're a shy woman, a natural listener with too much empathy for anyone but yourself. You'd let him speak, nod along, and then never get an opportunity to speak your mind because he wouldn't let you."

"Shut up."

Her eyes drop to Cassie's body. I'm getting through to her, unlocking a hidden part of her mind.

"It's a tragedy, isn't it? That two women here have been turned monstrous by their experiences. Poor Cassie. Poor me. We weren't loved. We were made, not born. Isn't that right? Isn't that what happened to you?"

"Shut. Up."

"Monsters made by men. That's what we are. Take the knife, Leah. Let it out at last. I know what's inside you. I know you're just as full of rage as I am."

37

TOM

It's the sound of the water that alerts him, but I crossed the stream close to him, not giving him time to react. By the time he turns around to face me, I'm lunging right at him before he can aim the gun. We fall into the snow together, my weight on top of him, the snow flattening to mush beneath us. As we fall, I try to push the arm with the gun away from me. But he pushes back, trying to raise his arm. I press the wooden handle of the hammer down on his wrist. His face strains.

I quickly assess his injury from the axe, noting the blood seeping through his coat by his left shoulder. As we're both struggling for the gun, I take my free hand and thrust it into the wound. Spittle flies from his mouth, his teeth clench together in agony. His legs scissor kick beneath my body.

"Let go of the gun and I'll stop hurting you," I demand. "Let go and the pain stops."

His face is red with the effort of keeping hold of the gun. His teeth set together. But when I push against his injury one more time, he lets out a cry of pain and reluctantly drops his weapon.

Still on top of me, I snatch up the gun and raise it, throwing the hammer into the trees. Then I aim the gun directly into his face. Owen's body goes limp beneath me. He lifts up his uninjured arm as if in surrender.

"Where's Leah?"

A grin stretches across his smug face. "I don't know."

Frustrated, I push the butt of the gun to the shoulder wound. Between screams, he makes an attempt to snatch the weapon from my hands, but I lift it higher, out of his reach. "You do know. I'm going to make this hard for you if you don't tell me."

The whites of his eyes are prominent. This time he doesn't smile like a Cheshire cat, he grits his teeth and remains silent.

"Didn't Isabel tell you that I killed Alison Finlay?" I say. "I know she figured it out. You're not the only one here who can take a life. If you don't tell me where Isabel has taken Leah, I'll end you, and it won't be painless."

"Maybe I'll show you," he says, "if you let me live."

I press the butt of the gun into his wound and he screams.

"No. That isn't an option. Tell me now."

"You're going to kill me anyway," he says. "So why should I tell you?"

This time I bring the gun down onto the bridge of his nose, and blood bursts from it. I lift the gun, ready to deliver another blow, but his hands come up in his defence.

"Let me go or I won't tell you," he says.

I bring the gun down again, smashing into his face.

"You die slowly or quickly," I say.

Owen's hands tear at me. In horror, I see that he's crying.

"Don't kill me, please don't kill me," he says.

"Tell me where Leah is," I demand.

"She's at the abandoned farmhouse," he says between

sobs. "The one on the moors near your cottage. Cassie Keats is with them."

"Who?"

"The little bitch cast to play Isabel in the movie."

"Why would some actress be there?"

Owen groans as I apply more pressure to his injury. "All right, I'm talking. Stop it." He catches his breath, blood and spit flying from his mouth. "Turns out she's an apprentice psycho. I helped them take the director up to the abandoned farmhouse last night. They're going to make Leah kill him, and then they'll probably kill Leah too. I don't know."

I lean back on my haunches, removing my weight from Owen's body. Then I slowly stand up, all the time directing the gun towards him.

"Don't kill me. Please, let me go. I told you everything," he begs.

I've never shot a gun, but I hope it's relatively easy. I can't imagine Owen keeping the safety on if he's in pursuit of us. Pulling the trigger would end this man's life and the world would be better for it. Owen has brought nothing but cruelty to the world. He helped his family murder James Gorden. He helped Isabel escape from prison. There's as much evil in him as there was my father. And me.

He shuffles up onto his feet, nursing his wounded shoulder. And slowly he backs away.

"You have to let me go. I told you everything."

"Did I say I'd let you go?" I say quietly, words almost stolen by the snow.

He ignores me and turns away. A few strides in, he begins to break into a limping run. I pull the trigger. The gun fires, the force of it rattling through my body. Owen drops to his knees, the blast hit him squarely in the middle of his back. He falls to the ground as I approach. Whether he's dead or alive, he's now incapacitated. I quickly go through his pockets and recover as many bullets as I can. Then I shove them in my own pockets and begin walking in the opposite direction.

On the way I see Seb staring out from behind his hiding place. One hand over his bullet wound. But I can't stay and help him. I have to go. If I don't go now, I won't get to Leah in time. Seb nods once, knowing that I'm not going to wait with him. He knows the same things I do. At least the police will be here soon. I have another job to do. I have to save my mother.

38

LEAH

"This man is your father, the one who raped you," Isabel says. "He's your son, the one who murdered an innocent woman because he wanted to see how it would feel. He's your boyfriend, the one who should be saving your life right now but isn't, and who hired a private detective behind your back." She pauses, licks her lips, turned on by her own intelligence. "Guess where Seb is now? I got Owen to pretend to be the investigator. He gave your lovely but quite dim boyfriend the address to find me. Seb might be there now, thinking he can save the day by coming after me. But he's wrong."

My heart sinks. "No."

"Owen is waiting for him."

She hasn't mentioned Tom. Perhaps there's still hope while Tom is out there unaccounted for. Isabel does appear to know about Tom's murder, but perhaps she believes Tom would side with her over me because of it. Or perhaps she simply couldn't get to Tom before she put this in motion, I'm not sure. Either way, I decide not to mention him. Let her forget about him.

"They've all let you down," she continues, her silver tongue working its way through my barriers. "And they will continue to let you down."

"Give me the knife," I say, holding out my hand.

Her eyes flash, but she hesitates. "I know you better than that, Leah."

A ripple of frustration passes over my body and I notice that I'm grinding my teeth together. Why is she always one step ahead of me?

"Hurt him with your bare hands," she says. "Punch him. Kick him. Gouge his eyes out with your fingers. If you want this knife, you have to earn it."

She's sick. This is sick. Neal's terrified eyes dart all around the ruin. He keeps making panicked bubbling noises through his gag. I let out a sigh. If I do this, I could buy some time, keep Isabel talking. I lift my right hand, open my palm, and slap him hard around the face.

Isabel starts to laugh. "Is that it? Is that your rage? A pathetic slap around the face. No, Leah. You can do much better than that. Or have you forgotten what you did to me? Have you forgotten the knife you plunged into my neck?" She caresses the scar at her throat.

I think about apologising to the man in the chair, but I don't. Instead, I close my fist and take a deep breath. When was the last time I hit anyone? Isabel in the cove was the only time I've ever truly been violent to another human being.

I withdraw my fist and Neal shakes his head, begging with his eyes. He screams as I connect with the cartilage of his nose. My knuckles throb, but I can't deny the release that spreads through my body. I do it again, and again. And then I kick him. In the ankle, then the calf. Then before I know it, I'm bringing my heel down on his crotch and he's screaming. He's crying and screaming and he's not Neal anymore, he's my father. I roll up my sleeves and bring my fists into the soft abdomen area, ignoring the screams. Ignoring the ripple of laughter behind my back. Finally, I stagger away, staring at the blood on my hands. Did I do that? Did I break his nose? I don't know whether to laugh, cry, or vomit.

I'm a mother, I think. I'm a mother and I did *that*.

A cold object is pressed into my palm, the cut one, dried blood and Neal's blood all mingled together. I'm gently pushed towards the director. Yes, I'm a mother, and there's a baby growing inside me. If that baby is a girl, I don't want this man to be around. If I kill Neal Ford, then one less sexual predator will be in the world.

But there will be one more killer.

Because of everything that has happened over the last few weeks, I hadn't actually noticed the sense of relief I'd felt when Tom confessed to me about Alison's murder. I was devastated that my son did something so terrible, but once and for all, my guilt was washed away. I finally knew for certain that I had not killed anyone. Finally. If I take this man's life, I will be a murderer again.

But this is different. This is taking a bad person out of the world.

"Do it," Isabel says. "No one will miss him. No one will grieve for him. He's nothing." She comes closer to whisper in my ear. "Take your power back. Take it. Remove this cockroach from existence."

I screw my eyes shut and open them again. Tiny, dark ovals begin to pour out of the snow.

"No," I whisper.

Isabel watches me carefully. I see her gaze follow mine. "What is it?"

"Cockroaches. Dozens of them."

She frowns. "It's a hallucination. Aren't you taking your medication, Leah?"

"No," I whisper.

There's a squawking above our heads. A magpie must have flown into the building. It comes down above me and I shield it with my arms. Flapping wings bat against my forearms and I hear a scream. The scream is from me.

"Stop that!" Isabel says. "It isn't there." Two hands grab my shoulders and shake me back to reality. "Whatever you're fighting against isn't there."

But I ignore her and try to slash at the wings fluttering around me.

"Focus, Leah," she says. "Kill the man."

Finally, my mind comes back to reality, and I remember that Isabel wants me to murder someone. Why does she want me to do this? Is this her way of toying with me before she kills me? Destroying my soul before mutilating my body? If there is a God, Isabel is evil. She's pure evil. An empty vessel filled up by Satan.

"I can't." I stare down at the knife. Now the change in medication is kicking in. At the exact moment I need to concentrate more than ever. A long line of ants dance across the edge of the blade.

"Yes, you can," Isabel insists.

I don't know what compels me to take a step towards Neal, but I do. He begins to shake his head. He's crying so hard that snot is coming from his nose. His eyes beg me to stop. *Please. Please.* I can make out muffled through the gag.

One thought seems clearer than the others. If I plunge the knife into Neal, the ants and the cockroaches will all go away. Everything will stop.

Neal's pleading is the first to stop, but I haven't stabbed him yet. He's listening. He turns his head sharply to the side, and I hear it too. There are voices outside the building. Young people's voices. Young people's laughter.

"This is it," someone says. "This is where it happened."

The dark tourists I warned Cassie about. My heart begins to thump. Isabel has heard them, too, I see her walk towards the entrance to the room. She's covered in Cassie's blood, a dirty knife still in her hand. I glance down at my own hands to see the clean weapon there. She gave me a new knife when she almost persuaded me to kill Neal. I wipe sweat away from my forehead. How close did I come to committing murder?

Isabel walks quickly, but not hurried, still in control. I have to help those kids because they don't know what they're walking into. More importantly, I need them to help me. They need to call the police. I follow Isabel, but not too close. Perhaps I can catch her off guard while she's focused on the walkers.

We step lightly through the house at the same moment the two young people walk in. My stomach flips over, the two teenagers are about sixteen years old, if that. The girl notices bloody Isabel before the boy and drops a part-empty bottle of vodka to the ground. She backs away, one gloved hand pressed to her chest, snow shimmering off her cagoul. Isabel says nothing, she simply slashes at the closest teen, the boy, catching him on the arm of his coat. I lurch into action, sprinting the last few steps. I manage to shove Isabel away from the kid before she gets her knife on him again.

"Run!" I yell.

The girl is already out of the door.

Isabel trips, but my push doesn't knock her to the ground. She uses that imbalance to dip low and stab my thigh. It's a deep puncture, and I can't help but scream. I grab the wound, applying pressure, watching in horror as Isabel directs her attention to the boy, now halfway to the exit.

He's not quick enough. She leaps at him, knocking him onto his back. I stagger towards them, but before I can reach Isabel, her knife lifts and plunges into his chest. It's the same as with Cassie, I watch her in a frenzy of violence, blood on her hands, face, clothes. For a split second I'm frozen. Stuck in a time when Tom was held by David Fielding and I was tied up able to do nothing, fearing that my son would be taken from me too soon. And then I spring to life. I pull Isabel away from the boy, who must be dead or close to dead.

She is momentarily dazed, and I try to stab her in the chest, but the knife hits the sternum, not cutting deep enough to kill her. She inhales sharply, the air in her throat like a last gasp. But it isn't a last gasp, it's nothing but shock.

I remove the knife and back away. The boy, somehow still conscious, drags himself forwards, managing to half crawl. He coughs up blood on the concrete and I have no idea how badly he's hurt. I want to help him onto his feet, but Isabel recovers quickly. I have one chance to get out of here and find help. One chance.

I begin to run.

39

ISABEL

Where she stabbed me is in agony, but my heart beats and I can breathe. I'm alive, that's the important part. More alive than I've been for a long, long time. But watching her stumble out of the house stirs rage inside me. *Come back, Leah, I'm not done with you. I have the small matter of taking your life to deal with.*

"Please don't hurt me again," the boy says, eyes leaking, body moving and squirming with blood seeping out of all his wounds. He'll be dead soon. I step around him to get out of the house.

There was another intruder who will no doubt have phoned the police by now. The irony is not lost on me. If I'd kept Cassie alive, none of this would have happened. She was supposed to help with any annoying interferences like this, but I have impulse control issues.

Emergency services response time is around eight minutes, but in a rural place like this, and given the snow, it could be much longer, somewhere between twenty minutes and several hours, I'm not sure. Let's say I have around twenty minutes. That's long enough to find and gut Leah. It might even be long enough to escape to the place Owen and I arranged to meet. But if I don't make it, at least Leah will be dead, and yes, she has to die, especially now.

The cold seeps down to my bones. It pierces the stab wound on my chest, and it's like being stabbed all over again. Visibility is terrible on the moors, and I can't run, because it hurts too much. But neither can Leah. When I stuck the knife in her leg, I was aiming for her femoral artery, but sadly missed. At least she'll be in pain now. There's no way she'll be able to run down to her precious farm this time.

I set off through the snow, blinking in the face of the blizzard before me. It's like walking through flying ice. The ground isn't particularly firm and my shoes sink and slide. Each step is blind. I could stumble over rocks, or I could step into a drift. I could fall on my face. This is all fine. I can adapt and overcome every time. I have the knife, I have my instincts, and I have a job to finish.

Leah knows these moors much better than I do. I don't want to admit it, but she has the advantage. I can't forget that.

Cold wind and snow hit my eyes, but I force them open. I force my chin up so that I can search for her. There's no swing of her long hair. No hint of a figure in the distance. Nothing. I take a slim torch from my coat pocket and check the surface of the snow for footprints. The stupid tourists have muddied the waters. There are several scuffs and half-filled footprints that could belong to anyone. I try to follow them as they change direction. What size are Leah's feet? Which shoes was she wearing? Hiking boots, I remember that. She had on a dark jacket that may be visible through the snow.

High up as I am, my torch should be able to find someone making their way down the path. But there's no one there. Leah is hiding somewhere. Did she crouch behind a boulder last time? Humans constantly repeat themselves. They act the same way in the same situations. Leah is no different to anyone else.

Then I see it. The drops of blood on the snow. I think of it dribbling from the wound in her thigh, all the way down her leg to the ground. I smile to myself. There we are. All I needed was patience. I knew everything would turn out well in the end. And now I'm finally going to end this.

40

LEAH

I t all came full circle. I think there has always been part of me that knew it would. My psyche knew, because it continued to lead me to the abandoned house on the moors. It had unfinished business with me. *Isabel* had unfinished business. Part of me knew we would end up at that house again, fighting for survival. And perhaps my body predicted that I would be hiding here, tucked away by a ravine in the moorland, crouching down where her torchlight can't find us.

The girl next to me wh impers and I shush her sharply before examining the wound on my leg. I don't mean to be harsh with her, but the world is silent apart from the snow. I don't know where Isabel is and what she can hear, but we can't take any chances.

I place my hand next to the wound on my leg. I was lucky she missed an artery. But the wound is over an inch deep and still bleeding. I quickly untie my shoelace and wrap it around my thigh, wincing at the pain, watching as the girl next to me silently cries. I smile at her, hoping that it helps, but she huddles there staring at me with wild eyes. There's smudged eyeliner travelling down to her nose, but still the whites of her eyes seem like an expanse in the darkness. Her chest rises rapidly up and down. I tie the laces and place my hand on the side of her cheek to calm her. She trembles under my touch. It's at that moment I comprehend that in this moment, I'm not panicking. I'm calm, because I've been here before. When I was here before, I won and I can win again.

"Did you call the police?" I whisper.

She nods her head.

They'll be on their way by now, though it won't be quick in this weather. This is an isolated area and I don't know which station they'll come from, especially if Isabel sent the police to a fake address.

"Sit tight," I mouth.

Last time Isabel was searching for me on the moors, she was bold enough to call my name. It was the middle of the night, Tom had killed her father, and I was hiding behind a rock somewhere. This time, she's silent, only the bob of torch-light through snow gives me a vague idea of where she is.

The way I see it, I have limited options. I could wait in this ravine and hope that Isabel doesn't find me or the girl next to me. I could get up and face her. We're both injured, but I don't know which of us is injured the worst. My thigh wound means that I can't run. I can walk quickly, but it's not enough if I want to fight her. On the other hand, I believe I stabbed close to Isabel's right breast, hitting bone. That has to hurt a lot. She must be almost as weakened as I am.

The other option is to try to lead her to the farm. Though this means possibly putting Donna's life in danger. But it could be possible. If Isabel sees me, she might follow me. She might decide that self-preservation is more important than killing me and simply run away before the police come. Isabel is clever. She knows that the girl will have a mobile phone, and she knows that the police will be on their way. Isabel knows she has limited time to either kill me or run away. The problem is, I don't know which option she's going for and I run the risk of not ending this once and for all. It would extend my life of living in terror, not knowing when she's going to strike. Could I live like that again?

I think of the baby inside me. I hope he or she is strong enough to live through this stress, both physical and emotional. If Isabel escaped, I could move away. Convince Seb and Donna to sell the farm, then find a nice apartment somewhere warm. South America, or Hawaii, or Australia. Tom could come with us and continue his atonement for what he did to Alison Finlay. Would that be paradise?

But as the snow continues to fall, I see a different path. I see myself looking over my shoulder, recognising Isabel's features in a stranger's face. New names, new identities. Moving a second or third or fourth time. A child constantly uprooted by my paranoia, smothered by a sense of my own demise. I see a child who will forever be a possibility to hurt me. Who could be used by a psychopath who does not possess the conscience needed to curb her desires. That's what I see.

I suck in a deep breath, force my brain to ignore the throbbing in my leg, and stand.

Almost immediately, the torchlight finds me, and I'm aware that I resemble a deer caught in the headlights of a car. Isabel's mouth opens slightly in surprise. She's closer to us than I thought she would be. Somehow, she was able to track us in this direction. I don't allow my mind to linger on that fact. I begin my descent towards the farm. I'm aware that this means luring a serial killer in the direction of Seb's mum, but

I'll have to cross that bridge when it comes to it. At least at the farm, I can get help. At least the police can find me. And maybe, just maybe, I'll have the upper hand on my own turf.

I glance behind me to see how far away she is, and, perhaps it's my imagination, but it feels like she's even closer. Her bottom lip is mashed between her teeth and one hand has hold of her chest. I can see that the movement is causing her pain, which is knowledge I can use if it comes to a fight. I try to speed up, but the sharp pain in my thigh makes me gasp. I grow light-headed. If I pass out before I get to the farm, this is over.

"You're too slow, Leah," she shouts.

I don't turn around, but I feel the light of her torch on my back. I grit my teeth and push harder, as hard as I can possibly go without feeling faint again. I still have the knife, I remind myself. I can still defend myself. She's no bigger than me and we're both hurt. *Keep going. Keep going.*

"When I catch up with you, I'm going to cut out your heart."

Keep going. Don't listen. Keep going.

"Have you ever seen what the Vikings used to do to their enemies?" her voice is muffled by the falling snow. She has to shout over the sound of crunching snow. But still she won't shut up. "They'd open up their ribs—" Her breath catches with the effort of moving. That sound frightens me because of how close she is. "They'd pull the lungs out so that they look like wings. Maybe I'll do that to you."

I want to engage with her because I know she can't do any of these things. She doesn't have time. It's tempting to shout back, to let her know that I see her empty threats and understand her desperation, but I don't. I put all my energy into walking. Until... the torch drops, and the light goes out. I feel the stirring of air by my ear. And then teeth sink into my left shoulder. A horrible shrieking sound echoes around the moors. It's me. I'm shrieking. Isabel yanks away and I half collapse to the ground. She spits a chunk of my flesh into the snow, and then the knife lifts.

41
TOM

Light fades, snow falls, and the fog lights come on. Through the blur of the snow, the streets begin to look familiar. But now that I'm away from the main roads and into Hutton village, there are abandoned cars everywhere.

I've driven a forty-minute journey in twenty-five, snow falling all around, managing to break every speed limit in a stolen Land Rover. For the first time in a while, luck was on my side. The Land Rover had been parked behind Owen's lodge, and must have been there for a quicker getaway, which didn't happen when he was injured by the axe. Seb's truck is still at the lodge, its windscreen now useless.

Six driving lessons in, I'm underprepared and breaking so many laws that it's a miracle I haven't been pulled over. But I don't care. I have to get to Leah. The snow won't hold me back, I won't let it.

My heart is hammering when I turn onto the country roads close to the Braithwaite's. Even though the snow is deeper here, the Land Rover handles it well. But reluctantly, I ease off the accelerator when I feel the tyres begin to lose traction. How long has Leah been left alone now? Long enough for Isabel to do whatever she wants to her. I glance at the shotgun on the passenger seat. I don't feel any remorse for shooting Owen. I'm pretty sure he's dead by now. The world is better off without him. Now it's time to take Isabel out of the world as well.

Finally, the turning comes up for the farm. I take it too fast and finally lose control completely. The Land Rover clips the gate post on the passenger side, spins, and then stops. I don't allow myself time to panic, I grab the shotgun, and get out.

Keep going. *Keep going.*

The farm is silent as I sprint down the lane. Snow has covered everything. The chicken coop, the courtyard. I trip over a stone and land on my knees, panting.

Get up.

Past the farm, now, the cottage coming into view. It's a long way up the moors to the abandoned house. I keep going, feeling the burn of my muscles as I continue up the hill to Rose Cottage. The lights are off.

Without my jacket, I'm freezing cold. Shivering down to my boots. The snow crunches beneath my feet. I make it onto the moors and stop for a moment to catch my breath.

The moors are silent. I lift the gun, hoping I've reloaded it correctly, and continue walking. My breath wheezes slightly from the run. I flex the muscles in my arms, trying to keep the heat in them, and at the same time force my mind to be sharp. How long has it been since Isabel jumped out at me at the campsite in Clifton? I let my guard down that night. It can't happen again.

But with every step, those thoughts of keeping myself together begin to fade away because there is a sense of foreboding about the general atmosphere around me. I scan the place, trying to put my finger on what seems out of place. And then I see it. Light. It bobs for a moment and then it goes out. Someone is out on the moors. Not walkers, not in this. Walkers wouldn't turn off their light. But someone who didn't want to be seen might.

I begin to jog towards the spot where I saw the light. There are no markers or moonlight. Snow catches in my eyelashes and hits my eyes. But I trust my feet, and I start to think through what's happening. If Leah was kidnapped by Isabel and Cassie, it would be unlikely that she'd be carrying a torch at the time. What would be more likely, is that Isabel, or her new accomplice, kept a torch with them in order to be able to follow someone in the dark.

My breath becomes laboured as I continue jogging. It's possible that Isabel turned off her torch because she saw me. I lift the gun and rest it against my shoulder, slowing slightly to maintain my control over the gun. I don't want to pull the trigger before it's time and waste my bullets. I feel like I'm close to the area where the torch went off when an ear-splitting shriek stops me dead. It makes my blood run cold. *Alison Finlay cried out when I killed her.* I shake the memory away and hurry towards the sound. Now isn't the time to feel guilt; it's time to generate the kind of rage that took me to the lowest, darkest point in my life. It's time to let out that killer again.

Isabel needs to die.

The snow eases slightly and my eyes adjust to the darkness. Finally, I see her through the darkness. Her small frame surprises me every time I see her. Perhaps I build her up to be a monster in my mind. There's blood on her mouth, at least I think it's blood. She's on top of a lump in the snow.

There are two sets of arms grappling for the same bloody knife. I stop dead, staring at the scene before me. Isabel is in the throes of her fight and hasn't noticed me. The slight reprieve in snowfall grows stronger again, making visibility difficult once more. It's Isabel, I recognise the shape of her body, the way she moves. But am I completely certain?

I make a decision. I lift the gun back to my shoulder and pull the trigger.

The bullet hits, and Isabel flies back. I lower the gun and run towards the fray. Leah lies in the snow, clutching the side of her neck. I help her sit up and see the blood seeping through the wound.

"I'm okay," she says. "The police are coming, but the snow..."

"I know," I say. I go to remove my jacket for her, but then I remember I left it with Seb. There's nothing I can give her now. Except, maybe... "Love you, Mum."

I stand, lifting the gun back to my shoulder.

Leah's mouth moves as though she wants to respond, but I walk back to where Isabel fell. She sprawls around in the snow, holding one arm with the other. The knife is still in her wounded hand. I lift up the gun and aim it straight at her face, and then I change my mind and direct it towards her heart. I want her body to be easily identified, so that the entire world knows that Isabel Fielding is dead. But when I pull the trigger, nothing happens. My stomach sinks. Isabel begins to smile. She lifts up from the ground and laughs. Her knife catches a trace of moonlight and when she moves closer to me, I see the blood all over her. At least some of it is her blood this time, not like the time she killed poor Maisie. Not like that. No, we've damaged her at least. We've made her feel pain.

I refuse to back away, instead I stand my ground when she comes for me. With the butt of the gun, I hit her on the right side of her jaw, but she twists herself so that it doesn't have the impact I was hoping for. She goes for my wrist, teeth sinking into my flesh. This is her stripped away, I think. Feral. Wild.

My skin is so cold that I barely feel the pain. At least until panic kicks in and I realise how much damage she could do. Before I can act, Leah knocks her away from me. It gives me a moment to regroup. I grasp hold of Isabel's hair and drag her onto her feet. Blood and spit bubble at the corners of her mouth. Her eyes are like two dark pits of rage. I've known that rage. This is like looking in a mirror for me.

"Tom!" Leah shouts. She sees the knife before I do.

It all happens so fast. Isabel screams in either pain or frustration or both when she plunges the knife into my hip. She first falls into me, but the shock of it all makes me let go of her hair. Leah attempts to either grab her or stab her, I'm not sure, and then Isabel begins to run, but not towards the farm, out towards the expanse of the moors.

Suddenly there are sirens wailing closer, but Isabel is getting away. She isn't exactly sprinting, but she's limping and groaning away from us. I can't rely on the police catching her. She needs to be dead. I begin to follow her.

She turns back, sees me, and manages to increase her speed. I glance down at the knife still stuck in the flesh of my thigh, right at the top near my hip. I could pull it out, but I think it might slow me down, so I keep going, ignoring the throbbing. It's torment, but I can't let her get away this time. This is it for us. This is how it ends. This is how I save my mother. And I know I have one advantage over Isabel. I know what Isabel has forgotten. I know exactly what she's running towards. A place she's been before. A place she'll never want to go again.

It's only when she's close to the edge that she sees the drop. But it's too late. She stops hurrying away from me and tries to turn, but I've gained on her, and now I'm moving even faster than she was. Now I have my arms outstretched. Now I'm shifting my weight backwards so that I can propel myself forwards. Now I'm connecting with her body, pushing us both towards the drop, pushing us both with all my weight so that we don't end up landing on the platform that I know is underneath this cliff. This is the place where Mum dropped Isabel. But this time, Isabel is going to die, because I'm going to make sure of it.

There's a scream, possibly two. I can't tell whether it's coming from Isabel, Mum, or me. We leave the safety of the snow and then there's nothing beneath us. It's like we're suspended in air until gravity takes over. It's not long, maybe a second, maybe less. She hits the rock first. Pain explodes all over my body. My head takes a knock. I hear a crack. A bone smashed, and I think it was part of my face. Breathing becomes difficult and a numbness spreads out to my limbs. Perhaps I broke my spine on impact. I don't have long. I look at Isabel. She's landed on her back, and I landed on my side, slightly to the right. It's only now that I pull the knife from my left hip. I don't even feel it.

"Please. Don't," she whispers through her bloody mouth.

I draw the knife across her neck, and then the world goes black.

42

LEAH

Time stops and my son is suspended in the air. Time stops and he has his arms around a girl. Time stops.

And then it starts again. A scream rips from my throat, almost as loud as the sirens down below. Blue lights flash. *Flash.* Tom tackles Isabel. *Flash.* They go over the cliff edge. *Flash.* I'm screaming.

I move as fast as I can to the edge of the cliff. I drop to my knees, crying into my bloody hands. I heard them land before I even made it to the edge. I heard the sickening thud. Slowly, I crawl on my belly until I'm looking over the edge, and then I strain my eyes, begging to see movement. There's nothing.

I wipe my tears, get to my feet and begin to walk along the cliff until I can find a place to climb down. It's all too steep. I yell out to the police below, waving my unhurt arm, then pointing towards where I believe Tom and Isabel landed.

"Help him," I cry, sobs racking through me. I can't help them. My body gives in and I drop to my knees again, but this time I can't get back up. The knife falls from my fingers. Someone's hands wrap around my shoulders and I fall into their body. The girl from the ravine, it has to be her.

Shortly after I hear the sound of boots on snow.

"At the bottom of the cliff," I shout. "My son is down there! We need an ambulance."

"Leah? Leah is that you?"

I lift my hand to shield my eyes from the light. DCI Murphy comes into view, covered in a thick coat and gloves. He swears when he sees the wound on my shoulder and calls someone over who must have a first aid kit.

"It's Tom. He jumped off the cliff with Isabel."

"I have officers down there," he says. "They'll find them. Now, tell me about your injuries. Tell me what else I need to know."

But I can't, because the slow realisation that Tom is dead seems to be spreading over me like the blood from my shoulder. Through a strange, thudding sound in my ears, I hear the girl begin to talk.

"There's a man tied up in the farmhouse. Isabel Fielding killed... I think she killed my boyfriend. I ran away." *Sniff.* "Then she came after us. We hid over there. A man came and he shot her, but it wasn't enough..."

It all fades away.

Murphy catches me as I fall forwards.

* * *

When the bright light filters in through the tiny gap in my eyelids, at first I think DCI Murphy is shining a torch in my eyes. But then I see the hospital lights.

I squint for a moment, adjusting to the brightness, and then I glance down at my hand, which is covered by a larger, stronger hand. Seb's hand.

He has tears in his eyes. He rests his head on the bed next to me and I try to stroke his hair, but when I move my other arm, a searing pain rips through me. That's when it all comes flooding back. It started with Jess Hopkins's dead body in the abandoned house. Then Cassie Keats and her betrayal. Followed by Isabel waiting for me at the farmhouse and Tom showing up to save my life.

And then...

I don't want to think about what happened after that, and yet I must.

When I say his name, I'm crying. Seb lifts his head and I don't need him to answer me, because I can see the answer on his face.

"I'm so sorry, Leah. He didn't make it."

I'm out of the hospital bed and on my feet the next day. It wasn't so much of an issue of whether I could or couldn't, I was always going to make this journey. My child could never be alone in such a place for any longer. Seb holds my hand as we make our way to the back of the hospital. DCI Murphy accompanies us. He's silent, too. His shoulders are stooped and weary, as are mine. Both men keep in stride with me as I limp my way through the long, stretching corridors. None of us came out of this unscathed. Seb has his shoulder injury. Murphy is clearly haunted by everything that has happened. But none of that matters because we made it, and Tom didn't.

He's presented to me as a sleeping man on a gurney. A white sheet covers everything but his face. There's part of his skull missing at the back. Someone has attempted to cover this, but the sheet has fallen back slightly. There's also a lump where his cheekbone and nose smashed. It almost makes me detach from the boy I used to know.

There are two other bodies in the room. Isabel and Owen.

The white sheets cover their faces, but I still feel their presence. But for now, it's Tom that occupies my thoughts. My boy. My son.

I remove my fingers from Seb's and place the palm of my hand on Tom's cheek. Cold. So cold. But touching him helps me remember. I keep my hand on his face and close my eyes. In my mind he's that same kid with the black hair – dyed in rebellion – eyeliner in his back pocket, band t-shirts folded in his cabinet. We could have had a life together, him and me.

I remember the way we'd put music on loud as we were doing housework. The horror films we watched together. The laughter we shared. All of that stopped when Isabel came into our lives. Maybe it can start again, in my memories; a time that should have lasted longer than it did.

"He died saving you," Murphy says. "He's a hero."

No, I think, my son wasn't a hero. He was complex. He was capable of great good, and great evil. He saved my life, but he took another. Murphy can never know that. I won't have his memory ruined as well as his life taken from me.

I clear my throat and face the detective. "I want to see her, too."

"Are you sure?" he asks. "She isn't in great... condition."

I nod my head. I've faced the worst life has to offer already.

I'm led to another gurney and a sheet is pulled back. Even though I was warned, I wince at what I see before me. Most of the blood has been cleaned from her face, but there is bruising all over her. There's nothing missing from her skull, but she's the wrong colour. Then I see the red line across her throat.

"Tom did that?"

Murphy nods.

"Can we keep that out of the papers?"

"I'll do my best," he says.

275

"He did what he had to do to keep me alive," I say.

I stare down at her, the small girl who made my life a misery for several years, who stalked me and my family, who desecrated my mother's grave, who taunted me, physically hurt me, psychologically abused me. I look at her lifeless face expecting to feel a surge of hatred. There is none. Nothing but pity and confusion. What did you see in me, Isabel? Was it a spark of specialness, or the kind of utter mundanity of which you had to take advantage? Was it a part of my personality that you could manipulate? Or was it a connection?

I thought you were the most innocent creature when I met you. There was a gentleness about everything you did. Even when I discovered the truth beneath the mask, that gentle side never went away. Did you know that, Isabel? Did you know that you could be gentle? Did you understand it? Did you know that there were times when I loved you, wanted to fix you, and the love didn't truly go away until I began to hate you? Did you know that I sent you books when you were in prison because I began to think you could get better away from your family?

It hurts to let those thoughts finally come to the surface. To face up to the fact that my feelings for Isabel were as complex as Tom's personality. She'll always be someone who hurt me and my family, but she'll always be the person I pitied, and she'll always be the person that part of me loved.

Goodbye, Isabel, I think.

I move back to Tom. "Can you move the sheet so I can see his hand?"

The coroner lifts the sheet. I wrap my fingers around his.

"Can you leave me for a minute?"

Seb kisses my forehead as the men filter away. It leaves me alone with death, somewhere I've been before.

I take a deep breath and begin. "Tom. This is what I

would have said to you if I'd been able to. It's what I should have told you years ago, so that you didn't overhear it. I'd say, I'm not your sister, I'm your mother. Your father is your father. I know it's scary, and confusing, but I need you to know. There was a night when Dad was drunk, right in the middle of one of his bouts. He was ill. He'd always been ill. And he came into my room at night. I'm not convinced he knew who I was or quite what he was doing, but it happened, and it was wrong, and I was devastated. I was young. Far too young to have a child.

"When I told your grandma, she was so angry with me. She didn't believe me. But when I told her that I didn't know how to be a mother, she told me that she would help me, and she did. I'm grateful for that, because I wasn't ready, Tom.

"I'm so sorry that I left you with them, knowing what a monster he was. *Is.* I should've stayed behind and taken care of you. But I didn't. It was the worst mistake of my entire life. That was the right time to tell you who I am so that we could live together away from them both.

"I don't think anything we did would've changed what Dad did to her. She wouldn't leave him, and he was determined to take it further every time he hurt her. I know you blamed yourself for a long time, but it was misplaced blame. You didn't do anything wrong." I pause, wipe away tears, take a shaky breath. "I always knew you were different, no matter how hard you tried to cover it up. I wanted to tell you that if you were gay, that was okay, and not to listen to anything a bully at school had to say. But I didn't know if you knew yourself and I didn't want to rush you. I wanted to be the cool Mum. Cool big sister, whatever I was to you, then. Maybe I didn't know what I wanted to be. But I wanted you to be happy, that much I know. You were the best of us. Sensible. Kind. Quietly strong. What I hate about Isabel is that she made you abandon those qualities for a while. I'm so sorry I didn't see it happening fast enough to stop what you did to that poor woman. I wish I hadn't been too ill to properly take care of you. I wish I'd been there for you, always. I know you found yourself on a dark path, I'm proud of you for coming back. For choosing to be better. You saved my life, you took two monsters out of the world, but I will always remember you as you were before any of this happened." I take my fingers, kiss them, and place them on his forehead.

43
LEAH

"Well, it looks like you're having a little girl."

The nurse gives my hand a squeeze, but I can't stop staring at the image on the screen. The wobbly, scribbled at the edges, image of our child. A survivor. She outlasted a serial killer. She lived when I tumbled down the moors, when I fought back against Isabel. She's strong.

"Would you like a photograph?" the nurse asks.

I pull my eyes away from the screen and nod to Seb.

"Great," she says. "I'll get that printed out for you." She removes the transducer and disappears from the room.

"Are you happy?" Seb asks, stroking the side of my face. His eyebrows are pulled up in concern, but even still I see the joy in his eyes.

"Of course, I am," I reply, laughter in my voice for the first time in a long while.

It's only partly a lie. I'm happy about the baby. I'm happy that I have a small bump now. But it's only three months since Tom's death, and I'm sad that I don't get to share this news with him. He'll never know that he was going to have a little sister.

"It's okay to be sad," Seb says, reading my mind. He kisses me gently on the lips. "I know you miss him."

"It'll take time, I suppose. I am happy, though. I'm just sad as well."

"Are you still okay for later?" he asks.

By later, he means taking the ultrasound photo to show his mother and brother at the farm. Josh needed a blood transfusion after what Isabel and Owen did to him. He also needed plenty of therapy to deal with the trauma. But like the rest of us, he's on the mend. We're all more fragile than we were before. At least Seb was reunited with his brother after we were certain he was dead. It was the one and only beautiful outcome after so much violence and pain.

Since Tom's death, which is how I think of that day, it's been tricky to work through everything that happened. But DCI Murphy has been a great help with piecing it all together.

It turned out that what Cassie Keats said about her past was all true. She did have a very unfortunate childhood which involved several foster homes. There was no way to corroborate what she said about one of her foster fathers, but I told Murphy everything in case it helped.

After searching her room, the police found a burner phone filled with messages between Isabel, Owen and Cassie. She'd been on Isabel's side right from the start. I don't think she ever intended to play Isabel in the movie; she wanted to act as Isabel, but in real life, not on screen. And her revenge on Neal was revenge on every man who had let her down throughout her life. What I don't think she fully understood was that Isabel and Owen were using her in the same way she'd always been used, and they threw her away like rubbish.

Cassie's claims against Neal found their way onto the internet via an anonymous source, which prompted three other women to come forward about his habit of slipping a pill into a champagne flute. Some online message boards speculate that it was me who leaked the information, and they would be right. Neal stands trial when the investigation into his crimes is complete. His face is disfigured after Isabel's torture, and he had a few broken ribs to heal, but apart from that he was fine.

He revelled in telling the police about the way I pummelled him with my fists. But despite his claims, no case was filed against me. Isabel had been holding the knife at the time, forcing me to do it.

Murphy and his team found Josh at the hotel and soon realised that they'd been tricked when Seb called from a second location. He then discovered that I had been taken to a third location and my life was in danger. But it wasn't until Tom got the address from Owen that he knew where to go.

After Tom shot Owen, Seb was found by police and taken to the nearest hospital. The wound didn't hit any arteries and after the bullet was removed, he was sewn shut. However, Seb has difficulty raising his arm even now, and doctors suspect that he might lose fifty per cent of the mobility in his shoulder. It means his farming days are numbered. *It's time to sell, Ma,* he'd said to her when he came out of hospital. And he said it with a smile on his face.

Owen died from the gunshot wound. He and Isabel were cremated in a quiet, lonely ceremony. The last of the Fieldings. I didn't go. I'd said all I wanted to say to my serial killer stalker. A young woman called Genna, Isabel's friend from prison, scattered their ashes somewhere quiet on the coast, surrounded by seagulls.

The boy Isabel stabbed pulled through but is suffering

from severe nerve damage. The young girl, his girlfriend, called Mia, came to visit me in hospital. She told me that she's given up obsessing over serial killers. I can't decide whether or not I believe her, but I email her every now and then to see how she's doing.

"Right, let's get you cleaned up and out of here," the nurse says as she bustles back into the room. "Here are your two copies. You can pay on your way out." She grabs a wad of tissue and cleans the gel from my bump. "You're both doing well, all your vitals are normal. But try not to get too stressed, okay?"

"I'm working on it," I reply.

She nods in approval.

I pull on my dress and Seb zips me up. I'll never get used to smoothing the fabric around my bump. The last time I did this, when I was pregnant with Tom, the sight of the bump made me feel sick. But now there's nothing but love. As I always do, when I think about the baby, I remind myself to think of my Tom, to send him love, even if he can't feel it anymore. I'll never stop loving him, no matter how he came into the world and went out of it.

"Ready?" Seb grabs my bag and I slip an arm through his, nodding my head.

"We'll meet in a few months to discuss your birthing plan," the nurse says. "And you'll get to meet your midwife."

"Can't wait," I reply.

She scans me, probably trying to detect sarcasm, but I genuinely mean it and she smiles. "Great!"

We make our way through the hospital corridors. As a former nurse, hospitals have always meant something else to me in comparison to other people. This is where I've made friends, learned my craft, helped those in need. It was in Crowmont Hospital that I tried to make a new start. But it was a false start because I didn't know I was ill. So much has happened since then that I barely recognise myself as we walk into the fresh air. I've lost people and that grief will never go away. But on a day like this, with the sun shining, the ultrasound picture in Seb's pocket, and his comforting arm around mine, I see a bright future. The darkness is behind me.

About the Author

Sarah A. Denzil is a *Wall Street Journal* bestselling suspense writer from Derbyshire. Her thrillers include the number one bestseller *Silent Child*, as well as *The Broken Ones, Saving April, The Isabel Fielding series, Only Daughter and The Liar's Sister*. Sarah lives in Yorkshire with her husband and cats, enjoying the scenic countryside and rather unpredictable weather.

To stay updated, join the mailing list for a monthly newsletter, new release announcements and special offers.

Printed in Great Britain
by Amazon

45858129R00169